Spinning
Away from
the Center

Spinning Away from the Center

STORIES ABOUT

Homesickness

AND

Homecoming

FROM THE
FLANNERY O'CONNOR AWARD
FOR SHORT FICTION

EDITED BY
ETHAN LAUGHMAN

THE UNIVERSITY OF GEORGIA PRESS
ATHENS

Most University of Georgia Press titles are
available from popular e-book vendors.

Printed digitally

Library of Congress Control Number: 2019945837
ISBN: 9780820356617 (pbk.: alk. paper)
ISBN: 9780820356600 (ebook)

CONTENTS

ACKNOWLEDGMENTS

The stories in this volume are from the following award-winning collections published by the University of Georgia Press:

Leigh Allison Wilson, *From the Bottom Up* (1983)

Mary Hood, *How Far She Went* (1984); "A Country Girl" first appeared in the *Georgia Review* (winter 1979)

Peter Meinke, *The Piano Tuner* (1986)

Philip F. Deaver, *Silent Retreats* (1988)

Christopher McIlroy, *All My Relations* (1994); "From the Philippines" first appeared in *Sonora Review* (spring 1984)

C. M. Mayo, *Sky Over El Nido* (1995)

Wendy Brenner, *Large Animals in Everyday Life* (1996); "Easy" first appeared in *Beloit Fiction Journal* (spring 1994)

Paul Rawlins, *No Lie Like Love* (1996)

Ed Allen, *Ate It Anyway* (2003)

David Crouse, *Copy Cats* (2005)

Hugh Sheehy, *The Invisibles* (2012); "Whiteout" first appeared in *Glimmer Train* (2012)

Karin Lin-Greenberg, *Faulty Predictions* (2014); "Miller Duskman's Mistakes" first appeared in the *Antioch Review* (summer 2014)

Monica McFawn, *Bright Shards of Someplace Else* (2014); "A Country Woman" first appeared in *Passages North*

Toni Graham, *The Suicide Club* (2015); "Hope Springs" first appeared in *Epiphany* (fall 2010–winter 2011)

Siamak Vossoughi, *Better Than War* (2015); "The World Is My Home" first appeared in *Sundog Lit* (September 2014)

Becky Mandelbaum, *Bad Kansas* (2017)

Kirsten Sundberg Lunstrum, *What We Do with the Wreckage* (2018); "Endlings" first appeared in *Ploughshares Solos* (issue 6.3)

A thank you also goes to the University of Georgia Main Library staff for technical support in preparing the stories for publication.

INTRODUCTION

The Flannery O'Connor Award for Short Fiction was established in 1981 by Paul Zimmer, then the director of the University of Georgia Press, and press acquisitions editor Charles East. East would serve as the first series editor, judging the competition and selecting two collections to publish each year. The inaugural volumes in the series, *Evening Out* by David Walton and *From the Bottom Up* by Leigh Allison Wilson, appeared in 1983 to critical acclaim. Nancy Zafris (herself a Flannery O'Connor Award–winner for the 1990 collection *The People I Know*) was the second series editor, serving in the role from 2008 to 2015. Zafris was succeeded by Lee K. Abbott in 2016, and Roxane Gay then assumed the role, choosing award winners beginning in 2019. Competition for the award has since become an important proving ground for writers, and the press has published seventy-four volumes to date, helping to showcase talent and sustain interest in the short story form. These volumes together feature approximately eight hundred stories by authors who are based in all regions of the country and even internationally. It has been my pleasure to have read each and every one.

The idea of undertaking a project that could honor the diversity of the series' stories but also present them in a unified way had been hanging around the press for a few years. What occurred to us first, and what remained the most appealing approach, was to pull the hundreds of stories out of their current

packages—volumes of collected stories by individual authors—
and regroup them by common themes or subjects. After finish-
ing my editorial internship at the press, I was brought on to the
project and began to sort the stories into specific thematic cat-
egories. What followed was a deep dive into the award and its
history and a gratifying acquaintance with the many authors
whose works constitute the award's legacy.

Anthologies are not new to the series. A tenth-anniversary
collection, published in 1993, showcased one story from each
of the volumes published in the award's first decade. A similar
collection appeared in 1998, the fifteenth year of the series. In
2013, the year of the series' thirtieth anniversary, the press published two volumes modeled after the tenth- and fifteenth-anni-
versary volumes. These anthologies together included one story
from each of the fifty-five collections published up to that point.
One of the 2013 volumes represented the series' early years, under the editorship of Charles East. The other showcased the editorship of Nancy Zafris. In a nod to the times, both thirtieth-an-
niversary anthologies appeared in e-book form only.

The present project is wholly different in both concept and
scale. The press plans to republish more than five hundred stories in more than forty volumes, each focusing on a specific
theme—from love to food to homecoming and homesickness.
Each volume will aim to collect exemplary treatments of its
theme, but with enough variety to give an overview of what the
series is about. The stories inside paint a colorful picture that includes the varied perspectives multiple authors can have on a
single theme.

Each volume, no matter its focus, includes the work of authors whose stories celebrate the variety of short fiction styles
and subjects to be found across the history of the award. Just as
Flannery O'Connor is more than just a southern writer, the University of Georgia Press, by any number of measures, has been
more than a regional publisher for some time. As the first se-

ries editor, Charles East, happily reported in his anthology of the O'Connor Award stories, the award "managed to escape [the] pitfall" of becoming a regional stereotype. When Paul Zimmer established the award he named it after Flannery O'Connor as the writer who best embodied the possibilities of the short-story form. In addition, O'Connor, with her connections to the south and readership across the globe, spoke to the ambitions of the press at a time when it was poised to ramp up both the number and scope of its annual title output. The O'Connor name has always been a help in keeping the series a place where writers strive to be published and where readers and critics look for quality short fiction.

The award has indeed become an internationally recognized institution. The seventy-four (and counting) Flannery O'Connor Award authors come from all parts of the United States and abroad. They have lived in Arizona, Arkansas, California, Colorado, Georgia, Indiana, Maryland, Massachusetts, Texas, Utah, Washington, Canada, Iran, England, and elsewhere. Some have written novels. Most have published stories in a variety of literary quarterlies and popular magazines. They have been awarded numerous fellowships and prizes. They are world-travelers, lecturers, poets, columnists, editors, and screenwriters.

There are risks in the thematic approach we are taking with these anthologies, and we hope that readers will not take our editorial approach as an attempt to draw a circle around certain aspects of a story or in any way close off possibilities for interpretation. Great stories don't have to resolve anything, be set any particular time nor place, or be written in any one way. Great stories don't have to *be* anything. Still, when a story resonates with enough readers in a certain way, it is safe to say that it has spoken to us meaningfully about, for instance, love, death, and certain concerns, issues, pleasures, or life events.

We at the press had our own ideas about how the stories might be gathered, but we were careful to get author input on the process. The process of categorizing their work was not easy for any of them. Some truly agonized. Having their input was invaluable; having their trust was humbling. The goal of this project is to faithfully represent these stories despite the fact that they have been pulled from their original collections and are now bedmates with stories from a range of authors taken from diverse contexts.

Also, just because a single story is included in a particular volume does not mean that that volume is the only place that story could have comfortably been placed. For example, "Sawtelle" from Dennis Hathaway's *The Consequences of Desire*, tells the story of a subcontractor in duress when he finds out his partner is the victim of an extramarital affair. We have included it in the volume of stories about love, but it could have been included in those on work, friends, and immigration without seeming out of place.

The stories in this volume on homesickness and homecoming center on a fulcrum point we all share to some degree—a place to ground oneself amidst the tumult of life, love, ambition, disparity, and fortune. During the compilation of the volume, a major theme emerged: that one's conception of home depends more on connection and affect than on blood relation or physical location.

This collection opens with Ed Allen's wistful "Wickersham Day," where the last remaining tenant of a rickety home reflects on the short-lived sense of community and belonging he found there. In contrast, Lunstrum's "Endlings" looks toward the future, as a doctor and her anorexic patient discover the necessity of adaptation in a hostile world. Both doctor and patient experience acute loneliness and learn that to feel at home, it may be necessary to jettison part of who you used to be.

The next two stories revolve around strained father-son relationships. The first, Peter Meinke's "The Starlings of Leicester Square," focuses on a father's plea to an estranged son for acceptance. The second, Toni Graham's "Hope Springs," tells the story of a man displaced from his native New York City who struggles with loss and aimlessness after his father's suicide.

Next is Christopher McIlroy's "From the Philippines." Desensitized and uncaring about the priorities of her high school peers and even her own family, Dierdre drifts through her routine longing to return to the family she came to love during her life-altering study abroad in the Philippines. This is a story of homesickness without the possibility of a homecoming. Yet we spy a ray of hope, as "From the Philippines" illustrates that home depends more on selfless love and fellowship than on biological linkage or geographical location.

What McIlroy writes in the way of despair, Mayo writes in the way of levity. "Sky Over El Nido" follows two Mexican prisoners making the best of a bad situation as they tell outlandish stories about their guards. The initial joking and distraction ends up creating a home with as much comradery and connection as can be found in any household.

We continue on to Becky Mandelbaum's "The Golden State," which reminds us—as in "From the Philippines" and "Wickersham Day"—that it is the people, not the brick and mortar, who make a home. A similar sentiment is found in Philip F. Deaver's "Geneseo," as the characters must decide for themselves where their home really is. In "South of the Border," which depicts a literal homecoming, the protagonist is homesick for a place that never existed. We hope that she eventually pursues her own path free from the emotional restraints her family puts on her.

The collection then shifts its focus to homecoming in "Miller Duskman's Mistakes," a story that dramatizes the necessity of community cohesion in the face of inevitable change. After Avery, the town sweetheart, falls for interloper Miller Duskman, the tight-knit town timidly accepts Duskman into the fold. What follows tests Avery and her community as they struggle to reconcile newness with their town traditions.

Some stories express the elation of returning home, and others depict the discovery of a home in an unexpected place. Often, as with "A Country Girl," stories on homecoming drive home the importance of finding the familial compassion and joy created amongst compassionate people. Following "A Country Girl" is David Crouse's "Crybaby," a masterpiece in atmosphere and character. Though the history between the central characters remains unspoken, its depth and authenticity push readers to acknowledge those who had a hand in making them the people they are today.

Next we have "Whiteout" and "Easy," both centered on troubled young people making a literal homecoming. We join in their anticipation of arrival, grateful for the solace and retreat that only a home can provide.

Monica McFawn's "A Country Woman" is a story about an extraordinary woman whose absence left a gap more significant than the contention created by her presence. Sometimes it is the memory of a place and its people, rather than the place itself, that gives a home its significance.

Homecoming is not always a joyous occasion. Philip Rawlins's "Big Where I Come From" shares much with "South of the Border" in that both follow protagonists who only return to their homes out of obligation. However, few would pity the protagonist at the end of this particular story.

Finally, Siamak Vossoughi's "The World is My Home" perfectly caps this collection. The stories in Vossoughi's collection *Better than War* narrate episodes that beautifully illustrate elements of human experience. Here, Vossoughi relays truths about the importance of compassion through the story of two young travelers who find themselves on the receiving end of much goodwill, suggesting that home is wherever we find people willing to share their bread and bed.

In "South of the Border," Leigh Allison Wilson writes, "I can go home again, again and again, each episode like a snowflake that sticks to your eyelashes. They melt and mingle with your tears. Take a memory, any memory, and it becomes an inviolable god, a sanity exactly according to plan. But those soft edges—those peripheral realities that blur, those landscapes that shift and rush past—those are the crucibles of emotion, and they flow headlong backwards beneath your feet. I come South only twice a year, once at Christmas, once in the summer. Each time is a possible fatal accident." Such landscapes of emotion keep us wishing to return home while we spin further and further away from center. As we tumble, we create pockets of community and belonging that keep us grounded—if only for a while.

In *Creating Flannery O'Connor*, Daniel Moran writes that O'Connor first mentioned her infatuation with peacocks in her essay "Living with a Peacock" (later republished as "King of the Birds"). Since the essay's appearance, O'Connor has been linked with imagery derived from the bird's distinctive feathers and silhouette by a proliferation of critics and admirers, and one can now hardly find an O'Connor publication that does not depict or refer to her "favorite fowl" and its association with immortality and layers of symbolic and personal meaning. As Moran notes, "Combining elements of her life on a farm, her religious themes, personal eccentricities, and outsider status, the peacock has proved the perfect icon for O'Connor's readers, critics, and biographers, a form of reputation-shorthand that has only grown more ubiquitous over time."

We are pleased to offer these anthologies as another way

of continuing Flannery O'Connor's legacy. Since its conception, thirty-seven years' worth of enthralling, imaginative, and thought-provoking fiction has been published under the name of the Flannery O'Connor Award. The award is just one way that we hope to continue the conversation about O'Connor and her legacy while also circulating and sharing recent authors' work among readers throughout the world.

It is perhaps unprecedented for such a long-standing short fiction award series to republish its works in the manner we are going about it. The idea for the project may be unconventional, but it draws on an established institution—the horn-of-plenty that constitutes the Flannery O'Connor Award series backlist—that is still going strong at the threshold of its fortieth year. I am in equal parts intimidated and honored to present you with what I consider to be these exemplars of the Flannery O'Connor Award. Each story speaks to the theme uniquely. Some of these stories were chosen for their experimental nature, others for their unique take on the theme, and still others for exhibiting matchlessness in voice, character, place, time, plot, relevance, humor, timelessness, perspective, or any of the thousand other metrics by which one may measure a piece of literature.

But enough from me. Let the stories speak for themselves.

ETHAN LAUGHMAN

Spinning Away from the Center

Wickersham Day

ED ALLEN

From *Ate It Anyway* (2003)

Getting the dog off the roof meant that somebody had to pull Danny's Land Cruiser up to the kitchen door, as close as possible to the edge of the house, then Danny would climb on top of the car, while Booger would walk back and forth, not quite understanding that he was on the roof, his long lips swinging, little pink potato buds of squamous cell carcinoma already growing around his mouth.

Danny would call Booger to him over the slanted asphalt, then balance him in his arms before handing him down to Kevin or Michael. Sometimes they forgot to close the door to Laura's room, whose window led to the roof, so that before Danny had even put the Toyota back next to the empty barn, Booger would have stumbled back up the stairs, into Laura's room, and out the open window onto the roof again, barking that shapeless flews-muffled foghorn of a bark out over the blue gravel of the driveway.

On Saturdays and Sundays they used to sit around outside the kitchen in old lawn chairs they had found in the garage, rolling joints in a bread-pan and passing them around as they looked east into the space between the farmhouse and the far subdivisions. Some weekends people's parents drove up to visit, with

1

food and furniture. Danny's mother was the bookkeeper for a home for the developmentally disabled, and she showed them an easier way to calculate each person's share of the rent and the phone bill.

One day, Laura's grandfather came up to the house, visibly frightened. He had just read a book by a psychiatrist named Immanuel Velikovsky, who believed that Biblical cataclysms had been caused by the planet Venus leaving its orbit and halting the earth's rotation—and that these things were going to happen again very soon.

They painted the kitchen bright yellow. They put up a calendar that Danny had gotten when he took a tour of the Molson Brewery in Kingston, Ontario, on which every day was a different Canadian anniversary that could be celebrated by drinking Molson: Joni Mitchell's first platinum record, the completion of the transcontinental railroad, the establishment of the Hockey Hall of Fame.

So they lived there, sometimes five people, sometimes eight or nine, some moving in, others moving out, cars loading and unloading. At night they stood around in the hard reflected yellow of the kitchen walls. They tried to drink whiskey sours, and they tried to play poker, but they ended up not being able to do either of those things very well. They always ended up with too many things cluttering up the table: magazines, the blender, sour mix, grains of dried sugar stuck to the tablecloth.

Playing poker, at least playing with any seriousness, was hard because they didn't know how to play any of the real poker games. All they knew were games like Cripple Creek Lowball or Upside-Down Pigs-in-the-Chute—usually with fives, suicide kings, and left-handed queens wild. If two or three different dealers named the same game for a few hands in a row, people would start to remember what the rules were, and some nights that would happen, but either way the result was usually the same; people won each other's nickels and quarters back and forth; by house rule no copper was allowed on the table.

A mystery: one day all the food in the house disappeared. Roy drew up a cardboard sign and tacked it on the kitchen door, warning the person not to do it again and saying that the state police had been called, but of course they hadn't. The man who had rented the farm before they moved in had said he was going to have them arrested for supposedly taking away the lumber from a collapsing outbuilding at the edge of the property, and Kevin had to spend an hour on the phone with the state police explaining what it was they hadn't done.

Another mystery: in the middle of a war, in the middle of a dope weekend during which they were celebrating John Diefenbaker's eightieth birthday, a white Lincoln Town Car appeared at the end of the driveway, moving very slowly toward the house. When they walked up to it, the inside of the car seemed as shadowy as the inside of a house with the curtains pulled—the father at the wheel with a hat on, his face old and rheumy-eyed, as he powered the window down.

What he said had something to do either with the fact that the family used to live in the farmhouse and that it made them sad to come back and see it—or that they were just driving around from house to house talking to people out the car window about a woman in Argentina who was about to be made a saint or maybe was one already; from the way this guy spoke, they couldn't tell. He never completely stopped the car, just steered across the blue gravel of the driveway so slowly that you could hear individual stones popping out from under the tires.

It was theirs only by accident; the ground around the house couldn't absorb water fast enough for the property to pass the percolation test, meaning that the real estate company Danny worked for couldn't get a permit to tear down the house and subdivide the property. So Danny rented it from them and brought most of his friends up to split the rent.

It had more bedrooms than they would ever need to use, but it was hard to make plans. Nobody knew how long it would last. For some reason it seemed one of those family subjects that nobody wanted to talk about. Kevin seemed to be the only one who ever got worried; maybe the others were on a higher spiritual plane and never had to make themselves nervous thinking about the future. When he tried to bring the subject up around the High-Low Day Baseball table, it suddenly would be his turn to bet or check, all the eyes looking at him, tired of reminding him, and then he would look down at his cards and forget the rules of the game.

Another crisis: The electricity got turned off because the power company had been sending the bills to the real estate company instead of to the house, and the bookkeeper there didn't know what they were for, so he threw them away. Suddenly one Friday afternoon they found out that they owed a thousand dollars. In the candlelight of a long weekend, they sat around telling jokes until they couldn't think of any more. Then they played Sorry, but every time Roy got a good roll, he crowed like a rooster, until nobody could stand to play anymore.

On another weekend, three of Danny's friends who had just come up on their motorcycles went into town for beer. On the way back to the farm, one of them lost control of his bike and was killed. Nobody back at the house even knew that anything had happened until the kid was already dead and the police called from the local hospital. Danny and Kevin and Michael and Roy and Laura and the two Judys sat around the table that night in the yellow light, not saying much, a quiet night, without poker and without very much beer. Nobody at the farm had ever met the kid who got killed. They sat around trying to understand what it was like to feel sad about somebody whose name you can't remember.

It was sad, but they couldn't sit there and be quiet forever. Later that night, after Roy had gone back upstairs and there was nothing to do but go back to playing Lowball Anaconda Whiskey Barrel—being quieter than usual but not solemn—Danny's dog, Booger, wandered downstairs with a note on a file card hanging on a string from his collar.

"Read it," Danny said, studying his cards.

Kevin didn't want to read it aloud, so he made Booger walk over to where Danny was sitting.

"DEAR MASTER," Danny read, bending down slightly to read the card attached to the dog's collar, "I SURE WISH YOU'D HELP ME LEARN TO STAY OUT OF OTHER PEOPLE'S ROOMS, BECAUSE OTHERWISE I'M WORRIED THAT I MIGHT GET MY FUCKING HEAD BASHED IN."

Another night, later into the spring, around the dope table, Danny and Kevin spent almost an hour trying to figure out what that day's Canadian reason to drink Molson was, which made it even harder than usual to concentrate on the card game. The calendar had it listed as "Wickersham Day" without explanation. Danny said it just had to be from a cartoon. It was early enough in the evening that the New York Public Library was open. Kevin called to ask, but the person who answered the phone said that they no longer answered people's research questions.

"It has to be something," Kevin said, but it was hard to concentrate over a cookie sheet full of dope seeds rolling back and forth. He kept forgetting to play cards, and it was always his turn to bet, and then he had to go back and figure out whether the hand he held was any good or not and whether or not the queen holding the rose was supposed to be wild this time.

Maybe it was nothing, an instance of a truly Canadian sense of humor. Maybe somebody just put it on the calendar on the least important day of the Canadian year, but it didn't seem that they would make a joke about one of their own holidays.

Just then Roy appeared at the foot of the stairs with a very calm expression on his face, holding a dustpan in his hand, which he tilted gradually until a piece of dogshit dropped onto the floor.

Kevin looked around—a fight, maybe. Everything stood still in the kitchen, the way it does when there is going to be a fight. But there was no fight, just Roy's footsteps softer than usual, up the stairs and slowly down the upstairs hall, to his room, where he did not slam the door.

"Maybe that's what Wickersham Day means," Michael said and laughed at a high pitch.

"I don't get it," Kevin said.

"It means you throw dogshit on the floor."

"I must be stupid. I still don't get it."

Some mornings everybody's toothbrush froze. One weekend Michael fooled around in the barn and managed to get the old John Deere tractor running. He drove it around the edge of the property several times, letting people sit on the broad seat.

"I'm giving pony rides!" he shouted over the popping bursts of the old two-cylinder engine.

One Saturday everybody got together and tore up the old kitchen linoleum to get to the wide pine boards of the floor so they could sand them and coat them with clear acrylic. The linoleum turned out to have been put there so long ago that the lead story on one of the insulating newspapers under it said that Mahatma Gandhi had been assassinated.

Kevin had a job all spring working in the warm cooking smells of a company that supplied frozen meals to a hotel chain in the Caribbean whose tourist traffic kept speeding up and slowing down. One day they started giving everybody in the plant all the overtime they wanted, and two weeks later half the people got laid off. Kevin walked around the property in the daytime and played poker at night, until he was called back to work again.

In the summer it went for two months without raining. In the fall there was a war. On the day they celebrated Dominion Day—a real holiday that he'd actually heard of—he walked up and down the driveway with the latest news bulletins hanging like ice in his scrotum and wondered what it would look like when the round explosions began blooming to the south.

No bulldozers came. Kevin got called back to his job twice in the same month, and both times he jumped up and down on the coated wood floor of the kitchen, the way the grand prize winner always did on *The $100,000 Pyramid*.

Instead of the percolation test and the surveyors, something happened that he understood less well. It became harder and harder to get enough people together for a game of Lowball Spit-in-the-Ocean. Fewer and fewer people sat around the table sifting through a bread pan of dope seeds, even on days when there were seeds to sift. Notes on various colors and sizes of paper started appearing around the kitchen, asking people to leave the sink as clean as it was when they got to it or to wipe the crumbs off the table after they had eaten something.

Then one day somebody moved out, and suddenly there didn't seem to be enough gravity to keep the rest of the place from spinning away from the center. Within days, and without anybody planning it that way, everybody that was still living in the house had found other apartments, and all the cars that still ran were being loaded for the trip.

Kevin walked around inside the house, deciding what he wanted to take with him to the place he was going to rent and helping the other people carry things downstairs when they needed it. Nobody seemed angry, not even Roy. They just seemed to be drifting around in a daze, as if there were no more air. If somebody tried to say something, nobody would be able to hear it.

It would have been nice, even this late, to be able to bring up the topic of whether or not it was appropriate to leave notes and what effect notes have on the dynamics of a shared living situation—but since the nature of notes is that they have to be anonymous, talking about the notes in front of other people would have violated the privacy of the person who put them up.

Maybe it was only Roy and one or two others; he never found out. All he knew was that he'd never left a note in his life and never would. Houses need ground rules about notes, which was a thing that Kevin could think clearly about only when it was too late. Somehow, to make a large generalization, notes always lead to somebody's throwing dogshit on the floor. Maybe it would be better in some shared living arrangements if people could on the first day start throwing dogshit on the floor and not have to bother with the long process of notes, but even then it was hopeless. All he knew was that it never works out when people throw dogshit on the floor.

On the last night, Kevin was chopping with a screwdriver in the freezer compartment to help one of the two girls named Judy get some ice trays loose. Her car didn't run right unless it was fully warmed up, so she had it going outside as she carried things around and got ready.

"What's this?" she said, holding a tray under the faucet. She picked a wet file card from the melted frost on top of the tray and read out loud in the quiet of the house:

"BECAUSE NOBODY IS CONSIDERATE ENOUGH TO REFILL THIS ICE TRAY, IT IS NO LONGER PUBLIC DOMAIN. PLEASE DO NOT USE."

"Darling Roy!" she said.

Kevin was about to tell her some of his conclusions about notes, but he decided that even broaching the topic would be itself a little too much like leaving notes, and in this case it would be twice as ridiculous, because they would be addressed to somebody who was not coming back.

Judy steered down the long driveway into the dark, her engine speeding up and slowing down as she gunned it to keep from stalling. Kevin was almost finished loading his own car for the move, but he wanted to stay for a little while, all by himself in the old house. Of all the things you can do in an empty house, Kevin couldn't think of a single one that would have been worth it. You can run around naked or you can break windows, but whatever you do, it's just an empty space, with all the lights on, and dirt all over the place that you will never have to clean up.

What's weird about a note like that is that Roy must have written it months ago. And although it's true that people should refill ice trays and also true that he was probably one of the ones who sometimes didn't refill it, it was strange, and it kept getting stranger, to think that when somebody writes a note, you can still feel how angry that person is even when that person has moved away and is no longer angry.

He promised himself not to bring along any dreary, used broken furniture, even if he didn't have anything else. For the first couple of weeks in his new home, he would be better without such things, even if he had to sit on a flat rock. Two houses don't make a sample, but people had left notes in both the shared-rent houses that he had lived in, and in both of those houses somebody had ended up throwing dogshit on the floor.

In the kitchen, the light was on, bright against the painted walls. Kevin looked and looked. Danny had taken the calendar, so there was no way to tell what Canadian day it was. The only thing he could be sure of was that people all over Canada, and to a lesser extent all over the United States, would be drinking Molson, popping open the ice-cold bottles, but for the first time in months he didn't know what they were supposed to be celebrating. Everything was solid yellow in the light. He flicked the switch and the house was gone.

Endlings

KIRSTEN SUNDBERG LUNSTRUM

From *What We Do with the Wreckage* (2018)

Dr. Katya Vidović stands outside the hospital courtyard gate, watching the Reptile Man exercise his pets. He has come to entertain the girls—her patients—who are prone to unnatural behaviors when left unsupervised. They've been known to pull out their own hair by the fistful, to tattoo their inner arms and thighs with the sharp points of safety pins, to slip into the ward's bathroom and quietly vomit the contents of their last meal. Now, however, they sit like angels, their angular bodies arranged just so on the courtyard grass, their spindle-fingered hands folded in their laps as the leashed tortoise lumbers forward before them and the copperhead looks on—languid and apparently bored— from its glass terrarium.

Katya has seen this routine before, but, still, there is something captivating about it. Something fascinatingly grotesque about the bodies of the animals the man brings to display—the vaguely indecent projection of the tortoise's long neck and bulbous head from its shell; the constant, flickering whisper of the copperhead's tongue. Last year the man, who himself is a small and balding curiosity of a person, brought a bearded dragon, its body spined in tiny teeth. Another year, he brought a frilled lizard with a headdress like a mythological monster. These are animals built for other worlds, their bodies armed for hardships that they—in their captivity—will never see.

From her place outside the gate, she looks on as the man tours the tortoise between the rows of girls. Prim-faced Natalie Fletcher, eleven years old, is bold enough to reach out and stroke the knobbly shell. Thirteen-year-old Kristina Berg titters. The animal trundles past them all, indifferent, awkward on the soft turf of the lawn, its front legs bent like inverted knees. As the tortoise moves, the Reptile Man speaks to it in a coo. He does his job with an obvious affection, efficiency, nudging the tortoise back to its crate, where he rewards it with half a watermelon. The fruit glistens, flush red, and the tortoise rips into the rind, its alien face dripping with juice.

To close the show, the man turns to the snake. From beneath a drape, he produces a cage, and from the cage, a live mouse. A ripple of interest stirs the girls, who sit up straighter, crane to see. "In the wild," the man says, "copperheads are incredibly efficient eaters. They require as few as one or two meals per month." He lifts the terrarium lid and drops the white ball of fur inside.

The girls go silent. The snake raises its head.

Katya knows what's coming—a methodical if artificial hunt, a strike, a laborious but bloodless swallow. The girls, however, lap it up. This is hunger as theater, eating as a feat of will.

Scanning them now, she sees the usual responses: Rebekah Silver is covering her eyes; Alina Culbert is hugging her knees to her chest; and near the back, the pair of twins admitted just this morning—nine years old, and the youngest patients Katya's ever had—are sitting side-by-side, grimacing.

Only Simone Hunter seems to look on without revulsion. Simone Hunter—twelve. Admitted last week. Malnourished, amenorrheic, tachycardic. Five-foot-four and eighty-two pounds. Katya thinks over the girl's chart, straining to pull up her mental register of the psychiatrist's notes. She recalls just one word, scrawled in her colleague's soft hand on the page's margin—*Obdurate*. Such an uncharacteristically judgmental assessment. These girls are often perfectionists, narcissists. They are usually anxious or depressed and typically determined in their disordered perceptions of their own bodies and practices. Still, it's a strong word from Dr. Moore, and what the girl could have said in session to warrant it, Katya cannot imagine.

On the lawn, applause erupts—the show is over. The mouse is vanished. The Reptile Man bows, begins to pack up. The girls unfold themselves from their seated positions and stand to file back into the hospital. They will take the elevator up to the ward. Climbing the five flights of stairs is too much physical exertion for them, though surely at least one or two of them will beg for it.

"Come," Katya says, and she opens the gate. She is so accustomed to them, sometimes she forgets how frail they are, but she sees it now as they angle past her—their hollow cheeks still pinked with the excitement of the show, their long arms downed in the fine hair of their starvation, their pronounced scapulas like rigid wings poking up from beneath the fabric of their shirts. An aerie of girls. Or maybe a quiver.

When Simone Hunter passes, Katya stops her. "Did you enjoy it?" she asks. "The show?"

The girl hesitates. She has a broad moon of a face, even as thin as she is, and dark, hooded eyes. She looks Katya up and down, her expression hard. "Who doesn't enjoy a spectacle?" she says. She smiles, then, polite, and Katya dismisses her to follow the rest of the girls inside.

Before Katya took this position in Seattle, she was a medical fellow at an American program for girls with disordered eating in Boston; and before that she was completing her medical training in Louisiana; and before that she was a girl herself, living with her grandparents in the top-floor apartment of a house in Zagreb. The house was three floors tall and painted blue. It had a steep-sloped roof, under which Katya's tiny bedroom was tucked. It was a cozy room, except at night, when the shadows of the street below arced up and played on the ceiling's wooden slats. "The owls' puppet show," her grandmother told her, though even as a young child Katya knew that this was an adult's game, an attempt to soften the nightmarish quality of the dark shapes— the fluttered silhouette of a wing and the slithered shadow of a snake—that she was sure she was not mistaken in seeing.

The room—and therefore the angled ceiling and the shadows on it—had once been her mother's. Katya's grandparents had lived in the apartment since their marriage, and they had raised her mother—their only child—there. When Katya's mother died the year Katya was eight, they took her in and gave her the bedroom and everything in it—her mother's old doll with the rag dress, a set of cloth-covered books in a language Katya could not read, a chest full of bridal linens that her mother had never used—and it was as if time inside the apartment retracted, rolled back like a measuring tape snailing into its case. Her grandparents became younger than she'd first believed them to be, and she became an old woman in a little girl's body. This is the paradox of death for the living, Katya learned then: it both stops and accelerates time. It both reanimates the past and fossilizes the future, and everything but the observable present becomes subject to the unreliable whims of sentiment or fear.

In response to this, Katya became a scientist, devoted to the world of the visible and irrefutable. Each day after her classes let out, she walked home through Maksimir Park. In the autumn, she collected specimens of fallen oak leaves to study under the desk lamp in her bedroom. In the winter, she noted what differentiated the snow tracks belonging to squirrels from those belonging to rats. In the spring, she liked to sit in the grass along the bank of the lake, waiting for the dark blots hovering beneath the surface to emerge and prove themselves nothing other than turtles. Once out of the water, the turtles had the amazing ability to arrange themselves—five or six or seven at a time—at near even intervals along the length of a fallen tree branch, their nub feet somehow gripping the slick bark well enough to keep them from falling. *How?* Katya wondered. The world was wide and curious.

At home she would report whatever she had seen to her grandparents over dinner, and they would reply to these benign, physical observations of the natural world with a cheerful encouragement and unwounded interest that seemed impossible for them when Katya's conversation veered toward more personal subjects—where, for instance, her missing father might be, or why he had left before getting to know her, or what correlation might exist between his sudden absence and the slower kind of vanishing her mother had wished for and that her cancer had finally achieved. There were never any answers to these questions, and so—her grandparents made it clear to her when she was bold enough to speak them aloud—it was better not to ask them at all.

She was sixteen when the war began, and whatever she might have asked didn't matter anymore. She was sent to relatives in France for a few weeks, then to a cousin in England, and eventually she made her own way to university in the United States. During Katya's last year of medical school, her grandmother wrote to say that her grandfather had died—a stroke. Katya had exams she couldn't miss, and no money, and so she mailed her grandmother a letter of apology and did not get on a flight home. Time passed. Five years later, another letter arrived, this one from her grandmother's friend, saying that her grandmother, too, was gone—a bad flu, pneumonia, grief. Would Katya come back now?

It was winter when she got this letter, late February of 2008. In Boston, there was snow on the ground—thin, granular, dirty snow. It lay in shrinking circles around the trees and the curbs and the front stoops of the brick houses. It clung in thinning patches to the roofs and sills and the crotches of trees. It made the city hard and tight, black and white. Katya did not love this place as she had loved the blue house and the park and the country of her childhood, but what did that matter, really? She had not been a child for a long time. She had lived half her life elsewhere. And what would be left for her there now? She had seen television footage of the war and its scars—the streets buried in the bones of old buildings, roofs collapsed into the cavities of attics, tanks maneuvering their metal flanks through once quiet neighborhoods. The landscape had changed, and she would be a foreigner there now after so many years away—so many years in the relative comfort of her expatriate life. Her grandparents had sent her away for her own good—her own protection—and she was grateful; but she'd grown too soft to live in the echo of such brutality. She was no longer suited to withstanding hardship or ugliness or pain. She'd be a performance of privilege there at home among the wreckage, the wrecked—her naïveté an obscenity, a shame. She could never return.

To her grandmother's friend, she wrote, "I have adapted to my life here." *Sućut*, she signed her letter. Condolences. She slicked the tip of her tongue along the envelope's bitter edge, sealing it shut.

Monday morning. Katya is doing her usual rounds. When she enters Simone Hunter's room, she finds the girl on her bed, a spread of books and papers fanned before her on the white cotton blanket. "What's this?" Katya asks, her voice enameled in careful cheer. She remembers the strange stare the girl gave her the other day at the reptile show, the spiked syllables of the word *spectacle* as the girl spoke it. She remembers Dr. Moore's odd note: *Obdurate*. "Are you drawing pictures?" she asks now though, holding her buoyant tone. "I used to like to color too, when I was a girl."

Simone issues a sigh, does not look up. "I'm working," she says. "Do someone else's check up and come back to me."

A flush of heat rushes Katya's face. "Why don't you show me your work?"

"I don't like to be interrupted. The nurse was just here an hour ago. Nothing's changed. I said come back to me."

The girl sits with her knees folded, her back rounded, the scallop of her spine visible beneath the weave of her sweater. She has braided her own hair, and the braid hangs limp over one shoulder, several oily strands coming loose at her face. The room smells faintly of her body odor, of the fermented sweetness of her ketotic breath, of her books—which must be old. She needs a shower, a shampoo, a morning of conversation with the other patients rather than this self-imposed cloistering. Katya makes a quick note of all this on her chart.

"Simone," she says, sterner now, "I have to do my job here."

The girl turns, frowns. "Fine, then. Look if you have to." She nudges some of her papers toward Katya.

The girl's handwriting is neat, exact. These pages, Katya sees, are notes—extensive notes. From one page, she reads.

- *Question: Correlation between rise in materialist culture and extinction of native animal species? * 19th and early 20th c. = U.S. industrialization.*

- *Question: Rise in extinctions during Anthropocene due to environmental change or animal bodies as commodities?*
  (Ex 1: California grizzly hunted as major predator of ranched cattle. Cattle a commodity.
  Ex 2: Western black rhino hunted for medicinal value of its horn. Rhino a commodity.)

From another page, she reads a long list that the girl has titled "North American Extinct Species."

Canis lupus fuscus
(Cascade mountain wolf)
Habitat: British Columbia, Washington, Oregon
Extinct 1940

Cervus canadensis Canadensis
(Eastern elk)
Habitat: Southern Canada, eastern and southern
United States
Extinct 1880

Ursus arctos californicus
(California grizzly bear)
Habitat: Cascade range, northern California
Extinct 1920s?

On a third sheet, the girl has collaged an even more detailed catalog of individual animals, a black-and-white photocopied image of each cut and pasted above a written description of physical characteristics and habits. *Zalophus japonicus*, a Japanese sea lion; *Ara tricolor*, a Cuban parrot; and at the bottom of the page, a striped creature on all fours, its face depicted in profile so that its wide-open jaw gapes huge and toothy, dangerous, one snap away from swallowing the hole punch in the margin of the page.

"*Thylacinus cynocephalus*, the Tasmanian tiger," Katya reads aloud. "Extinctions."

"These are all extinct?" Katya studies the drawing of the last animal—the tiger, tracing its long body with her forefinger. It's odd looking, disproportionate, not actually a tiger at all but a poor amalgam of several other beasts—tail of a jungle cat, body of a wolf, thick head of a dog bred for fighting.

"Benjamin," Simone says, still without raising her head. She taps the end of her pencil on the striped animal.

"You name them?" Katya asks.

Simone lifts her eyes. "They're not my pets. This is my work."

"Right," Katya says. She examines again the image and the print beneath it, which reads, *Marsupial. Nocturnal. Carnivorous. Last of line, Benjamin, died in captivity, Hobart Zoo, 1936.* "He looks—" She searches for a word. "He looks vicious. That mouth."

The girl snatches the paper from Katya's hands. "You think like everyone else."

The bitterness in her voice takes Katya by surprise. "I'm sorry," she says.

"Just go," the girl tells her.

"Simone," Katya says.

"I said go. I don't want to be bothered now."

In the hallway, Katya opens the girl's chart, writes, *Aggressive, defiant. Not adapting to hospital routines. Refusal to comply.*

At the nurses' station, she directs the nurse on duty to take Simone's vitals in ten minutes. "No longer than ten minutes," she says. "Don't let her put you out."

The nurse nods. "Is everything okay, Dr. Vidović?"

"Everything is fine," she says, and she walks at a clip down the hallway to the next patient's room, her pulse like a wing caught in her throat.

That evening Katya is late leaving the hospital. There's traffic and rain, the freeway a black slick studded by a never-ending train of taillights. Only when she pulls to a stop on the street in front of her apartment building does she remember that Jen has invited guests for dinner—a new neighbor couple from down the hall, Chris and Meg; as well as Tom from school and his most recent girlfriend. The thought of the apartment filled with so many people at the end of the day is exhausting. Who plans a dinner party for a Monday night? Katya lets herself into the building, shakes the rain from her hair like a dog, and takes the stairs up.

Inside, the apartment is lit up like a holiday. Jen has music playing in the sitting room—something international, chipper and taut with the beat of hand drums and maracas. The air is heavy with the smell of curry.

"Home," Katya says from the door, and there's a ring of welcome calls before Jen appears, red hair and pink face beaming with the warmth and light of the evening, to kiss Katya hello. Her mouth tastes of onions.

"You're late," Jen says. "We started eating without you."

"That's fine."

"Not really," Jen says, "but I couldn't keep everyone waiting any longer."

Katya follows her through the warm kitchen and into the sitting room, where their guests are seated cross-legged on pillows around the wide coffee table. Jen makes introductions and Katya nods. "Good evening," she says. "I'm glad you've made yourselves at home."

"Sit," Jen says, her hand at Katya's back, a little shove toward the table. "I'll make you a plate."

Katya would like to beg off, slip away into the bedroom and lie down for a few moments, but she takes the empty pillow and lets Jen bring her a plate heaped with rice and saag and a red lentil something that sears the roof of her mouth as soon as she takes her first bite. There are three bottles of wine on the table, a blown glass jug of water, small ceramic bowls of chutney and yogurt and cilantro—all Jen's touch. When she moved into the apartment two years ago, Jen brought with her this skill for the domestic, and it seemed a revelation to Katya, who had learned to live like a visitor wherever she went, never certain she'd stay long enough to belong to any one place again. Jen filled the apartment with the makings of a home, however—soft blankets and deep cushioned chairs, bright artwork on the walls, flowers in the clay vase on the coffee table, the scent of good coffee issuing from the kitchen like a love note every morning. "This is a treasure," Katya had told her then, "your homeliness." But it hadn't translated, the word *homeliness*. They had their first domestic quibble over the confusion before Katya was able to make clear her intended meaning: "You know how to make a home, and I don't. That's all. No joking. I need this. I need you." She had meant it then, even if now, tonight, she's finding the artifice of it all so wearing.

Over their wineglasses, the others make small talk. The old lady who lives up in 4B has hired a cleaning woman; the new grocery around the corner has an olive bar that's to die for; someone's sister has had a baby. The conversation twines with the music, and Katya allows the two to become one thread of noise, constant and indeterminate. Behind her eyes, she sees the yellow aura of a headache just forming. She tunes in again just as Jen lays her hand on Tom's arm, says, "You're so bad."

Tom shrugs. "I think the name's Arabic for *lofty*, if you can believe that. I looked it up at the start of the year. She's Syrian. Well, her parents are."

"What are we discussing?" Katya asks, and for an instant the others stare at her.

"Kat," Jen says. A sigh.

"I'm sorry," Katya apologizes. "I've had a very long day. Please just go on with your story," she says to Tom.

Tom smiles—broad, benevolent, showy. He strikes Katya as the kind of man who is never sorry to hold the room's attention.

Tom says, "I was just telling everyone about this student I have. Little girl. She's difficult. Stubborn—but I can't say that at school." He winks at Jen. "We're supposed to say 'independent' and 'a girl who knows her own mind.'"

"Ha," Jen says.

"It's all bullshit to make the parents feel better," Tom explains.

"Because really it's their fault, right?" Tom's girlfriend says. "Doesn't everybody know the kid is always the parents' fault?" She's been silent up until now. She's young—younger than the rest of them, anyhow—and has the glassy-eyed look of having had one too many glasses of wine. Katya can't remember her name from the introductions, but she looks strikingly like Tom's last girlfriend, so she'd likely confuse the name even if she could come up with it.

"Of course it's the parents' fault," Jen says, lifting an eyebrow, smiling. "But the teacher can never say that."

The music quiets for an instant and starts up again, this time with the calypso tin notes of a steel drum. The room throbs at its hard lines—the edge of the coffee table, the square outline of the darkened window. Katya touches a damp fingertip to her temple where the seam of the headache is now stitching itself tightly to her skull.

Finally, Katya says: "Maybe your girl is just surviving."

"What's that?" Tom asks.

"Your terror student," Katya says. "The one you mentioned. Her parents are Syrian, you said? Immigrants? Refugees? It's hard to be the only one of your sort among strangers. Maybe she's just surviving. Maybe she requires more empathy than you're accustomed to showing."

For a moment no one speaks, then Jen stands. "I have dessert. Let me clear away these plates."

Meg leans forward. "You're an immigrant also?" It's a statement, but she inflects it like a question, an American habit Katya finds grating. *Say what you mean and mean what you say*, her grandmother used to tell her.

"I heard your accent when we first met and thought maybe Russia," Chris says.

"Christ," Jen says from the kitchen. "Don't say that."

"I was born in Zagreb. I've been here for years."

"Where is Zagreb?" the girlfriend asks. "Is that Poland?"

Tom says, "And you feel like you needed to *survive*? That's the word you used, and I'm curious."

"Tom," Jen calls from the kitchen. "Could you come carry bowls for me?"

He continues, though. "I'm just interested. Because I am empathetic. I am empathetic to my kids, you know."

"You don't have to defend yourself to me," Katya says, shrugging. She wants to slip away to the bedroom, close the door, vanish.

Tom smiles, tight. "We're misunderstanding each other, I think, Kat. It's just interesting, your perspective. You have a unique perspective."

Kat, she thinks, taste of bile at the back of her tongue. "Of course," she says. "Of course we are misunderstanding each other. You're right." She presses a thumb to each temple, circles them once, twice. The calypso song seems to be doing laps around the room. "Does this song never end?" she asks. An uncomfortable laugh from across the table.

Meg turns to her. "We've talked about visiting Croatia, Chris and I. There are those waterfalls. *Plitvice*. Is that how you'd say it? The park. It looks beautiful. But we've thought maybe best to give it a few more years."

"I'm sure that park is beautiful," Katya says. "I've never been."

"Never been?"

Katya shakes her head. "Have you been to every park in America?"

"Do you go home often?" Chris asks.

"I was a child when I left, and there was a war. I haven't been back."

"Your family's here too, then?"

"There is no one left," Katya says. Her impatience throbs in her head. She looks to Tom. "I'm sure I was as beastly as your Syrian just after I left Zagreb. War doesn't allow for homesickness. What is there to miss when there's nothing recognizable left?"

"They've rebuilt, though," Meg says, chipper. "I've seen photographs of the region, and it's mostly restored."

I have not been rebuilt, Katya thinks, but she restrains herself from speaking.

For a long minute, no one says anything, and then Jen returns, a tub of ice cream in one arm and a stack of bowls in the other. "Who has room?" she asks.

Katya stands. "I'm sorry. If you'll all excuse me." She shuts off the music on her way out of the room.

For the rest of the evening, she waits in the bedroom, her head on her pillow and a cool washcloth on her face. She is there when Jen finally comes in, the last of the guests gone.

"That was rude," Jen says. "They meant well."

Katya rolls to her side and takes the cloth from her eyes. "People always mean well. I have a headache."

"Of course you do."

"I worked today. I'm tired. We shouldn't have parties on weeknights anymore."

"You had no obligation but to show up on time and eat. That's it."

"Come lie with me."

"I smell like the kitchen. I need a shower."

Katya watches Jen take off her clothes, walk to the bathroom nude. Jen has fair reddish hair and skin the pale pink of—*Of what?* Katya thinks. Of a sea rose, of a scallop's flesh. *Jakovska kapica.* Flavor of salt and brine, slick mound of meat like a pale pink tongue on the spoon of its shell. Katya made herself sick on such scallops one Christmas when she was small—their taste was so good. Her mother was still living then, and she had chided Katya about gluttony, about knowing when you've had enough, about self-control. "*Pohlepna djëvojka!* Good girls take less than they need." Katya's never understood what that was supposed to mean, virtue tied so senselessly to the absence of need. Only humans would entwine the two. Biologically, need is survival. Those who crave and seek and satisfy—they survive.

She gets up and removes her own clothes, opens the bathroom door to a billow of steam. Behind the glass shower door, Jen has her face dipped beneath the water's stream. "Why do you have to be so difficult?" Jen asks. "Why can't you just be normal, you know? Blend in? They're nice people, Kat. Really they are."

"I try."

"No you don't," Jen says. She has not lifted her face from beneath the water. "I need more from you."

"Look at me," Katya says, and Jen shifts, raises her head. "Your friends have made me lonely."

She waits, still, letting the splatters of water hit her feet while Jen's eyes decide.

"Please," Katya says.

"I'm angry."

"Please."

Jen sighs, and Katya steps into her arms.

Two weeks pass. When Katya arrives at the hospital for her Wednesday morning rounds, Dr. Moore is waiting at the nurses' station, frustration on her face. "What is it?" Katya asks, and they step into the small conference room and close the door.

At the table, Simone Hunter and her parents are already seated. The parents are exactly what Katya would have expected—slim and well dressed and the farther side of middle-aged. The father is spectacled, silver haired, wearing a suit. He'll be on his way to a bank or a law office or the boardroom of a tech company the moment this meeting is over. The mother is Simone plus forty pounds and forty years. Simone herself sits between them—sallow, skeletal—and every few seconds one of her parents looks at her with an expression of blinking fear, as if she is all their shared shame and anxiety caged behind bones and skin.

Dr. Moore begins. "Simone, as you'll remember, we agreed that you would gain at least two pounds per week." The doctor slides a sheet of paper from a manila folder on the tabletop—a copy of the contract all new patients sign at admission, agreeing to the nutritional and behavioral plans the program draws up for them. At the bottom of the contract, Simone's tight SH are faint on the signature line.

"That's not a contract; it's a punishment," Simone says.

"Simone," her mother starts. "We love you. Please."

Simone sits rigidly in her chair and does not turn her face to her mother. "You love me when I do what you want," she says.

Her mother looks to Dr. Moore, to Katya. "I'm so tired of everything becoming a battle. This is ridiculous. We're not her enemies." To her daughter, she says again, "We're not your enemies, Simone."

Simone's face is a stone. "And I'm not your lapdog."

A muscle flickers at her mother's temple and jaw. "I can't do this," she says. "I can't do this game of yours anymore."

Dr. Moore raises a hand, and they both go quiet. "Simone, I understand," the doctor says, "that you do not feel you have the control you'd like over your diet right now, but you do know that we are your team—all of us here—and we are not going to force you into anything unhealthy."

"Do you hear Dr. Moore, Simone?" her father asks. He leans toward his daughter but does not look at her—cannot, it seems to Katya, bear to look at her. When he straightens in his seat again, he is weeping silently, this tall man in his suit. He withdraws a square handkerchief from inside his suit jacket and wipes his eyes.

Dr. Moore turns to Katya. "Dr. Vidović, please explain to Miss

Hunter the next step in her treatment if she is unable to gain the necessary two pounds per week."

Katya swifts a strand of hair from her face, puts her elbows on the table. "It is simple, but—I will not lie to you, Simone—it is unpleasant. Do you know what a nasogastric tube is?"

"This isn't fair," the girl says. "This is not fucking fair." At her sides, her parents wince as if she's slapped them. "I'm not having a feeding tube."

Katya shakes her head. "It will not be for you to say."

Dr. Moore raises a hand again, stopping Katya. "Simone," she says, "you do have a choice now."

"You're liars," the girl says. The skin of her face has gone as hard as wax after the candle has been snuffed out. She narrows her gaze at Katya. "You will not touch me. Do you hear me? You will not touch me."

Katya meets her stare. "My job is to keep you alive," she says. "I will do my job."

"I think we can take it from here, Dr. Vidović," Dr. Moore says. "Thank you for making time in your morning to join us."

Katya leaves, closing the door behind her, and tells the nurse on duty at the desk that she needs a moment before continuing her rounds. She takes the elevator to the cafeteria, gets in line for a yogurt and a cup of coffee, finds a table in the corner where no one else is sitting. She's not hungry, but she peels the lid from the yogurt container and eats. The yogurt is thick and cold, the goo of fruit preserves at the bottom of the cup so sweet it makes the salivary glands at the back of her mouth ache.

One of the few things her mother would still eat even at her worst was jam—apricot jam spread on a wafer cracker; strawberry preserves taken a half-a-teaspoon at a time, like medicine; plum jam made from the fruit of the tree behind their house. Because of this, Katya's grandmother kept the cupboard stocked with jars—beautiful jars that glowed red and purple and translucent orange, jewels on the papered shelf above the breadbox. On Saturday afternoons, she and her grandmother often bought a flat of whatever fruit was at the market, brought it home, and stood at the stove boiling it down. *For your mama*, her grandmother would say. *For your mama's good health.*

Then later, in her mother's room, which stank with the florid, fermented smell of illness, Katya would lift a baby spoon from the jar to her mother's mouth, feeding her the preserves. *Please, Mama*, she'd beg again and again. *I need you to try.* And when it opened, she'd see against her will her mother's mouth, raw with sores, as pink and pulpy as a peeled blood orange, the tongue like a raspberry. *Click*, the spoon would sound against her mother's yellowed teeth. *Click.* A horrible sound, but it was necessary. For her mother's survival, Katya had to keep lifting the spoon, waiting for the swallow.

In the end none of it mattered, though. It was not enough. In the end, her mother needed nothing, was hungry for nothing, would eat nothing. She drank water that ran through her and came out in the bedpan as clear as it had gone in. "You see?" she'd said one day as Katya took the pan from beneath her. "There is nothing left of me. I'm gone. I've become a sieve. Nothing can hurt me, *moj mačić*. It all just passes through. Nothing can hurt me anymore." Katya had bent to kiss her mother's cheek and the skin was like wax paper under her lips.

In the cafeteria, Katya wads her napkin into a ball and gets up. "Get back to work." She says it aloud without intending to, then looks around, embarrassed, but there's no one near enough to have heard her.

In the corridor, she's waiting for the elevator up when the doors open and the Hunters step out.

"Dr. Vidović," Simone's mother says.

"My morning's quite full," Katya says. She reaches out to hold the elevator door.

"Just one minute of your time," the father says. His face is drawn, his pallor gray, his eyes still red rimmed from the crying.

"Okay," Katya says. A sigh. She lets the door close. "But I have just one moment."

"They've signed another contract," the mother says, outrage edging her voice. "The doctor—that psychiatrist—she's let Simone manipulate her. I love my daughter, but she lies, doctor. She's lying to you all. And she's stubborn. She's not going to eat now if she hasn't already. She won't change, and how long can we let this go on? Do you see what I'm saying? She's a danger to herself. That's why we brought her here. At some point, Simone simply has to be fed, whether she wants that or not." The mother steps close to Katya, grips her wrist with a cold hand. "You see what I'm saying here, doctor? She's a minor. I'm not even sure why we're letting her think she has a choice about this anymore."

Katya withdraws her arm, holds it behind her back. "I understand your concern, Mrs. Hunter."

"Do you?" the father asks. "Because it doesn't seem like that. It doesn't seem like anyone here is really doing anything productive."

The elevator dings.

"Take away her animals," the mother says. Her eyes are wide now and frantic. "Those drawings she does—her horrible books—they're morbid. They encourage her. Take them away until she agrees to eat."

Katya frowns. "I am not a schoolteacher, Mrs. Hunter. You should speak to Dr. Moore about your disciplinary concerns."

"You're not listening," the father says.

"I am listening. I understand your worry." Katya steps toward the elevator.

"You're leaving?" the mother asks. "You're just going to leave?"

"I understand your concern," Katya tells her. There's the

golden shush of the doors opening, Katya gets in, pushes the button for the fifth floor.

"That's not good enough. You need to do something," the father says. "We came here so you people could treat her. Why aren't you doing your damn job?"

"It is not that simple, Mr. Hunter," Katya says. There's heat behind her eyes, heat like shame prickling her cheeks.

"You're the doctor," the father says. "We trusted you."

"Yes," Katya says. She pushes the button once more. "You're right to trust the staff."

"Our daughter is killing herself." The father is near tears again, his voice pleading. To his wife he says, "Can nobody hear us?"

"I hear you," Katya says, and the doors close.

She presses her back against the wall, clutches the handrail. *Move*, she thinks, willing the elevator doors not to open on the parents again. *Move*. It takes what seems like several seconds before she feels the movement of ascension, the stomach-swirl of gravity's tug inside her body, and she can relax. "God," she says. Her heart is still racing. She tips her head back and catches an image on the ceiling. What is it? She's disoriented until she realizes she's looking at a mirror, seeing herself reflected—white wings of her coat, white round of her face. She lifts her arms to be sure, and the reflection follows her. Flap. Flap. It is her, after all. *A little bird*, she thinks. *A little bird trapped in a cage of its own making.*

That night, home late again, Katya finds a note from Jen on the kitchen counter: *Out to the movies with Tom. Plate for you in the fridge. Back late. Don't wait up. XOXO.* She takes the plate to the desk in the bedroom, opens the laptop, eats the ham sandwich while reading the day's news. Political unrest in the UK. A black man beaten and left bleeding for an hour on a dark street in St. Louis. A new mosquito-borne virus in South America. She remembers Simone's tiger then—what a horrible world, full of dangers, monsters. She wants to see how much liberty Simone took with her drawings, and so she Googles Tiger + Benjamin + Australia. Immediately, a strip of black-and-white images materializes on her screen. *Benjamin, the last known Tasmanian tiger. Captured 1933, died 1936.*

The animal is just as odd as she has remembered, just as the girl rendered it—long caninelike head and pointed ears; muscular, striped body; tail of a jungle cat. She clicks a YouTube link and watches BBC footage of the animal in its enclosure at the Hobart Zoo. It stalks back and forth across her screen. The enclosure appears to be small, nothing but a cement paddock, fenced on all sides. For an instant, the animal pauses in its pacing and looks into the camera, its eyes fixed, alert, undeniably frantic. It opens its massive jaw in—what? A growl? A yawn? A cry? There is no sound to this old film. The screen goes black.

Katya pushes refresh and watches the clip again and again and again. It is compelling, but why? And why, in particular, for Simone? What does the girl get out of all her note-taking and categorizing? Anorexics long for control—she knows this. And there must be some measure of satisfying control for Simone in the keeping of data. Katya remembers her own observations of the turtles and fish and foliage at the park as a girl, the safe certainty and constancy of fact against the frightening helplessness of her life in those years after her mother's death. Perhaps it is just this for the girl, too—control in order, self-protection in control.

She scrolls, lands on a nature documentary about Australians who believe they've seen Tasmanian tigers recently, living examples still eluding human capture out in the woods. "They're a menace," a pink-scalped man in a rain poncho says into the camera. "They're predators. They'd kill a child if they felt threatened or hungry. They'd terrorize our national parks." A voiceover contradicts the man, citing evidence of the tiger's weak jaws, incapable, even, of killing a sheep.

Katya chuffs at the screen. "Alarmist," she says into the empty bedroom.

She's still at the computer several hours later when the front door sounds—Jen home. Katya closes the laptop, gets up, and finds Jen in the kitchen, filling the kettle with water. "It's late for tea, no?" she says. She rubs a circle on Jen's back. "Why don't you come to bed?"

Jen turns away, pulls a mug from the shelf. "I'm cold. I couldn't sleep now anyway."

"I'll drink with you, then. The movie was good?"

Jen sighs. "I didn't see a movie. I just went to dinner. With Tom. We talked."

"Oh?" Katya says, though her stomach drops. It's dark in the kitchen, the only light coming in dimly from the hallway, and she cannot see Jen's face well enough to read it, to read what she is sensing beneath Jen's words.

"I'm not having an affair with him, if that's what you're thinking."

"I wasn't thinking that. My god, should I have thought that?" All the blood in Katya's body seems to rush to her bowels, hot. *Flee*, she feels her body thinking. *Fly!* She fights the impulse and forces herself to stand perfectly still.

"I just—. I don't think we're working anymore, Kat."

"I don't understand what you're telling me."

On the stove, the kettle blows a high, wet note, and Katya rushes to remove it from the burner. The cirrus of steam issuing from the spout scalds her hand before she can think, and she drops the kettle, pulls her hand close to her chest, cradles it.

"Jesus," Jen says, righting the kettle. "Are you okay?"

"I want you to tell me what you're saying. What your meaning is. I think I'm misunderstanding."

Jen shakes her head. "Don't do that. Don't play that game. Your English is perfect. You're not misunderstanding."

They drink their tea sitting side by side on the couch, not speaking. In her mind, Katya still sees the Tasmanian tiger pacing its square pen, turning, opening and closing its soundless mouth. It occurs to her that when the film was made, the animal was already the last member of the species. Everyone watching him circle his artificial den knew what the animal could not know—that there would be no more of him. He was the end.

"Why?" Katya says to Jen. "Have I done something wrong?"

"Oh, Kat." Jen's voice floats, disembodied in the dark room.

"It won't feel like home here without you."

"For a little while maybe. Not forever," Jen says. "You're barely ever here anyway. You'll get used to it."

"That's not fair," Katya says.

"No, it's not."

Katya gets up and crosses to the kitchen, dumps the last of her tea into the sink. "I should never have let myself become comfortable," she says.

"Stop it," Jen says. "Don't make yourself a victim. You've never been comfortable here. You've never acted like my partner in this—"

She nods at the apartment. "It was never really what you wanted anyway. I saw it the other night. You couldn't even sit through a dinner party. You can't do it."

"That's not true," Katya says. "I did want this. I do."

Jen stands. "I'm tired," she says. "I'm going to bed."

Katya watches her go. She feels the whole night rushing through her like wind down a vacant street. She cannot catch it. She cannot pull it back.

"You'll be fine," Jen calls from the bedroom. There is the *click* of the door shutting.

The next morning Katya wakes to find Jen already up and packing a suitcase. She'll come back for the rest of her things, she says. She's going to stay with Tom until she finds another place. It's best not to drag things out. They say goodbye at the door—a stiff embrace—when Katya leaves for work.

At the hospital, Katya arrives to the news that Simone's weight has dropped again and she must attend to the intubation before seeing any other patients. But, of course, the girl is stubborn. She refuses the NG tube. She refuses the sedative offered. She refuses to lie still. A second nurse appears at the bedside, then a third. One nurse holds Simone's right arm, one her right foot, one her left. She's given a sedative by injection. When Katya squirts the lidocaine into her nose, Simone turns her head and vomits a spill of yellow bile onto her pillow.

"Enough," Katya says. "This is enough, Simone. You must calm down." A nurse hands her a cool cloth, and she touches it to Simone's face. Another nurse brings a clean pillow and removes the soiled one. Simone's breath slows.

"That's it," Katya says, encouraging. "That's it, *dragi moj.*" The endearment comes out of her mouth before she thinks—a hush, fluttering up to her tongue from the deep of her mind. Her mother used to whisper it to her when she woke from nightmares as a child. It startles Katya, but she doesn't pull away. She strokes Simone's forehead. "You'll be fine," she says. "You can trust me."

"I never wanted any of this," the girl says.

"Look at me," Katya tells her, and when Simone does, she recognizes the dark gaze of feral panic, determined fear. "Just hold my hand now. You're not alone." The girl complies, her hand frigid, shaking, and Katya closes her own around it.

It takes no time after that. Katya is good at this part of her job. This is something, she tells herself—this steadiness in the midst of crisis. This is something not every person can manage.

"Lie back," Katya says when it is finished. She props another clean pillow behind Simone's back. "You need to rest now."

"Don't leave yet," the girl says, and Katya nods.

Through the fabric of her shirt, Simone's clavicle is a blade, a brace, a buttress. Her skin has the fragile, filmy look of tissue. Her lips are the pale gray of a winter sky.

Katya says, "You know, after you showed me your work, I looked for your friend, your tiger. I watched his movie, online."

Simone's eyes are heavy with the drugs, the exertion of her struggle and her submission, but Katya sees her listening.

"I've been thinking about him," she goes on. "He was beautiful. I've been thinking they should not have locked him up."

The girl moves her hand inside Katya's—agreement.

Katya thinks again about the tiger pacing round and round its square cell—about that look of fury and fear in his eyes when he faced the camera and opened his mouth. She wants to attribute virtue to it—emotion—but she knows better. There is purity in an animal's desire, though; there is benefit to following instinct. The tiger could not have grieved or yearned—could not have known that nothing waited for him beyond the fence. He could only know what kept him alive in the wild—self-protection, hunger, isolation. It was not his fault that his body, his mouth full of teeth, left him unsuited to the human world.

She looks again at the girl, but Simone is sleeping, her head dropped to one side, her jaw slack. Her breath smells with the sweet stink of wasting, and Katya is called back to her mother once more, her mother at the end. This same smell in the little room with the sloped ceiling. Owl's wing and turtle's shell. That bow of branches seen in double—the thing and its reflection—at the pond in Maksimir Park. Fine stone Xs of the stone-boned Zagreb cathedral ceiling at Christmas mass. These visions are in her. She carries them, just as the girl carries the facts she has gathered about her extinct species, her examples of life lived on the margins and in the gaps. Katya thinks: *Without the body, the world extinguishes.* She thinks: *Without the body to catch it, the world drains away and is gone.* This, maybe more than anything else, is what we are meant for—not our own survival, but this devouring. And perhaps the isolated, the lonely, the left-behind— those least suited to peaceable adaptation—are best at this particular kind of hunger. Perhaps, like the tiger, it is this hunger that always ends them alone.

The room is warm and still; and in the bed, the girl has begun to snore softly. Katya releases her hand and stands. Later, she will speak to Dr. Moore. Later, she will call the girl's parents. Now, however, she has other patients to attend to, other work to do.

The Starlings of Leicester Square

PETER MEINKE

From *The Piano Tuner* (1986)

"I understand," the boy said. They were looking at a snapshot of four generations.

"No, you don't," the man said. "This was snapped right here in Leicester Square, in front of the statue of Shakespeare, because everyone thought I was a writer. I tried, but couldn't do it. I'd sit all morning and bang out a few lines, and everyone said they were terrific, but no one would publish them unless I paid for it. So everyone said you need an agent to get published, but you can't get an agent unless you're already published. I was a great disappointment to your mother. She thought she was marrying the new Shakespeare because I won the Senior Poetry Prize. It all seems bloody stupid now. For five years I sat at that typewriter with my thumb up my nose while your mother supported us. Have you lost your voice?"

"Hello."

"Jolly good." He had signaled the waiter in the Swiss restaurant to come over. "This wine is wretched," he said. "Bring us something decent: a Neuchâtel red, chilled." The waiter said nothing, but picked up the bottle and padded off. It was clear he didn't believe the man, who was dressed, below his good sportsjacket, in jeans and filthy sneakers.

"This is you," the man continued, "on my lap. You were a fat thing, and your head came out like a zucchini. And that's your grandpa, who is still a fat thing, and that proper Englishman with the mustache and the stiff lower lip is your great-grandpa. Was. He never forgave me for marrying an American, and Jewish to boot. He told me it would never work out. Quite right, too. Would you like this picture?"

"I don't know," the boy said.

"Then to hell with it." The man crumpled the photograph and stuffed it in his cup of coffee, which spilled over the printed table-cloth. "If you don't want something hard enough"—his voice rose and diners at the nearby tables turned their heads—"then to hell with it."

The boy sipped his coffee and said nothing. He looked at the man steadily, without expression. He was a tall boy, pale, with brown curly hair and the faint beginnings of a mustache.

"That's what your mother did to me," the man said, "hard-hearted bitch. Sorry," he added, as the boy raised his chin. "She did the same thing with old Rex when he got flatulent, just chucked him out. Said she couldn't breathe the air and he was staining her nice little ruggies. Waiter!"

The waiter stood silently, staring at the tablecloth.

"There's been a terrible accident, a frightful accident," the man said. "This time I'd like an Irish coffee, put in a double scotch instead of whiskey." The waiter carried away the cup with the crumpled photograph bobbing on the surface.

"But she liked this square, all the birds, all the trees—that's why I thought we could meet here. You've changed, you're look-ing more and more like her. Little eyes. But you're tall—in two years I'll be a shrimp next to you. She liked these big ugly knobby trees with the peeling bark and a thousand starlings on every limb, and I liked all the theaters around them, so it was a spot we could get together on. What do you feel, sitting here?"

"I don't know," the boy said again. "Nervous, I guess." He paused. "But not *very* nervous."

"Yes, just like your mother. She was not very anything. That's American, I think." He leaned back, waving his arms and teetering in his chair. "But we're all Americans now. We queue up for burgers and milkshakes and pizza and *Star Trek VII*. Bloody joggers all over the city, knocking down old ladies and picking them up again, nice as pie. Confess, you're a jogger, am I right?"

"Yes," said the boy. "I'm on the track team at college."

"I knew it. You have that lean and hungry look that worried Caesar. Do you think too much? Are you a dangerous young man?" He pulled out a mashed pack of cigarettes. "What kind of young man are you?"

"Just average," the boy said. "Not dangerous. I'm studying to be an engineer."

"Yes, all American boys become engineers, don't they? It must be a law of some sort. They build and they knock it down, they build and they knock it down. I would think it's exhausting."

"I have to go," the boy said, beginning to rise from the table.

"No!" The man put his hand on the boy's thin wrist. "Please don't go, it's been so many years. I know I'm not doing this well, I'm out of practice, is all. Don't go." The boy sat down again, but perched on the edge of his chair like a fledgling ready to test his wings. "Do you know what I do for a living?" the man asked. "Does your mother ever tell you how I make the money I send?"

"She says you do all right."

"I sell mail and laundry chutes to apartment buildings. It's quite profitable, actually. Better than bloody sonnets or short stories, what a fool I must have been! Everybody needs them—chutes I mean, not sonnets. Letters and dirty laundry, that's what the world's about. But at twenty-one"—he patted his pockets, looking for the photograph—"who knows that? And I think I was the youngest man ever to reach the age of twenty-one, I was that silly. Your mother liked that for a while, staying up all night to see the sunrise, sitting in the park waiting for the starlings to come out, things like that. You know what I like about you?"

"What?" said the boy.

"You look people in the eye, that might be American, too: the English have trouble doing that. We tend to stare at a light fixture while we talk, haven't you noticed?"

"You look at your drink," the boy said, and the man laughed, beckoning the waiter. "A pint of ale to stare at," he said to the waiter. He winked at the boy. "Never mix, never worry."

"That makes white wine, red wine, scotch, and beer," the boy said. "You won't get sick?"

"Sick?" said the man. "I'm dead. Your mother killed me. She was a keeper-tracker, too. 'That's your fourth,' she'd say. 'That's our sixth movie this month, that's the tenth time you said that, that's the twelfth time you've gone to the loo.' She got tired of my spending her money, I suppose; it must have bored her, cheering me up all the time. So she went back to Newport, la dee da, and took you with her. Do you like America, really?"

"I do," the boy said, "I like it a lot. I've met nice people."

"They're nice if you're not black or Mexican or Polish, whatever. Your mother told me some stories."

"Just read the papers," said the boy. "I mean the English papers."

"Yes, people prefer their own, don't they? Paint your bum green and sooner or later someone will shoot you. Only natural, after all."

"I really have to go. I have a date."

"Listen, did your mother ever tell you what we did the first time I was away from you? I flew to America; we had this crazy idea that American publishers would like my work better than the English publishers did. I was only going to be gone a week. You were about two years old and we were afraid you'd forget me, so we made a dozen copies of my passport photograph and pinned them all around your crib, probably scared you to death. Did she tell you that?"

"What did the publishers say?" the boy asked.

"Never saw them," the man said. "I stayed at the Algonquin and got terrified by the whole thing. I'd look up an editor's address and walk around the building and duck in the nearest pub for a drink. Came home in three days. She had taken down the photographs. You had eaten one of them apparently. She never told you that?"

The boy was standing, shrugging into his jacket. He took the man's hand. "Good-bye," he said. "Take care." He strode off on long thin legs.

The man turned around to watch him. He struggled to rise, then sat down again, pulling out his wallet. "He's a good lad," he told the waiter. "Did you hear him? 'Take care,' he said. He has every reason"—he held the waiter's eye—"*every reason* to dislike me. And still he said, 'Take care.' I bloody well will, too."

Through the windows he could see the starlings swooping and swerving over the bright marquees, in and out of the tall plane trees, mirroring the dense crowd below as we surged toward our dim and irresistible destinies.

Hope Springs

TONI GRAHAM

From *The Suicide Club* (2015)

> Even though thou seekest a body,
> thou wilt gain nothing but trouble.
>
> —*TIBETAN BOOK OF THE DEAD*

Slater steps onto the front porch to scoop up the morning newspaper. When he stands, he finds himself looking up at the eaves, just above the mailbox. Only yesterday, there was a large wasps' nest there. He is embarrassed to admit to himself that he had not realized what the thing was. Living in Manhattan had not exactly made him an expert on Oklahoma entomology, unless one counted a nodding acquaintance with cockroaches. But he had received a sharply worded note from his mailman: unless he removed the nest, there would be no more home delivery.

He is so allergic to stings that he has to carry an EpiPen to avoid anaphylaxis, so he was chary of dealing with the nest himself, and he sure as hell was not about to ask his wife to do it for him. At first, when looking through the Yellow Pages for a bug-extermination service, he was unable to find any. He soon realized that the heading "exterminators" no longer existed. Bug killers were now termed "pest control" experts. Slater felt like a wuss for seeking one at all. He remembered his father going out on the back patio of their family home carrying a Louisville Slugger and, with a powerhouse swing that would make Bonds on 'roids look tame, sending a nest flying from the patio.

When the pest control van drove up yesterday morning, things grew rapidly worse: the exterminator was a woman. Slater was given the humiliating task of standing by while a petite female with a blond ponytail sprayed the nest with a can of something and then collected 125 ducats for being braver than the man of the house.

Though Slater had always thought his father was manlier than he was, he had not realized the old man was a stand-up guy until Poppy was gone. He and his sisters had often complained about what a coldhearted guy Poppy could be, and his suicide certainly seemed to confirm their opinion. Later, though, they learned that Poppy was a serial blood donor who had earned several plaques and a write-up in the Albany newspaper for record-breaking donations, that he had always given 15 percent of his income to Jewish charities, and that he had designated himself an organ donor. This last was not to be—the mandated autopsy interfered with Poppy's attempt to give part of his body to someone who needed it more than he did.

Slater and his sisters were stunned three months ago when legions of mourners showed up for Poppy's memorial service, people they had never before seen—weeping, all of them, as if these strangers themselves were Poppy's family. Droves of them approached Slater, tearful or sobbing, to tell him what a wonderful man Isaac had been, how he had chauffeured them around, cooked for them when they were sick, come to their kids' graduation ceremonies and bar mitzvahs, always weighed down with food and gifts. Their tears dried up momentarily when they began regaling Slater with tales of how funny Poppy had been, how he had been able to coax them out of their darkest moments with his good cheer and his hilarious jokes. Poppy, it seemed, was perceived by everyone but his family as a hybrid of Santa Claus, Robin Williams, and David Ben-Gurion.

Before retirement Poppy was a longshoreman, a thinking man's dockworker like Eric Hoffer. When he was young, he met Hoffer and even knew Harry Bridges, and he remained a staunch union man until the day he took his own life. Suicide or not, everyone else at the funeral seemed to have believed all along that Poppy was a mensch.

Now a lone wasp buzzes on the porch, flying frantically around the spot where the nest used to hang. The poor schmuck, thinks Slater, it went out for a while and came back to discover there has been some sort of wasp holocaust, leaving him alone in the world. Slater cannot help it, he feels bad for the creature and rather wishes he had not caved in to the mail carrier.

Back in the kitchen, he decides he would rather go out for breakfast and turns off the kettle. He knows his wife will sleep for at least another hour, so he leaves a note on the whiteboard: *Beth—Went to Sancho's—back soon.* Usually he vets students' projects on Saturday mornings before he and Beth go out for a bike ride, but he has a hankering for huevos rancheros. Granted, the eggs will be Oklahoma style, not Tex-Mex, so he knows the unmistakable flavor of ketchup will taint the dish. The "Mexican" restaurant in Hope Springs is a place called Siesta Sancho's, which has a red and green neon sign bearing a logo, the form of a man slumped against a wall with a sombrero pulled over his eyes, the prototypical racist vision of the lazy Mexican. The restaurant also sells T-shirts with the same snoozing image on the front. The shirts with the dozing, mustachioed, sombreroed Hispanic are pervasive in the town of Hope Springs.

He goes quietly into the bedroom, where Beth sleeps belly-down, breathing deeply, her gray-flecked black hair curtaining one eye, an arm flung across the spot where Slater slept. In the mornings she has begun to give off what he thinks of as a doughy smell, like sourdough bread except less appealing. Nothing that comes with aging is beautiful or fresh—this much he knows. And if Slater is repelled by his wife's yeasty smell, she has complained somewhat bitterly that he often "reeks" of garlic. Maybe her doughy smell and his garlicky smell commingle in their bed to mimic the scent of Texas toast.

Slater picks up from the floor a pair of Levi's and his Tool T-shirt and slips them on. Oh, shite, the T-shirt conjures a less-than-pleasant recollection. He wore the Tool tee on campus earlier this week, nearly late for teaching his senior seminar. While normally he would have worn at least an Oxford-cloth shirt and khakis, dressing in jeans and a T-shirt is acceptable in his department—the architecture professors never dress up the way some of the other faculty do. A few of the guys in English and in Theater are downright fops. But wearing the Tool shirt turned out to be a particularly unfortunate choice. As he rushed across the parking lot and toward the architecture building, he heard a girl, probably an undergraduate, say to her friend—not even bothering to lower her voice—"I bet he *is* a huge tool, too." Her friend laughed.

Was simply being a fifty-nine-year-old noticeably balding guy wearing a rock-band T-shirt reason enough to be considered a frickin' tool? Maybe he had heard incorrectly—maybe she actually said, "I'll bet he *has* a huge tool."

He puts on his Mets cap, glad that Beth is not awake to call him on the choice. She has often told him that most people are not fooled by the hat ploy. When she sees a man wearing a cap, she assumes the sartorial choice was made for one of only two reasons: he is very short and compensating by adding a hat, or he is bald. Well, what the fuck is he supposed to do: spray his bald spot with brown dye the way guys on TV do?

When he steps out onto the porch again, this time he notices that the neighbors have affixed yellow ribbons to the trees in front of their houses. Who are they mourning now? he wonders. He has noticed for quite some time that Oklahomans seem somehow to enjoy PDGs: public displays of grief. There is always a flag at half-staff in Oklahoma, often for some dead football coach or deceased Republican former governor. Just as, during the historical Oklahoma land rush, many cheated by sneaking in early in order to claim the better homesteads, now they rush to get to the memorial services "sooner," among the first to be photographed publicly sobbing. The Sooners come in droves, bearing teddy bears and plastic-wrapped bunches of flowers, weeping and mugging for the cameras.

He guesses that huge PDG exercises are the only thing other than football championships that provide a sense of glamour here. Whether this aspect of Oklahoma culture is a sad consequence of the Oklahoma City bombing he cannot say. He and Beth came here several years after the terrible disaster at the Murrah Building. Slater was offered an endowed chair at the university, and when he reluctantly but sensibly accepted, Beth left her New York job in advertising and opened a gift shop in Hope Springs.

The yellow ribbons are perhaps Iraq related, he figures. He and Beth are antiwar blue voters, living in a red state that is gung ho about the war. He remembers the yellow-ribbon type very well from the Vietnam War days. There was always a certain sort of person who loved wearing POW bracelets, loved *war*. In Oklahoma many of those people, older now, have young adult children who wear WWJD? bracelets, expecting the entire world to believe that, every second of every day, they are wondering what Jesus would do.

Slater seats himself in Sancho's and without consulting the menu orders a pot of coffee and the huevos. He has chosen a booth in the rear of the restaurant, his back to the wall so that no one can see his bald spot. He removes his cap, then remembers he forgot to bring the newspaper. Slater habitually carries a small notebook in his jacket pocket in case he thinks of something he needs to take care of or wants to make a quick sketch. He pulls out the notebook and a pen and begins to make some notes in order to pass the time—no, face it, Slater, in order to seem occupied, to avoid looking like a sad sack.

He has recently begun to find himself making lists, lists that serve no real purpose. He compiles the lists, then seldom peruses them again. He looks at the list he began last time he jotted in the notebook.

THINGS NEVER TO DO:

1. *Never answer the door to someone carrying a clipboard.*
2. *Never sit next to a midget on the bus.*

This one is certainly moot, as he has not been on a bus since they left New York. He crosses out the word "midget" and replaces it with "dwarf." After a moment he crosses that out too and writes "little person." Then he changes it back to "midget."

3. *Never trust someone who is always smiling.*

Slater now adds:

4. *Never call a pest control service—do your own killing.*

He looks up for a moment and is surprised to see walking into Sancho's the psychologist who runs the suicide survivors workshop. "Dr. Jane" they call her. He thinks her last name is something like McPhee or McMillan—it can't be McGraw, that's Dr. Phil, isn't it? Dr. Jane is the group facilitator, also a "suicide survivor." Slater has heard from friends who have been in rehab that the facilitators are always fellow addicts or fellow rape survivors or fellow something-survivors. Slater prefers the more antiquated terminology: "victim"—he and the others in the group are all victims of suicide, no matter if the word "survivor" is now the preferred nomenclature.

Dr. Jane is ordering coffee, and he cannot help but catch a good view of the back of her. She wears one of those ruffly knee-length full skirts he has been noticing on campus, but he can see that she has a nice ass for a woman her age, and her tanned legs are still shapely. He knows that when she turns toward him, she will have cute little painted toenails emerging from her sandals. He feels himself stirring like some jacked-up seventh-grader drooling over a sexy high school girl, and his face heats. He is still married to Beth, has been married to her for thirty-some years, will probably always be married, and Dr. Jane is aware he has a spouse. He pages through the notebook, not wanting her to see him staring.

She passes by his table on the way to her own, her eyes not visible behind Jackie-O sunglasses, and as she breezes by (yep, there are the red toenails), she only nods slightly, with a tiny trace of a close-lipped smile of acknowledgment. Damn—he did not realize until now that he has some sort of crush on her. He figures this is no different from the crushes students develop on their professors; he has heard about what shrinks call "transference."

Metallica's *Black Album* plays on Slater's car stereo as he drives home from breakfast. He turns up the volume even louder, the sound thumping through and from the car the way the gang-bangers at home drove around, glaring out their car windows at anyone who dared to object. He presses the lever to open both front windows, treating his neighbors to a sweet taste of metal as he drives down his own block. When he pulls into the driveway, he spots a man who appears to be in his twenties, jogging along, wearing running shorts and a Siesta Sancho's T-shirt, accompanied by a Doberman. The guy slows to a walk and stares Slater down. He and the dog are both lousy with muscles.

"Got that cranked up kind of loud, huh?" the guy says. His face wears no expression: he is either naturally poker-faced or making an effort not to show his cards. Is his question a benign inquiry, or is it a challenge? Slater is not sure.

"Rock on," Slater responds.

"Sure thing, old-timer," the jogger says, then canters off.

I ought to kick his ass, Slater thinks. It is not a serious thought, but he feels the sting: *old-timer*. He has become a codger, Slater realizes, a schlemiel.

Beth is sitting at the kitchen table when Slater enters. In front of her rests a ceramic pot of what smells like mint tea, and she sips from a cup as she watches the tiny Sony tucked into a niche on one wall. "How was Sancho's?" she says, her gaze still fixed on the screen.

"Ketchupy."

Beth asks if he thinks the weather is okay for a bicycle ride, but Slater finds he has lost his zest for exercise. "Hon, would you mind? I wanted to watch the Mets game this morning, and then I need to do some prep work for the Price Tower trip." In fact, he had planned neither; he just wants some time to himself.

"Price Tower?" Her expression registers no recognition.

"Beth, I told you, I'm taking my undergrads to Bartlesville this week—a field trip to the Frank Lloyd Wright building."

She says that oh, yes, now she remembers about the Price Tower trip but then returns her attention to the TV and says, "Will you look at that, Dave?"

When Slater follows her gaze, he sees a wedding cake on the screen. Beth picks up the remote and turns up the volume.

"—entirely out of Krispy Kremes," he hears the TV person say. Apparantly a woman in Muskogee is selling wedding cakes made from Krispy Kreme doughnuts. What is more notable, it seems the woman can barely keep up with the orders for wedding cakes made of doughnuts and is looking to expand her facilities. Beth laughs good-naturedly.

Slater says nothing. This is the woman with whom he occupied the administration building at Columbia during the student strikes in '68, the black-haired antiwar firebrand and fellow sds member, the woman with whom he expected to be arrested. But on the evening of the second day of the building occupation, Beth's period arrived a week early, leaving her sitting in a pool of rancid red fluid, some of the other students around them whispering and looking sideways. That was the end of their revolutionary stint; Slater had to wrap his jacket around Beth's waist and escort her out of the building, where media people rushed them, wanting to interview them about their defection from the cause. His father had been so pleased to learn that Slater was going to be a part of the student strike that Slater was never able to admit to him that he and Beth had made a premature exit.

Slater drives to downtown Hope Springs to pick up some items for the field trip to Bartlesville. He buys a case of Mountain Dew and a Styrofoam cooler at the Discount Depot, then stops at the pharmacy to pick up some Tylenol and enteric aspirin and a box of Band-Aids. But when he tries to pull open the glass door of the pharmacy, nothing gives. He takes off his shades and reads the sign on the door: *Closed for Memorial Day. See you tomorrow.* Annoyed, Slater heads back to his car, realizing he will need to make a sortie into Walmart. But suddenly he sees something that takes the breath out of him: an old man wearing an American Legion cap, sitting in a lawn chair on the corner, selling paper poppies. Slater feels gut shot, even lurching to one side, off balance. *Poppy.*

Nearly every time he has to reveal to someone the oppressive fact that he lost his father to suicide, the first thing the person says is "How did he do it?" People ask horrible questions, rude and gruesome, and do so with benign, even consoling looks on their faces. Slater has to wonder if he himself might have asked such terrible things, before he became a "suicide survivor." Slater continues to be stunned that rather than offering a politely sympathetic phrase such as "I'm very sorry to hear that, Dave," they seem to perk up—their voyeurism kicks in immediately. The only thing folks want to know about is the morbid details: did he blow his head off, stab himself in the heart, jump off a bridge, drink drain cleaner? What was that song from the seventies?—"Just blow out your brains, James; jump off the Brooklyn span, Dan; gas yourself in the car, Gar; swallow cyanide, Clyde."

And if asking Slater to furnish the grim details of the means of death is not enough, the next question is inevitably "Did he leave a note?" Why does anyone care, and what does a note have to do with the death of one's father? Is someone's terrible demise supposed to become a source of entertainment?

Fine, cough it up for everyone, he has decided; serve up the ghoulish details on a plate; give them the complete personal horror show. No, there was no note, folks. Poppy's goodbye consisted of messages left on the answering machines of David and his sisters. "Sorry I missed you," Poppy said. "Love ya."

That "Love ya" was the closest his father had ever come in Slater's entire life to saying *I love you, son*. His father had never once said the words "I love you" or even "I'm proud of you," not a single time in Slater's lifetime.

How did he off himself? Slater wishes he could report that his father blew his brains out, a death both dramatic and masculine, a real crowd-pleaser. But no, Poppy never owned a gun, much less shot off his head like Hemingway or even like poor old Hunter Thompson or that kid Cobain. Poppy's death was more like Marilyn Monroe's, an uncharacteristically womanly mode of death. He simply swallowed an entire bottle of barbiturates, crawled between the sheets of his bed as if he were retiring for the night, and expired. The family knew Poppy had been despondent since Mom's death, but they did not learn until after his exit that he had been diagnosed with a malignancy in one lung; Poppy had not chosen to share the bad news with his family. Couldn't he have just had chemo like everyone else?

Beth had been astonished the first time she heard him refer to his father as Poppy. They were still students at the time, only just beginning to become a couple, when in conversation he mentioned Poppy.

"Poppy?" she said, not even bothering to hide her laughter. "Goo-goo Da-Da."

Slater explained that the name Poppy was not a diminutive of Papa but rather referred to the brilliant red flower. Like most men in his age demographic, Poppy had served in World War II. Every year on the eve of Memorial Day—in those days not yet celebrated on Mondays—he came home from the docks wearing a bright paper poppy on his lapel. Slater and his sisters found it hilarious, their father wearing what seemed to them to be a corsage. Mom shushed them, explaining that veterans sold the poppies to raise funds for disabled soldiers, and that Dad was being patriotic. Still, they had begun calling him Poppy after that, and the name stuck.

He pulls his wallet from his back pocket and buys five poppies from the old veteran.

Sorry I missed you.

After waking, Slater lies in bed and halfheartedly considers masturbation, remembering a crudely humorous slogan he once heard: *After fifty, never trust a fart or waste an erection.* Well, he has not yet pooped his pants, but the few spontaneous erections he has now more often than not go to waste. Maybe he has been dreaming about that attractive shrink.

He has not for a fairly long period of time felt himself seriously tempted by an extramarital affair. He and Beth put all that behind them long ago, after some calamitous dalliances in the seventies. In any case, the cheery Baptist women who populate the town are not to his taste. Even if he could stomach them, they wouldn't consider a Jew—he might as well tattoo the mark-o'-the-beast on his forehead. There is no synagogue in the town; he and Beth have to drive an hour and a half to Tulsa during the High Holy Days.

Slater kisses off the possibility of morning onanism and instead gets out of bed. Beth has kicked the blankets and sheet away from her in the night, and her nude body lies motionless on the white bottom sheet like a cadaver on a slab. He cannot help but stare at her thinned-out pubic hair. Where there was once a luxuriant thatch, now there is only the gauziest webbing, her sex revealed like a baby's.

In the bathroom, he decides to change the cartridge in his Quattro and to use some of Beth's aloe moisturizer after he shaves; tonight is the weekly meeting of the grief support group.

Slater observes his hairy chest in the medicine cabinet mirror as he shaves his chin. One cannot ignore the ratio of hair loss to hair growth that is seen on aging bodies. The more hair Slater loses from his head, the more grows on his chest and back, and as for the nose, fuhgeddaboudit—he has had to order one of those trimming devices from the Sharper Image. They say bald men are more virile, so he can perhaps understand the growth of body hair, but what about his ED, as they call it in the pharmaceutical ads. In the three months since Poppy's death, he has been unable to have an erection with Beth. He resorted to ordering Viagra from the Internet, and he and Beth had sex successfully one time about a month ago. The stuff worked great, but it gave him such a blinding headache that he never risked it again. Hell, he read somewhere that even Tommy Lee had tried Viagra, and that the drummer suffered the worst headache of his life.

Beth's sex drive is no longer what it used to be, either, and she too suffers from the inverse hair issue. Though she has barely any pubic hair, he has caught her in the bathroom ripping hair from her upper lip with wax strips, and shaving her toes in the tub. A velvety growth of hair coats her neck, and her formerly pristine thighs now sprout dark hairs. Whoever came up with the expression "aging gracefully" was entirely full of crap.

"Metaphorically at least, he died in my arms," a woman in their circle of metal folding chairs says. She is from Los Angeles. Slater has wondered fairly often why so many of the members of the grief support group are originally from outside Oklahoma. Well, if being devastated by a suicide is what it takes to introduce Slater to some other expats, so be it. He has come to cherish these Wednesday evenings, even though there is bound to be a lot of weeping every week, sometimes his own. The metaphor woman owns a bookstore in Hope Springs, and her fiancé blew his brains out in their bedroom. Slater's chest burns with pain for the poor girl. Those who commit suicide are in fact murderers; Slater has long known this to be true.

The woman herself now addresses this very issue. She tells the group that her little son from an earlier marriage, an eight-year-old boy who had been very fond of his future stepfather, said to his mom, "Reed thought he was killing himself, but really he was killing all his friends." Much nose blowing ensues in the room, and Slater's eyes sting.

Dr. Jane volunteers commentary on the possibility of the woman's son obtaining some counseling, but Slater cannot concentrate on what she is saying. Rather, he finds himself looking again at Jane's bright toenails, pink this time, easily visible in her thong sandals. It's not that he has a foot fetish; rather, he finds looking at her lovely feet quite a bit easier than looking at her up-tilted nose or directly into her eyes. Now that he realizes he is hot for her, he feels self-conscious. Slater does not wish her to find his behavior "inappropriate," nor to think of him as some sort of randy bastard, even if that's what he is.

But now Slater feels like a kid in grammar school, because while he has been inattentive, it seems Dr. Jane has steered the conversation elsewhere. "David, what about you?" she says.

Slater feels his ears flame as if he were under a sun lamp. He is embarrassed that he missed the switch in topic. The fact that she called him David instead of Dave heats him up a bit; sometimes using one's proper name instead of a customary nickname seems the more intimate choice. His groin burns hotter than his neck, and for a moment he thinks he feels dizzy.

"Searching," Jane prompts him. "Did you engage in those behaviors?"

He cues right in—just last Wednesday they had been talking about "searching behaviors" in the bereaved. It seems that after one loses a loved one, particularly if the loss is unexpected and sudden, the aggrieved person begins searching for the lost one, walking about the house in a daze, looking under the blankets on the bed, opening closets, and even looking into the bathtub. Equally prevalent is the desire to wear clothing of the deceased. Newly bereaved people are often seen wandering their houses in a fugue state, wearing the lost one's bathrobe or sweater. Sometimes they open the front door and peer out, as if the dead person is simply tardy and any minute will appear on the porch. This all takes place during what Dr. Jane terms the denial phase of grief.

Slater reports that, no, his situation did not mirror the woman's, as his dad was not living with him and Beth at the time of his death and thus Slater had no reason to look for him. Someone else picks up on the conversation and begins to share her experience. But what Slater has not told them is that there was an odd incident, one that frightened Beth. The night after his sister telephoned to tell them about Poppy, Slater walked in his sleep. Beth found him pacing up and down the hall naked at three o'clock in the morning. When she turned on the light, apparently he looked past her with unseeing eyes, and in a voice she later described as "unearthly" he said, "Poppy?" She had to touch his shoulder and tell him several times, "Dave, you're sleepwalking, everything's okay, come back to bed."

He engaged in sleepwalking one other time in his life, when he was four years old. His father went into the hospital for a ruptured appendix—whisked from the house by ambulance attendants and not coming back that evening. The toddler Slater was found by his mother in the middle of the night walking the house in his yellow jammies, making an eerie moaning sound that awakened her. In fact, he can still, more than half a century later, remember his mother picking him up in her arms and carrying him back to bed after he murmured "Daddy?" several times. In the morning, she told him he had been sleepwalking and reminded him that Daddy was in the hospital but would be home very soon. He does not share these recollections with the group; he keeps things to himself, his father's spawn.

What he encountered that night when his mother discovered his nocturnal roaming was a floor made of air, through which he was about to plummet; a cataclysm; the imploding of the universe.

When the university van brings them home from Bartlesville after nine, the students are still talking to one another sotto voce or listening to their iPods, but Slater is wiped out. Field trips are not as invigorating as they used to be when he was a young assistant professor at Pratt. He thinks of all the corny old jokes the borscht-belt comedians used to make about the legs going first. Too bad this turns out to be true—his calves began throbbing while he and the students were still walking Price Tower.

"Did you know that the most common post-disaster injury is cut feet?" one of his students says to her seatmate. Slater is unable to hear the whispered response.

Once the van has pulled into the lot outside the architecture building, Slater makes sure all the students are safely out of the van and into their cars, then climbs into his own car, his knees cracking like adolescent knuckles. God, he feels like he could use a nightcap, but this is a college town and he does not wish to run into any of his students in a bar. He opts to go up instead of down—caffeine rather than alcohol—and stops the car in front of Sancho's.

In his car in the darkened parking lot, Slater's view through the restaurant's enormous plate-glass window is unobstructed. Sancho's blazes in front of his eyes like a brilliant outdoor movie screen, and he feels as if he is back in his childhood, sitting in the backseat of the family car at the Pageant drive-in theater. And it is not Liz Taylor or Pier Angeli who stars in this movie but a more current leading lady: Dr. Jane sits in profile, backlit like an ingénue, sipping from a cup. He recognizes her by her upturned shiksa nose, adorable.

Fatigue renders him loopy. His mind swings from its hinges for a few moments, his thoughts careering into irregular space: I wish for just one day I were not married to Beth. I wish I had hair like Stone Phillips—if he's not wearing a rug, the guy must have had a transplant. I wish I were named Stone instead of Dave. I wish I still lived in New York. I wish I had been a better son. Please, God, let me find a way to get Jane into bed with me and not get caught. God, send Poppy back, if only for a day, an hour.

He watches Jane take a few more sips from the cup. One last thing slides into his mind as it reels along askew, something he once overheard one student say to another as the pair walked across the quad: *You can't pray for what you want. God is not a short-order cook.*

Slater knows he should go home to Beth rather than approach

Jane in Sancho's, but he resists the sensible part of his brain, the part that would have him wimp out. I'm going in, he decides—I'm not a eunuch yet. He first takes a whiff of his underarms, just in case the long day in Bartlesville has rendered him rank. He seems to pass muster, so he gets out of the car and approaches Sancho's.

He decides that rather than letting on that he has seen Jane through the window, he should make the encounter seem like a bit of serendipity—he does not want to come off as a stalker. He will casually order a cup of joe and then walk by her table, ostensibly on the way to a seat further in back. If she does not ask him to sit down, he will assert himself, say, Might I join you?

But after he has the coffee in hand and turns away from the counter, something changes. Jane has seen him and is smiling, has even raised one hand slightly in greeting. He wonders how her face looks so young—he is fairly sure she is about his age. Beth posits that Jane has "had some work done" and points out that Jane's hands look much older than her face.

She seems glad to see him. Her teeth are so white, he thinks. He feels himself smile, too, and strides toward her table, but—oh god, this cannot be happening. It's one of those cartoon moments, a scene enacted myriad times in Hollywood comedies, the smile-over-the-shoulder scene, a bit of cheesy slapstick. It seems she is in fact smiling at some guy behind Slater; the smile and the little hand raise are for the other man.

He hears Poppy's voice in his ear: *Tough it out boy. Never let 'em see you sweat.* He will not let Jane know what has just gone down. He pretends he has only now noticed her and nods in what he hopes is a businesslike manner as he passes her table. Once he is seated, his face engorged with heat, he takes the opportunity to scope out his competition, who is now seated at Jane's table, facing Slater.

It would have been too much to expect that Dr. Jane's companion appear effeminate or perhaps homely or even mildly handicapped. No: the bastard could give Johnny Depp a run for his money. He has dark hair, enough for five men, and wears a tight red T-shirt and Levi's, the red shirt inflaming Slater's ire, the showy son-of-a-bitch. And not only does he appear to be far more handsome and fit than Slater, he also appears to be tremendously younger; the guy looks barely thirty. For one goofy moment, he thinks maybe the guy's her son.

But no, Jane and sonny-boy are doing what the entertainment programs on TV call "canoodling," nothing flagrant, but a lot of looking into each other's eyes and a bit of fingertip touching.

What was I thinking? he wonders. I'm done, the guy with the Doberman had it right when he called me "old-timer." My parents are dead and I'm flat-out next in line for the Slater family plot. And there will be no one behind me in that grim queue. Maybe we should have had kids; at least some of my DNA would remain in the universe. No wonder I can't get it up: I'm kaput.

In the car on the way home, Slater attempts to tamp down his distress by turning up the volume on the radio, the Oklahoma City NPR station. The first thing he hears is the interviewer asking someone described as a scientist/professor, "So, are you saying that the invisibility cloak may no longer be simply science fiction?"

The man answers, "Yes, you could actually make someone invisible as long as he wears a cloak made of this material." It seems the guy is in the process of creating a cloak made of what is termed metamaterials, which can be tuned to bend electromagnetic radiation and visible light in any direction. The scientist claims, "We think we can present a solid case for making invisibility an attainable goal."

When Slater was nine years old, one of his uncles gave him a radio-controlled whoopee cushion for his birthday. The thing looked like a typical accent pillow and could be strategically placed for the chosen mark to sit on. The young Slater could control the device from another location, causing deplorable honks of flatulence to issue from the unsuspecting sitter's behind. The first time he tried out the device on his parents and sisters, everyone in the room laughed when he cried out, "It's a dream come true!" But the real dream-come-true would be an invisibility cloak. Since early childhood he has had a persistent fantasy of walking the earth in a mantle of invisibility.

The wind has picked up, and as Slater drives home he can see that it's about to rain. A loud, sharp crack of thunder causes him to flinch. But the thunder booming above him also initiates kinesis of his mind. He finds himself transported back to the first time he can recall hearing thunder, before he even knew what it was. He was at the time about the same age he was when his father had the appendectomy and had felt not exactly frightened but surprised when he heard a peal of thunder above the family home, as if a convoy of trucks was driving across the roof. His father explained to him then about thunder and lightning and took him to the window to observe the lightning flashes. He told his son that soon rain would begin to fall.

When Slater asked how his father knew this, Poppy told him that rain inevitably followed thunder and lightning. "When it starts to rain, can I go outside?" he asked Poppy.

His father said as long as he cleared it with Mom, that would be fine. His mother dressed Slater in a slicker, red rubber boots, and a sou'wester rain hat, and he stood at the window until he saw the rain begin to fall. Poppy joined him then, wearing a Giants sweatshirt and a hard hat. He held young Slater's hand in his callused paw and led him out into the garden. They sat on deck chairs near the lilacs and honeysuckle, faces upturned, Davey Slater opening his mouth to catch the raindrops.

In the driveway in front of his house, Slater sits in the car in the rain, staring at the porch light that Beth has switched on, feeling immobile and heavy as if his body is a sack of meal. His heart breaks for a moment when he spots that poor wasp still circling on the porch, slow to get the point that he is now homeless.

He sits at first inert in the car, but before he knows it, his notebook is out and he is making a list beneath the glare of the dome light:

THINGS TO DO IN THE INVISIBILITY CLOAK:

1. *God forgive me, but: follow Dr. Jane home and get the goods on her—is red shirt her lover? Does she look as good naked as she does with her clothes on?*

2. *Wear the cloak to the grief support group and listen to what they say about me when I'm not there.*

3. *Follow Beth—see if she has an alternate life. Does she have some man with billows of hair, who never smells like garlic?*

4. *For this one, need time machine as well as invisibility cloak: Let me be with Poppy when he dies. If I cannot change what happened, at least let me be there to prevent my father from dying alone.*

Slater stops writing, then rips the page from the notebook and crumples it. He does not wish anyone ever to learn of his base wishes and pitiful regrets—let him put an invisibility cloak around those.

He thinks of Dracula. Dracula wore a cloak. And Superman, though his was more of a cape. If Slater wore a Superman cape, he could fly through the sky with his arms out in front of him like the young, unmaimed Chris Reeve, perhaps carrying a Lois Lane (or a Dr. Jane) in his arms, a hero. Or he could don a darker cape, the Dracula stealth cape, which he could wrap around his creamy prey before he sank his teeth into her lovely stem of a neck and took them both all the way, all the way to eternal life.

Suddenly Beth appears in the driveway and raps her knuckles on the driver's side window. When he rolls down the window, Slater sees his wife is weeping, her nose streaming and eyes red. He looks at her, at first uncomprehending. But then he realizes, my poor Beth, she knows the man she married might now as well be a thousand miles into the stratosphere.

"Come inside, Dave," she says. "You've been sitting here for half an hour." The rain has become a soaking downfall, and Beth's hair hangs in wet sheaves, lightning illuminating her face like a flashbulb shot capturing a catastrophe. "It's just the grief," Beth says, "the grief, that's all it is."

He leans out the car window, reaching toward Beth, the cold rain soaking his outstretched hand. His wife's weeping has a muffled quality, as if she cries behind a partition. She seems far away, pearly in the downpour like a Las Vegas stage illusion.

What is vivid in this moment is Slater's vision of what might be possible. He sees himself now, flying back to the scene of that dismal afternoon, this time wearing his invisibility cloak. He swoops down on the casket before the ghoulish undertakers can lower his father into the soil.

From the Philippines

CHRISTOPHER MCILROY

From *All My Relations* (1994)

Deirdre's Philippine snapshots were late. Every day they failed to arrive, Deirdre's friend Curtis told her, she grew dizzier. Her gray eyes glittered. Her freckled complexion flushed pink. The soft waves of her auburn hair burst into a fiercely becoming curly frame around her head. She talked incessantly, though not about the Philippines, since by now everybody but Curtis refused to hear about it. She had spent a semester and summer there, as an exchange student.

When the final bell rang, Deirdre edged down the ramp, books clamped to her chest, in a surge of 2,500 other high school students. She felt assaulted by bulges—the boys' prodding crotches, the girls' nipples encircled by blonde flips and Izod alligators. Deirdre hated their touching her. Her first months home after the Philippines, she'd needed only to close her eyes to be shinnying up a date palm with Chacho or ladling Mama's fish stew, her back to the warm oven. Now she felt in the midst of her recurrent dream: waking on a beach that came alive, a moving carpet of crabs, feathery and spiky, intimate with all of her. As the students squeezed down the ramp, a boy pushed himself against her buttocks. Deirdre swung her looseleaf binder back in a hard uppercut. She heard a grunt. When she knelt at her locker, a girl was saying above her, "Who would you kick out of bed, Erik Estrada or Sugar Ray Leonard?"

"Good-bye Erik," another answered. "Give me brown sugar every time. Who would you kick out of bed, Billy Zoom or Billy Idol?"

"*Whom*," Deirdre said. "Wignorant itches. *Whom* would you kick out of bed. Think of womb. That shouldn't be any trouble for you."

Home, no mail. Her father squirmed in his armchair and sipped from a highball glass, watching TV. He'd sat there for eight years, since rheumatoid arthritis had forced his retirement from City Maintenance. The living room belonged to him. No one else was allowed to use it.

Deirdre filled her silver pint flask from the half gallon of Seagram's in the kitchen and drove into the hills.

Thickets of mesquite gave way to saguaro forest as she hiked up the mountain. Below her, trails meandered through muted green desert in a scene as delicately complex as a Japanese watercolor. Soon Deirdre was in the Philippines. At first she couldn't capture the matter-of-factness of true memory. The tropical vegetation was impossibly shaggy, the colors blaring purples and greens. Then she was swimming in slow motion, water flowing over her back. Crisp stems of water hyacinth parted beneath her fingers, the petals brushing her face. Her host Filipino family—Mama, Papa, Chacho, and the three sisters—flitted through the trees, their white underwear iridescent. Afterwards they lay on the bank, Chacho asleep, his head on Deirdre's knee.

Swallowing from her flask, Deirdre sat against the trunk of a palo verde and put her hands to her temples. By almost closing her eyes she could see Chacho as a mountain hovering in the distance, huge. His lowered lids were sloping faces of rock, his mouth a soft crease in the earth. Floating over the desert, the Chacho-mountain swept back and forth, erasing the gray and glass bits of the city, the cars with hundreds of setting suns reflected off their roofs, the chatter of her high school halls.

With delight, Deirdre recalled reading Kahlil Gibran aloud with Chacho: "When you part from your friend, you grieve not; for that which you love most in him may be clearer in his absence, as the mountain to the climber is clearer from the plain."

She walked back down the trail into the dusk, singing. After she could no longer see them, she could hear her feet on the stones. The long curve of lights marking the boundary of the city was the Manila shoreline. The far mountain range, absorbed into the dark, was the ocean. A few birds, she thought, would still be flying over the obsidian water.

In the kitchen at home, her mother gave her carrots to wash and peel, broccoli to trim. Deirdre held the lumps of vegetable under the streaming tap. She felt dazed, and the light hurt her eyes. Her mother hurried from stove to refrigerator to counter to oven. From long practice, the two cooperated well and had little need to talk. Mrs. McGuire seldom spoke, as a matter of habit. Turning from the sink with her pots of vegetables, Deirdre bumped her mother, carrying meat loaf in a pan. The broccoli tipped onto the floor.

"Sorry, Mom."

"We'll wash it. We won't tell anyone."

Deirdre giggled, but her mother already was past, opening the oven door.

Deirdre set the table and, when dinner was ready, served her young sisters. They were beautiful and untrustworthy; Deirdre constantly covered for them. One stole money from her mother's purse. The other would not do *anything*, not clean her room, help with the dishes. She cried when asked to put away her clothes.

Deirdre brought her father a plateful of food. "They're in it now," he said, pointing to the TV. "No one's going to get them out of this one."

His arm knocked the highball glass to the floor. "Get me another, sweetheart," he said.

"Ha, ha," Deirdre said. Often, despite her sharing the Seagram's, her urge was to spit in his liquor. Resisting, she would feel sick with herself for the thought. She returned to the dining room, sat down, and began to eat. But her father yelled until her mother made him a 7 and 7. Furious, Deirdre said nothing for the remainder of the meal.

Curtis was late picking her up. Deirdre walked back and forth in her room, reading Gibran's "On Friendship" from an imitation parchment scroll, a gift from Chacho. The JV game had gone into double overtime, Curtis explained when he arrived. He was the school paper's assistant sports editor. Deirdre tucked the scroll in her back pocket, and they drove toward a boondocker in the desert, drinking rum.

"I never told you the weirdest thing that happened to me with Gloria," Curtis said. Deirdre and Curtis had carried on their six-week friendship by exchanging monologues, hers on the Philippines, his on Gloria. Curtis was driving fast up First Avenue, and badly, as usual. Twice he yanked the car back from the dirt shoulder. Sometimes he drove with his right hand on the wheel and his left waving out the window, sometimes with his left on the wheel and his right arm around Deirdre.

A month ago, he told her, just before the breakup, he'd sneaked the car by pushing it out the driveway and down the block, then gone to Gloria's. He woke her by tapping on the bedroom window.

"She had on her nightgown, which was just a little lace here and here, and even in the dark I was just thiiis close to seeing her through it." Curtis had admitted that he tried to look down Deirdre's blouse and the back of her jeans whenever possible. "She put on her fur coat and came out the window."

On their way to the desert, she'd tickled his neck and stuck her tongue in his ear, Curtis said, but when they parked, it was the same as always: neck, arms, and legs below the knee, O.K. Shoulders and back outside her clothes, O.K. Period. "We're kissing and I'm going crazy, and all of a sudden I realize I'm embracing, stroking, really digging my fingers into this thick fur. I feel like I'm making love to a big muskrat. I ask her, hey, whose perverso movie is this?"

"I don't know what's wrong with Gloria. If I weren't the Frigididity Queen, I'd be raping you every second," Deirdre said kindly. Curtis might have been called peculiarly handsome, tall and slender, with pointy features, thick white-blond hair, and dark circles under his eyes.

"Say 'frigidity,'" Curtis said.

"Frigididity." It was Deirdre's policy to fracture words suggesting sex.

"Say 'tits.'"

"Bazoozums."

"Say 'ass.'"

"Hindnickels."

"Excellent. Say 'vagina.'"

"Virginia."

"That's the girl. I was thinking, the reason they haven't sent the pictures is probably because it's harvest time or something."

"That was November," Deirdre said. "It's almost Christmas." She didn't want to talk about the mail. After three letters a week from Chacho, now no letters in five weeks.

From the top of the rise in the dirt road they saw the party, two bonfires in a dry swimming pool, part of an abandoned, reputed Mafia resort of the '50's. A couple of dozen natty teenagers danced to a boom box between the fires.

Deirdre soon was drunk again, with the accompanying tension that left her face lopsided and pugnacious. She was concentrating on Chacho's theory of sex: with abstinence, the sexual fluids would rise up the spine into the head, creating a dynamo of spiritual energy. "The face glows," he'd said, "like yours." While the tape was being changed, she climbed onto the diving board. Shadows of flames played over the pool like a negative of sunlight on water. The board felt very high, and slender like a bending reed.

"What do any of you know about friendship?" she said. "The Filipinos understand friendship. Your *kasama* is your friend for life! *Pingsarili*—you would translate that as 'privacy.' That's what I used to think. But Pilipino has no word for privacy. *Pingsarili* is like loneliness. Imagine a people whose word for privacy means loneliness. Friendship!"

"Oh, Christ, Deirdre," someone said. A bottle broke against a far wall.

From her back pocket, Deirdre pulled the scroll of Gibran's "On Friendship." After reading, she replaced the parchment in her pocket and recited the whole from memory.

The others began singing loudly.

"Friendship is staying up all night on the beach, just talking," Deirdre shouted. "Friendship is giving everything, your secrets, your voice, your language, and getting everything in return. Friendship is touching for love, not tutti-frutti. 'Let there be no purpose in friendship save the deepening of the spirit.'"

The diving board sagged and bounced. Below Deirdre, her companions' faces looked as remote and featureless as pebbles. "Come sit with me," Curtis was saying, and, his arm around her shoulders, he led her to the pool steps.

How many acres did the family farm? he asked. What was the growing season? What were the major crops of the Philippines? His pointed nose and sharp chin darted toward her with intense earnestness. Deirdre wasn't fooled. She knew he quizzed her to disguise his boredom with the Philippines. She didn't care. Boring everybody gave her a sense of accomplishment and pride. Curtis at least tried to be interested.

Deirdre explained the planting of rice. She remembered ambling home astride the carabao, led by Chacho, how she could lean forward and grip the animal's sweeping horns, like tremendous handlebars, and rub the forehead, broad as a slab of moss-covered mahogany. Chacho's brown feet squashed into the mud, guiding her through green rice plants and rich brown earth, paddies that seemed endless.

"Do the women ever work in the fields topless?" Curtis asked.

"The old grannies, maybe, in the hills."

"Did you ever work topless?" His forehead contracted into cobwebbed lines, his eyes squinted eagerly.

"Mother of God," she said.

"My dick hangs down the left leg of my pants, and I notice that everyone else's is on the right," Curtis blurted. He rolled and lit a joint, but something was wrong and one side of the paper flared up like a jet of natural gas. "My guess is that it won't function properly. Go in crooked. Gloria knows her sex, she would have caught that right off. There's the problem."

After they'd gone together six months, Gloria had told Curtis she'd slept with a quarterhorse trainer she picked up at the track. The man, a Canadian, moved on with the racing circuit, but Gloria said since she was in love with him there was no point in seeing anyone else.

"Unzip," Deirdre said. "Show me."

"What?"

"Come on."

Curtis turned his back to the bonfire, hunched forward, lowered his fly, and cupped his hand around, without touching, his exposed penis.

"It's fine," Deirdre said. "No problem."

"But how would you know?"

"My father leaves his lying around carelessly sometimes. Yours is much more appealing, believe me."

Curtis finished his smoke. "This makes me nervous," he said. "I'm going to move around." He hopped the pool steps two at a time and began loping along the rim of the pool, circling it twice with high, floating bounds. His white hair stood on end, settled, rose, fell. The black circles made his eyes look enormous in his white face.

On Deirdre's front porch, Curtis suddenly kissed her on the lips. Startled, she allowed his tongue in her mouth. Her mouth gaped open, slack, until he put his hand on the seat of her jeans. She stiffened. Her saliva took on a metallic tinge. She thought of his hands in fur, a dead animal, his fingers breaking through desiccated skin and tufts of hair. A line of teenagers embraced, the girls in their pleated skirts crumbling, clothes collapsing to the concrete floor of the swimming pool. "Good night," Deirdre said. Pushing off Curtis's chest, she backed through the door.

Her father sat in the dark facing the gray slush of the TV screen. The pale light traveled up his legs, to his open fly and his penis, which pointed straight at his head. True as a compass needle, Deirdre thought. She hurried by.

Sitting on her bed, chin in hand, she thought of how Chacho, when he talked most seriously to her, would lie on his elbow and pluck at whatever was beneath him—grass, reed matting, sand. He had long black lashes. His eyes were soft; if she touched them, they would feel like the bodies of bees. Beauty in her life, Deirdre reminded herself, was a sign of favor, and Chacho was beautiful.

Deirdre woke at four in the morning to go to the bathroom. The kitchen light was on. Her father's armchair was empty, so he was spending the night in the master bedroom. Her mother, naked except for a black lace bra, an old birthday gift from her father, stood by the kitchen sink. Deirdre retreated into the shadow of the living room. She hadn't seen her mother naked that she could remember. Her mother reached for the cutting board and laid it on the counter. She turned, passed from Deirdre's view. The refrigerator door opened, shut. Her mother brought bread, a head of lettuce, mayonnaise, and luncheon meat to the counter. She spread mayonnaise on the bread. Her belly and buttocks were round and white, too soft, even baggy. Afraid, feeling unbearable tenderness, Deirdre ran into the kitchen. Her mother shrieked. On her knees, Deirdre embraced those soft parts of her mother, pressed her face against them, the fluff of pubic hair.

"How can you let him have this?" she said. "How can you give it to him?"

Her mother, frozen, holding the knife and a slice of ham, stared at her. Then her eyes, as large and clear as Deirdre's, but blue, shifted vaguely around the room. She stepped free and returned wearing a robe.

"*Go to bed*," she said. Deirdre stood, wanting to resist, but the robe stymied her. She could think of nothing to say.

To help herself sleep, Deirdre remembered wrestling Chacho's sisters in the pond. The girls clambered over her back, and she toppled forward. Chacho's arm shot around her waist, breaking the fall, and the tower of people collapsed on Papa and Mama on the bank. For a moment, the children squirming over her, Papa grunting underneath, Deirdre hadn't wanted to move, to leave the warm, wet flesh against her skin. The tangle rolled over on itself. The girls yipped. "Yaaah," said Chacho. "Ou ou ou," Papa said, punching and prodding the mass of flesh as if molding a great ball of dough. Smelling again their moist, common scent, Deirdre drowsed.

Friday there were no letters. Deirdre went to bed early and slept until Saturday noon.

It was time to check the mail. Her father waved. Cheerleaders were kicking long diagonals across the TV screen, the tips of their feet disappearing beyond the edge of the small picture tube.

Outside, a kite, rising on the unseasonably warm breeze, showed red against a fat bank of clouds. A packet from the Philippines lay in the mailbox. Deirdre slit the envelope with her fingernail and unfolded Chacho's note. He apologized for the delay. Papa had forgotten to send in the film, and then processing had taken longer than anyone could have imagined. He apologized for not having written. He was engaged to be married. The girl was a Christian Chinese, daughter of a grocer with connections to a department store chain in Manila. Chacho had never spoken to her. Papa and Mama were very enthusiastic, and he must obey their wishes. It was difficult for him to tell her this. He would write more later. He closed *"Iniigib kita"*—I love you.

The kite dipped in the pale sky. The bright winter sun seemed to have leached color from everything—house, trees, the bicycle on the lawn. Deirdre refolded the note and with great care tried to put it in her shirt pocket. The shirt had no pockets. Deirdre let herself into the house. She saw her father's bladelike face, small ears tight against his crew cut, the shriveled, twisted feet, and hatred clenched her stomach. She locked the bathroom door behind her, feeling enclosed in hatred like a vault. Sitting on the edge of the tub, she scraped her father's razor across her wrists until blood dripped onto the white porcelain. Then she began to cry. Running the bathwater to hide the sound, she staunched the blood with a washcloth. The wounds were only shallow scratches.

She called Curtis. He was covering a basketball invitational in Phoenix, because the sports editor was sick, he said, and of course she could come.

Wearing a long-sleeved blouse with frilled cuffs over the Band-Aids, Deirdre sat against the door in Curtis's front seat. Curtis smoked a joint, seeds sizzling and popping as they chugged along the freeway in his '51 Plymouth. The night before, he'd taken speed and lain awake reconstructing every minute he'd spent with Gloria. For an hour and a half he delivered the history to Deirdre, jerking the steering wheel back and forth in time to the music, cursing cars that passed them—"Dog's ass. Carnal intimate of rats."

Deirdre refused the puffs he offered. Watching his face, the most expressive, she realized, that she'd ever seen, she made a fascinating discovery. There was a wonderful beauty in the harshness of that face. Deirdre felt odd. Each moment was fragile, elongated. She couldn't remember where she lived, the number of her house, or what it looked like. The desert outside her window was unfamiliar. She couldn't judge if it were pretty or drab.

A swerve of the car threw his cigarettes on the floor. When she bent to retrieve them, he asked what was in her pocket.

"My photos." Deirdre broke the seal on the envelope and removed the prints. They were stiff colored artifacts in her hand. Chacho cutting green peppers into likenesses of the family, Papa with his cigar and big ears, Mama's bun and wide skirt, Chacho's floppy pandanus hat, Deirdre's backpack like a hump. Deirdre and Chacho reciting his Pilipino translation of "On Friendship," their mouths open exactly the same width on the same word. The sisters catching a frog. Chacho and Deirdre, late for Mass, running down a pink dirt path overhung with gray-green foliage, feet barely blurred. Each held the other's hat in place, his hand on her white lace chapel cap, her hand on his pandanus.

Deirdre tossed the photos on the seat. "You can look at them later," she said.

Curtis glanced at her, said nothing, and lit a joint.

Early for the game, they drove down a broad, shady boulevard. Above the treetops, a violent pink and orange sunset flamed the glass of a double-decker mall, the Phoenix smog curling like smoke.

Curtis needed more cigarettes. A series of turns took them into a black ghetto. Children popped wheelies on their bikes. People talked in doorways. The buildings were dingy and decayed. A tattered billboard showed an airplane flying into a glass of beer. Lying against the brick wall of a lounge, a man threw a tennis ball in the air, catching it without changing the position of his hands.

"Brrr, this is sad," Curtis said. "I shouldn't feel good in a place like this, but I do. Isn't that terrible? But Gloria and I were so close when we were sad. When she was depressed, she'd call, and we'd want so much to be together, but it would be too late at night and we couldn't. It was a sweet thing. I love her so much," he said, banging his hands on the steering wheel. "That's why I wanted to touch her. It would have been enough to feel the skin of her back. I always wondered if she has a nice back. That's important to me."

"I'm sure she does," Deirdre said. "Gloria has lovely bones."

"What's wrong with me? Six months, and then the first time she meets this Canadian horse mugger—I hate Canada. I read the hockey box scores every day to see the Canadians lose. I want them to lose every one of their games."

"It makes me angry that Gloria treated you so badly. She needs a good kick." Deirdre's voice rose. She was trembling.

Curtis looked at her again. "Do you want a drink? We could have someone buy us a bottle."

Deirdre shook her head.

The gym was like an old hangar of yellow wood. Deirdre studied the rows of bleachers. Their existence seemed arbitrary. She might look away and back, she thought, and half would be gone. It was all a matter of pure chance. The buttocks of the players looked like sea sponges. Deirdre was unaware of the action until midway through the fourth quarter when, their team ahead by twenty points, Curtis lit a cigarette.

"Idiot," she said. "Do you want to get thrown out?" She crushed it on his bootsole.

Only when they were on the freeway home did Deirdre re-member, "Chacho is getting married."

"No," Curtis said. "I don't believe it. Oh, honey." He squeezed her arm tightly.

"We said we were never going to get married. Everly-Neverly Brothers never." Though she'd drunk nothing, her tense jaw pulled her face lopsided. Bare sticks of growth flashed by in the headlights. The vastness and emptiness of the desert sky, with its dull distant stars, terrified her. "He doesn't know her. He doesn't like her."

"Chacho must be miserable. He'd do anything to see you be-fore it happens."

"I think I'm going to put my head in your lap," Deirdre said. She lay on her back, knees huddled against the seat. Curtis fin-gered her hair and stroked her cheek.

After a few miles, she unhooked her bra and put Curtis's hand inside her blouse. The weight of his hand made her feel the mo-tion of her breast, vibrating with the hum of the engine. She felt the car decelerate and stop, the engine dieseling. She opened her blouse to Curtis and looked at him. He gazed at her with-out blinking. He was barely smiling, but the corners of his black-rimmed eyes turned down and his forehead was deeply lined. Covering her breasts with his hands, he bent to kiss her.

Deirdre averted her face. "None of that," she said. "Go ahead. A gift." Muscle knotted her jaw. Her teeth were clenched. She un-fastened the buttons of her jeans and arched her back to strip herself. She heard part of Curtis bang against the steering wheel as he lowered himself onto her. It wasn't their bodies touching, Deirdre thought, but only a bridge from her to him.

Curtis's boots scuffed against the door. Occasional passing headlights swept across the interior of the car. Deirdre tried to hear Chacho's voice speaking of the sexual juices' ascent up the spine, their opening like a flower in the head, tried to see his hands illustrating the expansion of energy. But instead all she could see was a woman, not herself, yet leaving her body, racing into the glare of traffic. Holding her long, white, ugly breasts in her hands, the woman thrust them into the headlights, against windows of the passing cars. Metal grazed her. Headlights bore down on her. She lunged and dodged among the cars while the traffic broadened, a half dozen lanes wide, a dozen, a river of yellow lights. Now she was struck, broken on a hood, tossed to a roof, thudding from fender to door to bumper to windshield, flung from lane to lane. Deirdre's heart slammed against her chest and her breath tore in her lungs.

"It's O.K.," Curtis was saying. She was lying on the floor. His arms were under her, lifting her towards him. "Take it easy. You jerked right off the seat, that's all. We were already done. I got out in time."

Deirdre's naked body felt gray and dead in a film of moisture. To herself she smelled like the clots of dust in a vacuum cleaner.

"You look so wonderful," Curtis said. His face was smooth, lines at last relaxed. He kissed her breasts and draped her clothing over her. She allowed him to kiss her lips.

Driving home, Curtis said, "I have a vision of the Philippines." He described a long sweep of beach, ocean a blinding blue, thatched huts, and hundreds of brown people making love. Like bundles of driftwood, they were strewn along the sand, receding into the distance until they were only dots.

Deirdre's mind was blank, and so she saw only Curtis's couples, arranged symmetrically like a pattern for giftwrap, rolling by on an endless sheet.

Curtis walked her to the porch, pressing her hand. As she opened the door, a streak, a yellow ribbon of clashing noise and light, entered with her, but it faded. The living room was dark. Looking toward her father's chair, she saw that he had slipped to the floor. Suddenly she wanted everything to be different, that he would be healthy again, that she could even remember him healthy. But her memory of that time was always vacant. She lifted him by his armpits and set his stiff back into the hollow left by his years of sitting. He batted at her weakly.

In her room, Deirdre concentrated on the image of Curtis's wondering face, a new emblem. She couldn't lie down. Instead she found she must sit upright, knees drawn to her chest, while the yellow river of noise and light roared around her bed until morning.

Sky Over El Nido

C. M. MAYO

From *Sky Over El Nido* (1995)

> Rosita conceded that torturers playing
> *trucco* with their prisoners was weird . . .
>
> —MARGUERITE FEITLOWITZ,
> "NIGHT AND FOG IN ARGENTINA"

Figueroa was the fat one. He was the one who always remembered the maple syrup (colored Karo, actually) on Sundays.

We would call to him through the bars, "Figueroa, Figueroa, did you forget the maple syrup?"

For some reason, Figueroa thought this was tremendously funny. When he laughed he would lick his teeth and his belly would jiggle. Sometimes he had to hike up his trousers—with his left hand; he balanced our tray of waffles with the right.

Guzmán was the one with pimples: large pus-filled boils on the back of his neck. His nose looked like a beak. He kept a kerchief in his back pocket.

"Fuck the maple syrup," Guzmán would sneer as he stalked down the corridor. "Fuck it. Fuck you." His heavy black boots would thud by, then echo like the hard flaps of a trapped bird.

To pass the time, Diego and I told each other stories about Figueroa. My story began like this: Figueroa lives with his mother, in a two-bedroom bungalow that smells of soap and lemons. They listen to public radio together, and he cooks her waffles. Figueroa also washes and irons their sheets, and makes their beds. He sweeps the floors, rinses the dishes, tends the herb garden. After a late supper, he takes her rheumatic Pekinese, Adolph, for a walk around the block.

Diego's story went like this: Figueroa lives alone, in a little room with a low ceiling, a sixth-floor walk-up. Figueroa has to use a bathroom that is down the hall. He has a closet full of women's shoes, all stolen. He subscribes to a foot-fetishist magazine, which arrives more or less every other month, in a brown paper wrapper.

"What is the name of the magazine?" I asked.

Diego was thoughtful.

We smoked.

The striped shadow cast by the window stretched across the floor. It inched up the gray blanket on Diego's cot. It touched his pillow.

"*Pump,*" he said.

On Tuesday, Figueroa brought us our dinner: oatmeal with chunks of broccoli stalks. We have been here for many years. We are not sure how many.

"Why not *Spike*?" I said. I picked out the chunks of broccoli and ate them first.

Diego slurped his oatmeal. Diego always leaves the chunks until last. He said, "*Stiletto* perhaps."

On Wednesday, Figueroa brought us our lunch: boiled rice with sauerkraut. Our cell is lit with a dim 60-watt bulb, but we both spotted the bruise on Figueroa's left cheek. It was the size of an owl's eye.

While we were eating, Guzmán came up and shone his flashlight on our faces. "Bon appetit," he said sweetly. "So sorry you couldn't share the breast of pheasant in mushroom sauce." Then he stomped down the corridor, clanging his flashlight against the bars.

I began: "It was a dark and stormy night."

"Was it?" Diego licked his fingers.

"I thought I heard rain last night, didn't you?"

"No."

On Thursday, Figueroa brought us our lunch: hot dog buns with golf sauce. His bruise had turned light green, but it was the same size.

We ate.

I continued: "After Figueroa had taken Adolph the Pekinese out for his evening walk, they were soaked. Adolph looked like a used kitchen mop. This aggravated his rheumatism. He made a wee-wee on the corner of Figueroa's mother's living room sofa. Figueroa yanked the leash. He said, 'No! Bad doggy!' and smacked Adolph on the haunch. Adolph growled and leapt up. He bit Figueroa on the cheek."

We smoked.

Diego said, "And so, Adolph bit the cheek that fed him. So to speak."

Figueroa brought us our dinner: deviled kidney on saltines. Figueroa's bruise was still the size of an owl's eye.

Diego said, "Figueroa was sitting on his rumpled bed in his one-room apartment on the sixth floor. It smelled of stale laundry and old newspapers. He read a personal ad on the back page of *Pump*. It said, 'I have nifty little feet, soft as English rose petals, and on my left foot I have an extra toe.' It gave a telephone number. Figueroa called. A deep voice answered. He immediately thought: Oh my God, this is a transvestite. But then he told himself, Figgy old boy, it's just that she's been smoking unfiltered cigarettes all her life."

Figueroa brought us our dessert, a Twinkie. It was my turn to pull the Twinkie apart. I have rather less talent than Diego; my half had more creme filling.

We heard the buzzing noise, like a bumblebee in front of a microphone. A woman screamed.

It stopped. We smoked.

Diego continued: "So Figueroa made a date: Monday night, at her apartment. He arrived, she let him in. She was wearing big black orthopedic shoes. He knelt down and unlaced them. She *did* have an extra toe on her left foot! Her feet *were* as soft as English rose petals! Figueroa was in ecstasy! He lifted her up and took her over to the bed. He brushed his lips over her ankles, he kissed the soles of her feet. He darted his tongue between her toes. He nibbled and sucked the twisted little extra toe." Diego coughed. "I cannot go on."

"Go on," I said.

Diego lit another cigarette. He exhaled, and we watched the thin smoke filter through the bars of our window. A cluster of stars winked in the twilight.

"Afterwards, the woman went to sleep," Diego said. "Very carefully, very quietly, Figueroa slid open the doors to her closet. She had rows and rows of stiletto-heel pumps, all covered in blue silk. Each heel was as long and sharp as the bill of a heron. 'How can I ever leave?' Figueroa asked himself. 'How?' He climbed into her bed. He rested his feet on her goose-down pillow, next to her face. He felt the whiffs of her little snores on his insteps. He cradled her rose petal feet and began to dream."

On Friday at dawn Guzmán threw a pail of icy black water through the bars. It landed on the cement floor between our cots.

"You want coffee?" he screamed. "Lap it off the floor!"

We spent the morning watching the coffee evaporate.

By lunchtime there was only a bark-colored splotch.

Diego said, "When Figueroa would not leave, the woman popped him on the cheek with one of her stiletto-heel shoes."

We smoked.

An airplane passed by, the sound of its jet engines arcing across the bowl of the sky. We searched our window, but we could not find the plane.

There was no lunch.

I said, "Birds of a feather don't always stay together."

There was no dinner.

On Saturday, Figueroa brought us our dinner: soft-boiled eggs. His bruise was a livid yellow. He watched us eat. He had a benevolent expression, which made me think of his mother's herb garden. In a sunny patch of her garden, behind the forest-green iron lawn furniture, she would keep tubs of basil and borage and sage. Insects hum and buzz around a clump of gladiolas; a robin has its nest up in the crook of the roof. Watercress sprouts from coffee cans scattered under a leafy walnut tree. (Adolph would be tethered in the garage.) And in the kitchen, on a ledge over the sink, tiny clay pots of rosemary, chive, and lemon balm rest on saucers.

Diego winked at me and wiggled his toes.

Figueroa held out his hand through the bars. It was hammy, hairy. We passed him our eggshells. He smiled and licked his teeth as he balled his fist, crushing the shells. Then he walked down the corridor.

We smoked.

Figueroa was back. He hiked his trousers. "Inge!" he called. A little girl, perhaps ten years old, came shuffling up. She had a pixie cut, and her eyes were set close together. She curled her hands around the bars, delicate as the claws of a wren. She stared at us.

Figueroa said, "These are the ones I've been telling you about, Princess." He pointed. "This is Diego, and the other one . . ."

"Hernán," I said.

"Diego and Hernán," Figueroa said. "They like waffles with maple syrup." He laughed that big belly laugh, his thumbs in the belt loops of his trousers.

The little girl blinked. She said, "Pleased to meet you."

Figueroa patted her on the head. Then he took her by the hand and led her away.

On Sunday morning we heard loud clattering footsteps. It was Guzmán and Figueroa, together. Figueroa carried the tray of waffles and a small white pitcher with our maple syrup.

Because Guzmán was with him, we did not call to Figueroa through the bars about the maple syrup.

Guzmán squeezed the back of his neck. Then he whipped out the kerchief and dabbed at it. "You can go now," he said quietly. "The Governor says you are both free to go."

This had happened before. "Figueroa," I said, "did you forget the maple syrup?"

Figueroa passed the tray to Guzmán. He held up his trousers with both hands and began to laugh. Guzmán hurled the tray against the wall. Shards of crockery flew through the clammy air like a spray of stars.

Figueroa laughed and laughed, until his face turned red and tears welled in his eyes. The syrup ran down the wall, sweet rain oozing through the plaster.

The Golden State

BECKY MANDELBAUM

From *Bad Kansas* (2017)

As these things go, we left Kansas on the hottest week of the year. A red rash burned over the weather map as Alec and I shoved everything we owned Tetris-style into a U-Haul, which we then dragged across the prairie and desert, completely bypassing the pretty parts. In Denver I suggested a day hike, but Alec ruptured his Achilles tendon playing Ultimate Frisbee in college (an injury I never entirely believed), so anything athletic was strictly out of the question.

The drive carried on, all garbled talk radio and forest green mile markers and Alec listing off things we needed to do once we got to California: buy a box fan, change our mailing address, get a parking permit. Boring, boring, boring. Around Vegas I asked if he'd ever go hiking with me. He turned to look at me, revealing soft pockets of darkness under his eyes. He hadn't slept the night before—at dawn I found him sitting upright in the hotel bed reading *Les Misérables*, shoveling ranch-flavored corn nuts into his mouth.

"You're free to go hiking without me," he said.

"But I want to go *together*."

"We'll do other things together." He was using his lecherous voice—he reached over and squeezed my thigh. "Did I mention I'm glad you're coming with me?"

"Well, nobody wants to move alone."

He kept his eyes on the road. "That is the kind of comment I will choose to ignore."

I was not without a point. So far, he'd seen to it that the move lacked all romance. He put a deposit down on the house in California without consulting me and then fell asleep an hour into our going-away party, snoring away on the sofa as my friends and I danced to "Girls Just Want to Have Fun" on the coffee table beside him. Most of our conversations over the past few weeks had revolved around how to best pack his dishware. At one point I asked if he thought I was his assistant. "If you were my assistant," he said, "I'd be paying you."

I turned and watched the desert spit out tumbleweed. It was just like in the spaghetti westerns, all red sand and saguaros. About every other minute a semi came hurtling past us, plastic truck nuts swinging from the trailer hitch.

Already, I missed Kansas.

California was supposed to be better in every way: better food, better weather, better people. In movies, the West Coast was a utopia of beaches and liberal politics, hippies high-fiving scientists at the farmers market. Meanwhile, redwoods and cheap tacos and Yosemite! My Kansas friends feigned jealousy, although they too were heading out for other lands: Madrid, Seattle, a rustic lodge in the Rocky Mountains.

Alec had his own campaign, whose main platform was that California was not Kansas: no snowstorms or tornados or governors trying to arm children with rifles. Plus, he'd gotten a job near Sacramento, teaching French literature at a university. The job didn't pay well, but it was—back to his main point—very much not in Kansas.

The university town was not by water or mountains, but somewhere vaguely between—the Central Valley. "It's the best of both worlds!" Alec promised. He had promised many things over the course of our relationship: that he would only smoke cigarettes after sundown, that I could borrow his car without asking so long as I was sober, that he would love me ferociously. This was his word: *ferociously*. So far, he'd made good on everything, which I credited to his advanced age. He was twelve years older than me and had been my French teacher.

Technically he was a lecturer—he had his eyes on tenure that would likely never be his, because as much as he wanted to be French, the truth was that his real name was Alex and he came from a poor farming town in upstate New York where people ate pigs' feet and married their first cousins. That his life and career were turning into something of a failure was entirely his problem, and yet sometimes it felt like my own. I'd just graduated with a degree in linguistics and couldn't think of anything better to do than follow him. What was a young woman supposed to do with her life? The answer probably should have been: Anything! Everything! She's politically liberated! But something in my gut—perhaps fear masquerading as love—was urging me to stick with Alec. Plus, I had very little money.

"You're making a big mistake" was what my mother told me.

"But I'm in love," I said.

"Love has weak legs. You'll see."

I told her I'd prove her wrong, but I could hear the uncertainty in my voice. At this point, the doom feelings were compacted into a small kernel, located somewhere behind my belly button.

Our house in the Central Valley cost three times more than the one-bedroom we'd shared in Lawrence and was, I should mention, not really a "house." Granny cottage, they called it—whoever *they* were. At best, it was a room in which someone had accidentally left a sink and a toilet. At worst, it was an architectural side note to the larger, two-story mission-style home in which a history professor and a veterinarian lived with their litter of blond offspring. We were there to help pay the mortgage.

Inside, Alec's head scraped against the ceiling, where a network of cobwebs stretched from corner to corner like prayer flags. In the kitchen, I put my arms out and twirled like a ballerina, my fingers grazing the cabinets. There were two rooms, one of which was the bathroom. An image came to my mind of a mastiff and a dachshund forced into a gerbil cage.

"Cozy," Alec said, and forced a smile that read: *Do not panic or girlfriend will panic.*

I said, "As a womb. Or a very, very small, overpriced home."

We got to work unpacking and ended up making okay-but-sort-of-forced love on the kitchen linoleum. This is how we discovered the cockroaches. I'd never seen one up close before. Kansas had all sorts of critters—millipedes, brown recluses, cicadas—but nothing as Kafkaesque as a cockroach. Like a rotted thumbnail with legs.

"They say when the world ends, it'll just be all cockroaches and Twinkies," Alec said. He was naked, dust on his thighs.

"Where do you want to be when the world ends?" I asked.

He stared up at the ceiling, thinking. "Maybe the ocean. Watching the waves." He turned to look at me. "What about you?"

There was only one answer I could think of, and because I didn't know better, I figured it must be the truth. "I'd want to be right here," I told him. "With you."

Alec started school and I started researching the state of California, specifically the Central Valley. I had the time—the days had begun to stretch outward in all directions, expanding along with the cosmos. The mornings were temperate but by noon the house was an inferno; there was no air-conditioning unit (the house being not really a house), and so I grew to worship the monstrous box fan that stood by the window, whirring like a jet engine. At night, Alec grew damp with sweat so that sleeping with him was like sleeping with a man-sized baked potato. My time in bed was spent wrestling with the sheets, dreaming of house fires and prairie burns. Most of my REM cycles came in the languid afternoons, when I'd fall into naps deep as a miner's hole. When I woke up—startled by the sound of an ambulance or the feeling of sweat gliding across my stomach—I had to crawl my way back to reality, back to the scorching surface of my new life.

My research paid off in a bad way. I learned that California was running out of water, that there were too many people compressed into too little space too far from natural water sources. Even in Kansas, I'd been complicit: the production of a single California walnut required five gallons of water, and I liked to eat my walnuts by the handful.

I learned that the college town had played host to a series of freak tragedies: stranglings, decapitations, body parts Saran Wrapped and left in Dumpsters. Even nature seemed bent on retaliation. More than four people had died after driving into the same eighty-year-old magnolia tree. Further research suggested the tap water might cause organ cancer and that rabid bats roamed the treetops after sundown.

Where had Alec brought me? Better question: Why had I let him?

The first week, Alec came home before dinnertime, tired and grumpy. His office was hot, and the students were stupid.

"I thought this was supposed to be a world-class public university," I said.

He brought a tub of mint chip ice cream from the freezer and hacked at it with a fork. He was on a medicine that made him crave sugar—on more than one occasion I'd caught him in bed at dawn, a salad bowl of Lucky Charms in his lap. "They're just rich kids who want to stay rich," he said. "All they really want to do is design drugs or build robots. They just need my class for the language credit."

"You're saying not one of them actually cares about learning a new language?"

Something flickered in his eyes, a premonition of danger. "There's one girl—her father's a diplomat. She already knows Italian and Spanish. It's like teaching a fish to drink water."

"A girl?"

He shoveled more ice cream into his mouth. "Don't worry, she's probably gay. They're all gay here. Or Marxist."

I grabbed the tub of ice cream, brought it to my face, and licked the surface.

"Gross," Alec said, yanking the tub from me. "What's the matter with you?"

"It's mine," I said, pointing to the ice cream. "Everything I touch is mine."

He winced. Sometimes this happened: I played baby, he played dad. "Have you thought about looking for a job?" he said. "They're hiring at the cafeteria."

"I have a degree in *linguistics.*"

"And my barista has a PhD in philosophy. Get over yourself." He stood and took the ice cream to the living room, which meant he relocated it about a yard east of the kitchen table.

"I want to take a class," I called to him. "I'm wasting my potential here."

He did not look at me but instead turned on the television. "It's your life. Do what you want."

I decided that academia was stupid, and so I signed up for a woodworking class I planned to pay for with the rent money I would withhold from Alec. I'd recently read an article in the *New Yorker* about a novelist who claimed to have learned everything she needed to know about writing from her years laying brick in

Indiana. Surely woodworking would open up some dusty cellar door in my soul, revealing a room of glittering treasure.

The class was held in a Presbyterian church. I thought of Jesus and Santa's elves and wooden crosses, wondering if there was something inherently spiritual about carpentry, or if Jesus just happened to be good at making stuff.

I'd expected plaid-wearing twenty-somethings, but the class was mostly old men and New Age moms. We started with introductions. When I said I was from Kansas the class let out a collective coo, as if I'd admitted to being a puppy with a serious case of kennel cough. "You're sure not in Kansas anymore," one of the old men said. An invisible puppeteer gathered his wrinkles and pulled his face into a horrifying grin.

We were starting with birdhouses. Our teacher was a middle-aged man with a red beard and hands like two T-bone steaks. He came up behind me and showed me how to sand down the edges of my wood. Inhaling his aftershave, I pressed my butt into the crotch of his blue jeans and closed my eyes, thinking all the while about the diplomat's daughter. Was she skinny? Blond? Could she build a birdhouse out of scrap wood? The teacher cleared his throat and went to help one of the moms beside me. After class, he handed me my tuition check and said it'd be best if I didn't return. *Prude*, I thought, and ripped up the check.

Outside, a boy from class was waiting near the curb. "What'd you think?" he asked. He was young, maybe my age, with a hipster mustache and a tan baseball cap that said bluehorn winery.

"Not for me. I decided to quit."

"Same. I already know half the stuff anyways—I just figured it'd be a good way to meet people. You know?" He smiled in a way that suggested I was the people. He then asked if I wanted a ride. A nearby bank sign read 104 degrees, so I followed him to his rusted Civic. A sticker on the bumper read KEEP TAHOE BLUE. Inside, something had eaten away a golf-ball-sized hole in the floor. As he drove, I watched the road go by between my feet.

"So are you digging it out here so far?" he asked.

I realized it was the first time anybody had asked me this. Even Alec had avoided the question, perhaps to avoid an answer that might require some action on his part. "Not really," I said. "I know that may be hard to imagine."

"Not at all. I understand—you're homesick."

"I'm not homesick."

"Then what are you?"

"I'm just not comfortable here. I'm not a Californian."

"Maybe you should go to the ocean," he said. "That's what all the fuss is about. Check out Point Reyes if you get the chance."

We were at the "house" already. He pulled over and let the car idle so that he could jot his name and number onto an In-N-Out napkin. Theo was his name. "I work the farmers market if you're ever around," he said. "I'm the honey man."

"Honey man," I said. "That's sweet."

He was blushing as I got out of the car. Inside, I put the In-N-Out napkin next to the toaster, so that Alec would find it.

The next day, I dropped Alec on campus and took his car to Point Reyes. The drive was all metal and tension. Aside from the traffic, the road kept curving and expanding and turning into bridges. In Kansas, you could close your eyes and take your hands off the wheel. Count to fifteen Mississippi.

I found a trailhead and walked a handful of miles until the Pacific appeared on my left. *Holy shit*, I thought, *that doesn't end until Japan.* There was blue water and wheat-colored sand and cliffs taller than the tallest building in Wichita. Land, I now saw, was like pie. Who would settle for just the middle when the crust was the whole point? I felt bad for Kansas, that everything in it was the same: land, land, land. The occasional mosquito-infested watering hole. And then me, my family, all my history, and everyone I'd ever loved. If there was a map that glowed in the places where I'd loved and been loved, it would burn bright in the center, surrounded by darkness. Perhaps a lazy squiggle would mark the route Alec and I took on I-70. Perhaps not.

I scrambled down the trail to a waterfall. This close to the water, I felt the first inkling of claustrophobia. It occurred to me that the openness of the sea was a lie: the ocean was not space, it was the opposite of space! It was a wall, a cage, a no-man's-land promising imminent death.

Nearby, a group of people had congregated around a beached seal. It took me a while to realize that something was wrong with it. It was craning its neck in a sickly way, as if trying to break itself in half. Without warning, it began to convulse. White foam streamed from its mouth as quickly and voluptuously as soft serve. It was going to die, and these people were going to watch it.

"It's having an orgasm!" a young man yelled.

Around him, the women squealed in joyful disgust. One raised her phone to take a picture.

Leave it alone! I wanted to shout, but had the ridiculous suspicion they would turn to me and know I was from Kansas. *You're not even from here*, someone, probably the kid wearing the pink bandana, would say. *This is just how we do things. It's ocean stuff. You wouldn't understand.*

Later that night, Alec laughed when I told him the story. We'd just made love and were in bed, face to face. He'd been sweet that evening, making lasagna for dinner and then massaging my feet, which were sore from the hike. After dessert, we unpacked a box of candles and lit them in the bedroom. It smelled like our apartment in Lawrence: vanilla and mint. In many ways, it was the best night we'd had in the house yet.

"Your friends used to shoot squirrels with pellet guns," he reminded me. "You didn't find them morally bankrupt."

"That's different. These people at the beach were malicious. And anyways, those guys used to make squirrel stew."

"Squirrel stew isn't a thing."

"I'm telling you—they made stew. They weren't killing for sport."

"All right. Your friends made stew. Either way, you just hate the people here because you think you're tougher than them."

"I do not."

"You do. You think they're soft because they eat avocados and go surfing. And like you're some hardened warrior just off the Oregon Trail."

"None of that's true!" I regretted raising my voice. I wanted to stay nice, for the evening to retain its kind trajectory. The mint candle was still burning on the nightstand, casting a friendly orb of light onto the wall. *Help me, candle*, I thought. *I'm losing him.*

"Have you discussed any of this with the napkin man?" Alec asked. My stomach dropped—I'd forgotten about the napkin. About Theo. I wanted to undo it, to take it back and throw it in the trash. "I don't know anything about a napkin man."

"You don't know anything about that napkin on the counter?"

"I do not."

"Did you think I wouldn't call the number?" He looked at me hard, unblinking. "You fuck with me, I'll fuck with you back."

The words made my throat ache. "That's not a nice way to talk to the one you love."

"I'm tired," he said, turning away from me. "Some of us went to work today."

I held my tongue, pressed my fingernails into my palms, where they left little frowns of pain.

If Alec wanted me to work, I would work. For the rest of the week, I swept and mopped and ran Q-tips along the baseboards. Once everything was spotless, I started cooking elaborate meals that smelled so good Alec had no choice but to eat them. On Friday, I thought I'd try the farmers market, which blossomed in the center of town in the evening, while Alec held office hours.

I walked along the crowded produce stalls, making a point to eat as many samples as possible. I touched everything I could, running a lazy hand along phalanxes of pluots and cabbages. Like he promised, Theo was at the honey table, surrounded by plastic bears filled with golden liquid. We made a plan to meet at the ice cream stand a half hour later, when he had a break. Before moving on to the pickle stand, I tapped the cap of every honey bear on display.

As it turned out, Theo had turned twenty-three since I last saw him. He bought me a scoop of coconut ice cream with one of the two-dollar bills his grandmother had sent him for his birthday. She lived in Oregon. Every year she sent him fifty two-dollar bills and a nickel for good luck.

"I've heard nice things about Oregon," I told him. Cone in hand, I was steering him away from the market, toward campus. Toward Alec.

He looked at me like I'd just mentioned his childhood best friend. "I *love* Oregon. My dream is to start an organic farm outside of Portland. I have loads of friends who live there. They just love it. There's so much to do, and the food's incredible." He went on like this, as if Portland were paying him to advertise.

"Why don't you just go there, then?"

It seemed the thought had never occurred to him. "I don't know. I mean, I'd need to find a place. Save some money. I guess it just doesn't seem like the right time." He glanced shyly at me and smiled. I pulled him toward the French building, where Alec happened to be walking out with a redhead. She wore a white bow in her hair, like a dove had flown into her head and died there.

Alec saw us from across the courtyard and shot me a nasty look. "This the napkin man?" he called.

"Only if that's the diplomat's daughter," I called back, and then pulled Theo back toward the market. The moment was over before it even began.

After a few minutes of silence, Theo said, "Was that your dad?" I usually laughed at this type of question, but now it just made me sad. "Yes," I said. "That was my dad."

"I didn't know you moved here with your family."

"I did—we're very close."

"He looks like Vin Diesel in twenty years."

"I'll tell him you said that."

Before we parted, Theo asked why I'd never called him. I told him I was sorry and then gave him Alec's cell number—which technically he already had—and told him to text me if he was feeling lonely. I wanted Alec to get whatever message Theo had to send me, to understand that even though I'd followed him across the country, my loyalty was not to be taken for granted.

Alec beat me home. He was watching a French movie, all accordions and lovers rushing up to one another in brick alleyways. I hated when he did this—my French was terrible and he refused to use subtitles.

I went into the kitchen, where I was determined to make a cheese soufflé. Soufflés were Alec's favorite—he would have to apologize if he wanted to eat any.

"I'm making a soufflé," I called to him. "Cheese, not choco-late."

Like clockwork, he appeared in the kitchen. "What was that stunt on campus?" he asked. "Who was that dude?"

"A friend."

"A friend? You have friends now?"

"Yes. His name is Theo and he's my friend. What about the redhead? Is she your friend?"

"She's my *student*," he said. "They're this weird thing you get when you're a *teacher*."

"I see."

"You think I'm fucking her," he said.

I looked up at him. "No, I don't. I *know* you're fucking her."

"Well, I'm not. She's my best student."

"Once upon a time, I was your best student."

This was supposed to be a joke: I'd barely done the homework in his class. One time, I turned in a receipt for a Wendy's milkshake and he handed it back to me with a bright red A+ across the top. He smiled at me, the cute smile where his green eyes went twinkle-twinkle. He may have been oafish and bald, but he was attractive in a Viking-meets-Mr. Clean sort of way.

"I'm mad at you," I said, getting the eggs from the fridge. "I don't like it here."

"I know you don't."

"So what are we going to do about it?"

He sighed, turned off the twinkle in his eyes. "What do you want to do?"

"I should probably go home, right? That would make the most sense." As soon as I said it, I knew it wasn't what I wanted. Like any_one without a backup plan, I wanted the original plan to work out.

"It's not even winter," he said half-heartedly. "Maybe you'd like the winter?"

"It doesn't even snow here. I looked it up. What kind of place doesn't snow?"

"It snows in the mountains. We can go to the mountains and see snow."

"I don't want to go see snow like it's some relic in a museum. I want it to actually snow. I want it to rain. I want the sky to do something, anything at all." I was suddenly tired. The "house" was hot, the air thick and fragrant. There were orange trees in the yard and in the evenings they let off a sweet, sickly odor.

Alec took me into his arms. He used to smell like a thunderstorm, but they didn't have the same laundry detergent here, and so now he smelled like nothing. He had always reminded me of thunderstorms, the mixture of rain and wind and power. We'd spent our first week together in bed, spring storms raging outside. During the days, I worked at the university's map library, and he'd come visit, bringing peanut butter sandwiches and sodas. We'd play the map game, in which one of us would name a town on a map and the other had thirty seconds to find it. In the evenings, we'd walk back to his apartment, where we'd watch movies and eat take-out, wait for the room to flash yellow with heat lightning.

He didn't feel the same in California. How could he be like a thunderstorm when there were no thunderstorms to compare him to? When I looked at him, it was like a layer had come off, revealing some muted version of the Alec I'd known back in Kansas. I wondered what he saw when he looked at me.

As he held me, I closed my eyes and pretended like we were back home. In the morning, we'd walk to the bakery around the corner and split an order of biscuits and gravy, share a mug of coffee. We'd go back to his apartment and make love, do a crossword, read books. I realized all of this was possible in California— there were biscuits and gravy, bakeries and crosswords. But it wouldn't be the same. It couldn't be.

"Are you tired?" he asked.

I nodded, my tears dampening his shirt. *I miss you*, I wanted to say. "Let's go to sleep," he said. "Forget the soufflé."

We shuffled to bed, where I immediately fell asleep. At some point in the night, Alec left the bed and went to sleep on the couch—he'd done this once before, saying it was cooler there than in the bed, where I radiated heat.

In the morning, I put on a red tank top and gathered my hair into a ponytail. Wearing my hair up gave me a headache, but every time I did it Alec complimented me. *You've got such a pretty face*, he'd tell me. The morning felt sad, and I wanted to look pretty for him.

In the kitchen, he looked up from the table and squinted at me. I waited for him to compliment my hair, but instead he said, "I got a dick pic at one in the morning. Guess from who?"

I bit my lip.

He had a piece of paper in front of him, which he slowly pushed toward me.

"What's this?" I asked, although I could read what it was: a ticket from Sacramento to Wichita.

"We'll get you some big suitcases so you can check a couple bags. Everything else, I'll mail you." He looked down at the ticket, ran a hand over his head.

"Is it the girl?"

"No."

"Then what is it?"

"It's everything. It's every minute since we got here."

I was trying not to cry. "Do you still love me?" I asked.

He sighed, looked again at the ticket. "It's like every day, I'm trying to take a goldfish for a walk—nobody's really enjoying it."

A moment passed in which my body floated outside of itself, bumped against the ceiling like a helium balloon. Then he said, "I thought putting your hair up gives you a headache."

The room grew dark, a tint of gray swallowing everything it touched: the table, the walls, Alec. As quickly as it came, it left, restoring the house to a mocking brightness. Closing my eyes, I imagined my first breath of air in Kansas. It would be cold already, a layer of frost twinkling on the sidewalks. My mother would collect me from the airport in her minivan, the same old lightning bolt crack in the windshield. She would not say anything—she wouldn't have to. We would simply drive off through the saddest, ugliest city in the world, a city of Burger Kings and pawn shops and antiabortion billboards and residential streets bursting with plastic playground equipment and ratty front yards patrolled by toddlers in dirty diapers, snot dripping from their grimy little noses—noses their mothers would die to protect. Inevitably, my mother would turn to me and smile. Put a warm hand on my knee and squeeze three times. *I. Love. You.*

Geneseo

PHILIP F. DEAVER

From *Silent Retreats* (1988)

At dawn Jerome Slater came down the tall, chipping stairs of the carriage house apartment, down to the idling white Camaro in the drive. Behind the wheel, Janet messed with her gloves and he saw the frail blue-white skin of her hands. In the short time he'd known her, a few months, this was what he always noticed—her pallid, almost transparent color. The skin of a woman can make you wonder what you don't know about her.

Sometimes she would stay the night, and if she did she always dressed very early in the morning, and, thinking he was still asleep, she'd slide out the front door and soundlessly descend the rickety stairs. He would climb the ladder to the skylight and watch her as she hurried down the long back sidewalk through the trees, furtive and alone like a neighborhood cat.

He climbed into the car.

"Morning." He pulled the car door shut and slid down into the bucket seat.

"What's the matter?" she said. "You still up for this?"

"You've got rust on the back quarter-panel."

"You're speaking of the car?" She looked at him, smiled. "It's old, give me a break. Do you still want to go?"

"Tell you later," he said. She registered alarm, so he quickly leaned over and kissed her. "Yes, I still do."

They went down Scott Street, turned right onto Main, rumbled north past the college and into Tuscola's business district. The streets were brick and combined with the steel belts in Janet's radials to create a washboard effect. At the four-way stop downtown, Janet said, "Last call." She spoke staring straight ahead. "I'll whip a U-ey and you'll be home in sixty seconds."

"Don't make me keep reassuring you," he said. "I'm going."

Downtown was deserted except for a cluster of cars at the donut shop. She drove on.

Jerome had first met her at Gabby's, a tavern out on the township line. Out there they called her Geneseo because that's how she had introduced herself. He'd observed her from a distance then, as she charmed the construction crews and the guys from the chemical plant, the few professors from the college who ever went out there and, of course, the farmers' sons and all their country girlfriends. She told them long stories about rock and roll, and sometimes she'd even bring her twelve-string and sing old protest songs.

But also sometimes she would get too much to drink and she'd cry, her hair dragging in the water puddles left by her last four bottles of beer. Or halfway through the evening she would make a telltale switch to vodka, retreat to a corner. She had, it turned out, regrets about her former life—whether for having lived it or having lost it, Jerome was not always too clear.

Her former life: Janet had lived in what she called an "intentional community" for quite a number of years; within the past year, she had come to Tuscola to live, leaving her husband and daughter behind.

"Look at it like this," she had said, very good-naturedly. "Remember when communes were in? Back to nature, all that? Someone must have joined them, right?"

Fact was, Jerome knew several people out of New York who'd joined Virginia and Tennessee communes.

"The place was called Geneseo," she said. "On that land the women were all called places. I was an early one there and was named after that very place. Make sense?"

When he first met her, Jerome probably didn't believe half the things she said. Yet she sort of grew on him over the months. She was so soft and likable, and so feisty. Who knew where she'd been in her forty years, or who she'd been with? Who knew where her stories ended and the truth began, as she rambled on about things? Her clothes betrayed an obsession with her life many years ago, beads and shawls, jeans and workshirts. She held him with a kind of desperate, childlike "help me" stare, very level because of the sharp, even brow line against the pale skin. He knew someday he was going to draw those sparse lines of hers and remember her forever.

Now, Janet was heading back to Geneseo to reclaim her daughter, Barbara, and she seemed reassured that Jerome was willing to go, too, and they were heading north out of town. At the hardroad she turned left—the gates were down at the Illinois Central crossing. In a few moments a slick chrome Amtrak flew by.

"That's the famous City of New Orleans," she said. "Steve Goodman's dead, did you know that?"

"No," Jerome said.

"Don't you like music?" Janet turned onto Highway 45. She handed him the map. "You're the co-pilot—get me there. It's along the river."

Jerome wasn't used to getting up this early. "What river would that be?" he said.

Janet laughed, slammed a Beatles tape into the tape player. *Abbey Road*, pretty loud. Jerome pulled it out again. "What river?"

"The Mississippi, dorkus. Maybe I better navigate."

He put the cassette in its case, the case in its holder on the console, and went back to scanning the map. For a while they were quiet, and Janet put the first miles behind them at sixty-five.

"How about Steppenwolf—I've got everything they ever did in that box."

The vent window on his side whistled, and Jerome tried tightening it. Then he found himself forgetting the map and watching the barns fly past. Each barn was a different weathered color and bent shape, bent into its surroundings. Janet slammed in a Richie Havens tape. *Alarm Clock*. Here comes the sun. Recently Jerome had taught a summer class in painting at the college. "Don't bring me pictures of barns," he told them.

"Goddamn," he muttered.

"What's wrong?"

"I forgot the thermos. I had it ready. Walked off without it."

"Big hairy deal. Who needs it," she said, reaching behind Jerome's seat, "when we have each other." She pulled two cans of Stroh's out of a Styrofoam cooler, set his on the console, opened hers. "Cheers, my friend! We're on the road!"

It was a good state, Illinois: the middle. Here was the future population of California, Bimini, New England, Alaska, the cities of Texas, being nurtured up in these little farming towns: Strawn, Forrest, Neoga, Watseka, Kankakee, Urbana, Rockford, Plainfield. In the city Jerome had known many artists and Soho-dwellers who'd come from towns like these in the middle states. In fact, his ex-wife, a New York architect, had been raised in Waverly, Iowa.

"There's a picnic table on the spot. Find Galesburg . . ." Janet was reaching over and pointing at the map, trying to hold her beer and drive with the other hand. They swerved a little. "Then find a little town named Joy—it's west of Joy—and don't say 'Aren't we all,' because I've heard all possible Joy jokes. Find the picnic table."

"I found Geneseo."

"That's Geneseo the town, not the commune. The commune isn't on the map. Look for a picnic table on the river."

"Now we have three Geneseos?"

"It's a bitch, right? Can you handle it?" She laughed.

He traced the river north from Hannibal with his index finger. "I fixed that damned thermos and then forgot it."

"You're unusual, all right," she said, turning up the music.

The plan was to bring Janet's little girl back to Tuscola to live with her. There were unknowns. For instance, Janet didn't know how things were going at Geneseo these days.

"When I think of places like this, I keep thinking of Jonestown—the congressman's films and all that," he said.

"Of course, you do," Janet said. "How 'bout the commune in *Easy Rider*, remember it? That was a *real* beaut."

She sipped her beer. "The CIA has a plot going with the news media to make these pinko communities look pinko." She laughed. "I love this. You're gonna learn so much." She was smiling and gestured big, a joyful arm-wave that let the car swerve again.

"So tell me about it," he said, reaching back to locate the seat belt. He fastened it.

"My husband, Will . . . I've told you about him, right? He's something. I just hope he's sensible about this. God, that just reminded me of my dream last night." She was staring straight ahead.

"Wonderful."

"You think I talk too much, right?" She smiled right at him. "Tell you what, this was a strange dream. I woke up to a knocking on the door downstairs. Three or four raps, then a pause. Three or four more, pause. No telling how long it had been going on while I was asleep. So I woke up then—I wasn't really awake, just in the dream—and I went to Barbara's room and woke her up. I said, 'Barbara, someone's knocking at the door in the middle of the night.' And she sat up. There she was, except she was about fourteen. I saw what my little eight-year-old will look like when she's a teenager—this is weird."

"No kidding."

"Barbara was sleeping in this guest room in this strange part of the apartment I've never been in—it doesn't exist, actually. She wasn't wearing any clothes." Janet stared ahead as though she were back in the dream. "Amazing."

"Incest," Jerome said, jokingly. He turned down the music.

She looked over at him but then she went back to it. She had her forearms resting over the top of the steering wheel, leaning forward. "She was under a blanket or bedspread or something. I was glad that she was with me again, even though so much time had gone by and she was older and I'd missed—you know—a time in her life."

"Guilt," Jerome said.

She gave him another look.

"Sorry."

"I said, 'Someone's knocking on the door and it's the middle of the night.' Her bed had a window right above it. We could look out and see down in the front yard, but we couldn't see the porch because the porch roof hid who was down there knocking. A couple of more times the knocking came, and we lay on the bed together, real low, watching out the window. Then the knocking stopped and we saw this young woman. She was dressed like—I don't know—like Florence Nightingale or something, that kind of era—the bonnet, you know?—and all in black? She was hurrying away, I mean walking real fast, through the shadows and stuff—where could she have been going?—so fast I almost couldn't see her in the dark, almost couldn't focus on her, but I saw that she was carrying these flowers and they were black. Black flowers."

Janet was quiet for a while. She stared up the road. Finally, Jerome said, "Guilt. And death."

She punched him on the leg good-naturedly, then opened her window and chucked the can, rolled the window back up, and opened another beer.

He looked up the highway, trying to think of a way to change the subject. "Why didn't you bring Barbara with you when you left the place?"

"I didn't know what in hell I was doing—I was just getting out." Janet ran her fingers through her hair, shook her head. "I don't know. Don't ask me that. I was nuts."

The road was narrow, the old kind. The grass grew right up to the edge. The land was fairly flat, so the road was straight. In his mind, Jerome sketched it, stick and ink, the very subtle contours of the retreating tree lines and pastures, the clusters of houses, the receding road in the flatness. He wrestled with the colors in his mind, trying to paint it. In this season, the values were close, tans and grays, blacks and browns. In art school he'd drawn and painted a lot of landscapes, efforts he had long ago ditched.

Janet cut back the heat. She reached up on the dashboard and found a picture, which she handed to him. It was a wrinkled-up Polaroid of a little blond girl next to a tire swing. "I need this little girl in my life." Now there were tears. "Anyway," she said, wiping them, "Geneseo's an anarchist community, founded by libertarians. That was the name of the game in 1969 or whenever. The main guy's still there—Stephen Boyce."

Jerome was still looking at the picture.

"These communities, if you're wondering, aren't all drugs and free love like the CIA says. They often turn out to be more rigid than ordinary society or whatever. Believe that?"

Someone passed them in a van, honking. She stared into the cab as they went by. "Speed on, hell ain't half full." She toasted them with her beer. "Sometimes we'd get kids from Chicago or St. Louis, and they'd think they wanted to join. But they wouldn't work. We'd always split over what to do about it. One side believed that if these creeps wouldn't work they should be gone. And you had these other people over here who believed in the 'process' of anarchism. Very big idea. They believed the kids should be allowed to stay and that the process of community would convert them to work and the cooperative life."

They went on up the road a while. They were coming into the west side of Champaign. Jerome said, "So tell me about Stephen Boyce."

"He's like . . . the main person."

They shot under a sign for Interstate 74, and Jerome pointed her onto the cloverleaf. The van ahead of them was gone. Janet rolled down her window and chucked the can.

"As he gets older, he settles down more and more. He's a father figure there now. Beard's getting gray, that sort of thing." She smiled. "He's a literature buff, however, and big on Kafka, so anything can happen. He makes money for us by giving speeches about community and communes and stuff."

They were passing an enormous salvage yard with piles of old cars.

"I have a friend there named Clay City. Forgot her real name. May seem odd to you, but she's just Clay City to me, plain as day. She runs the school. Has a son there about Barbara's age. She and I were tight—she used to be a teacher, in the world."

Jerome put the picture of Barbara back on the dashboard. "A very pretty little girl," he said. He reached to cut the heat, discovered she'd already done it, and cracked his window. He heard her pop another Stroh's.

"She had been a teacher—out in Kansas somewhere. A terrible thing happened to her."

"Isn't that usually the deal? Something terrible has happened, so people join a commune?"

"You're so smart," she said, raising her can in a toast, smiling at him. "You're going to learn so much."

"Will I learn how the old hippie rationalizes throwing these cans out on the highway?"

She looked over at him. "Sorry," she said. She took a deep breath. "*Anyway.*" She smiled at him. "So anyway, Clay City was living with her sister, both of them teaching. But Clay City was dating someone, and one day she found out she was pregnant. And listen, this wasn't any of that sexual revolution 1960's shit—it's just something that happened, you know? Like it happens?" She stared at Jerome. The car swerved again. "Men don't understand this stuff, and I'm not kidding. Why do I bother? Anyway, she was ashamed, and you can bet she was never going to get an abortion, and so she headed back to her parents' home—somewhere, I forget—leaving her sister in Kansas to teach. She'd be back when the baby was born. Well, it's incredible, but while she was home having her baby, her sister, alone back in Kansas, twenty-seven years old, something like that, died. Believe it?"

Janet looked over at Jerome. "She just died in bed. Do you believe it? What kind of luck is that? Very rare virus, the doctor said." Janet wiped the rim of her beer can with the elbow of her jacket. "Well, of course, Clay City had a theory that God was getting her for her sin. A sort of divine scarlet letter, only hardball." She gulped down some beer. "I'd think it myself, and I'm not Catholic, never been to church a day in my life. Anyway, she reacts by following some extreme religious guys, a bunch of movements and groups. She was up in Winnipeg for a while, following some wise man named Murray. Then she heard about Geneseo and it sounded a little broader in scope, but was still shelter. So she packed up the kid and came. Stay there 'til she dies, too."

Jerome stared up the highway.

"The community group is very logical for some people," she said.

"You didn't find that, though."

She gulped her beer. "Actually, I did for a while. But like Will says, 'Some folks don't fit nowhere.' I kinda stopped fitting."

They drove north and west. Sometimes they were quiet for a while, and it seemed to Jerome like Janet was averaging ten minutes per beer. A couple of more times she swerved, so he suggested they stop at a Burger Chef for coffee. They arrived about the same time as a chartered bus loaded with Illinois State University students. Feeling rowdy, Janet exchanged one-liners with some of the boys. While she went to the bathroom, Jerome carried their coffee to the car, splashing it on his hand and shirt. He decided he would do the driving unless she argued against it, and sat behind the wheel. He dabbed at the spilled coffee with napkins. Traveling with Janet made him feel married to her. Jerome's ex-wife, Erica, still lived in the city with their little boy, and for some reason now he was missing them both terribly. He wondered how anyone in his generation ever stayed married.

He watched Janet come across the Burger Chef driveway. She knew he was watching, and it changed something in how she held her shoulders, the expression at the corners of her mouth.

The warmth of the coffee seemed to refresh Jerome, but Janet leaned her head back against the headrest, looking out the window away from him. Finally, she was asleep. The day had become warmer with the last warm weather of the year. He tried to imagine what to expect when they arrived and to prepare for it. After a while she was awake again, but still they said nothing for nearly an hour. Then they were coming through the town of Joy. Hovering just above the town's business district was a large steel ball propped atop four legs—the water tower. "Joy" was painted on it in big black block-type letters which loomed over an IGA, post office, drugstore, and police station. They parked in front of a Rexall drugstore, and Janet ran inside for aspirin. Outside, leaning against the car, Jerome watched the pantomime of Janet in the drugstore through the front window.

When she came out, she wanted to drive. They pulled away from the curb and in a moment they were back in the country. "Will's a good person," she said after a while. "He'll let her come with us."

They turned onto a country road and white gravel dust flew

up behind them. The land was now very hilly. They plunged into a parklike area, deep in beech trees and shade, with ravines first on one side of the road, then the other. They crossed ravines on old iron bridges. Old farmhouses were decaying in every hollow.

"There's your picnic table, from the map," she told him when they came into a picnic ground. "Geneseo community maintains this for the state. Pretty good job, eh?"

Soon they came up out of the trees. There was a gate and a simple handpainted sign: "Geneseo, Intentional Community, founded 1968." Several kids came running to the gate. Jerome was now leaning forward in his seat, watching. Two swung it open and the others clamored up around the car, smiling and shouting at Janet.

"Hi, Mick," Janet said to one of them. "Is Stephen here today?" The air felt so good coming in through Janet's window that Jerome rolled his own down. As he did so, he heard the gate swinging and craned his neck just in time to see it latch shut again behind them.

The little boy pointed toward several barns clustered in the distance, off to the right across the grassy field. "At the dairy barn," he said.

"Thank you. You're getting very big," she told him. "Where's Barbara?" she asked, and the boy gestured back in a different direction. "Thanks, Mick," she said to him.

All the buildings seemed scaled down. There was something new about most of them. They were made of rough sawn wood on the outside, stained dark, with decorative detail that seemed almost nineteenth century in style. Janet was driving across the large field toward the barns on a two-rutted grass path, grasshoppers jumping on the hood and butterflies scattering. The grass was brushing hard underneath the car. It was nearly noon and the sun was warm, the sky blue as crystal. For a distance the children chased along behind them, laughing loudly. Jerome could hear a bell ringing, like the yard bells they used to have on farms.

Presently Janet pulled up to one of the barns and stopped the car. She stared at the big double doors, closed, and took a deep breath. "He's in there," she said. "I'll be back in a minute."

She climbed out, disappeared into the cool, abrupt shade of the building. The sunlight on the windshield and dash was so bright Jerome couldn't look toward the barn. He stared off to his right, to a stand of trees in the distance.

After a few moments, a tall clean-shaven man came out with Janet. He seemed very friendly to her, chatting as they walked toward the car, laughing warmly at one point, his hand on her shoulder, her arm around his waist. He came to Jerome's side of the car and leaned down.

"Hi. I'm Stephen. Brought Janet back to us, looks like." They shook hands. Jerome didn't say anything, but smiled cordially at him. "Maybe you'd like to come in and get some water or something, look around? We've got to head over and find Barbara and her dad."

"I'd like him to come along," Janet said.

"Look," Stephen said to Janet, speaking over the roof of the car, "this is a family thing, Geneseo. There's no problem with Barbara leaving. But it's Will—we should be sensitive to how he feels about this."

For a moment everyone was still, saying nothing and not moving. Then Stephen opened Jerome's door, and Jerome found himself almost automatically climbing out of the car, Stephen sliding in. He looked up at Jerome. "Half an hour, give us. We won't be long."

Over the top of the car, Janet told Jerome, "I'll be right back." He was looking for some signal from her. Nothing came. She was absorbed now.

He stood outside the barn. Stephen looked large in the passenger seat, next to a very thin and frail Janet. He leaned back, his arm reaching all the way behind her on the back of the seat. The white Camaro slowly turned around in deep grass and headed off the way it had come, the exhaust rising up out of the grass behind it.

Jerome went into the barn. Inside were several cows, and on the other side it was open to a large pasture where many more dairy cattle were grazing. There was a pump and a tin cup like he hadn't seen for years. He pumped himself a drink of cold water, then a second one, washing away the sour taste of the morning beer and coffee. The cows watched him as he looked around. After a while he went outside. The south side of the barn had a painting of John Lennon on it, painted in dots like a Lichtenstein, only in black and white. "In Memoriam" was printed at the lower edge. Each dot was the size of a silver dollar. Jerome needed to get off a ways in order to really see the picture. He decided to head toward the clump of trees. The sun was warm on his back as he walked. Erica, his ex-wife, came into his mind. If they had lived in a situation like this, maybe they'd have survived. No, he thought, she depended on the city, and, really, so had he back then. Judging from the amount of work he was getting done these days, maybe he still did. He thought of the painting he had going right now, felt a wave of discouragement about it. Right now it felt a little irrelevant.

At the edge of the clump of trees he looked back at the Lennon painting on the barn. It was a close-up of the last Lennon we knew, gaunt, amazed at being forty, wire rims on the long bony nose, singing into the microphone, eyes half shut.

Looking into the woods, Jerome spotted a small pond among the trees and a house on the other side. The house seemed large and peculiarly modern, but sunken in among the foliage as though it too had grown there from roots. He sat in tall grass at the edge of the pond, in a large square of sunlight blazing down, high noon. He watched the house and occasionally looked back toward the barn, half a mile behind him, to see if the car had returned. He thought about little Barbara. This was what she knew, had always known. It was sad to be a part of showing her the larger world. It was bound to disappoint.

Presently Jerome heard the bell again, ringing off beyond the barns, and soon after that two men came out of the house and hurried along a path that led right toward him. He couldn't tell whether they had seen him or not. His heart sped up, and he bent farther down until he thought he might be completely obscured by the tan grass. The two men passed him, heading out across the field. They seemed like monks, their hair short, their work clothes ill-fitting. And there was something about their silence as they walked fast, side by side, first among the tall trees, then out into the sunlight, crossing the field toward the distant rise.

He walked closer to the house. It was a large cottage, older than the other buildings. As he approached, a woman came out. Right away he thought he might know who she was. She was wearing an old dress that was long.

"Hello," Jerome said, going to meet her. "I'm here with Janet."

"I know," the woman said. "I can see the gate from the other side of the lodge. Her famous white car." A smile. The two of them were standing under gray beeches, oaks red and brown. Jerome could sense their branches arching high above him.

"Am I trespassing? That bell rang and I thought . . ."

"The bell is how we put out word if someone is needed," she said. "You aren't trespassing. I love the sound of it, don't you? You can hear it for miles. Stephen got it from a school that was being torn down in Rockford. It was made in the Netherlands. The new school probably uses buzzers." She looked at him. "Did you find Stephen?" Maybe there was some tension in the question.

A woman appeared in shadows on the steps of the cottage, another at the window. Jerome felt as though he'd come into a herd of deer, gentle, wary. Any sudden move might cause them to leap away.

"Well . . ?" He gestured back toward the dairy barn. "Stephen and Janet went off that way somewhere, to find Janet's husband, I think. Stephen was at the barn—they went off that way." Jerome pointed again. "They wanted me to wait."

"We all know to find Stephen at the dairy barn if it's a workday," she said.

"Why's that?"

"It's just true. The cattle are his project. Will's not well, I assume they told you." She extended her hand to him. "My name is Madeline Eisley. I'm called Clay City here." She smiled. "It's so your old boyfriends won't ever find you. That's what we always say among ourselves."

"Like Sister Mary Fatima?"

"Exactly," she said. She looked around. She gestured toward the other women, watching from the cottage. "We almost never get visitors. Can you tell?" She tried to wave them out into the yard, but they wouldn't come. "Janet's name here was Geneseo. Somehow it fit. You get used to things."

In the awkward pauses, Jerome looked out over the pond. Clay City looked back toward the cottage, where her friends continued to watch.

"We know you're here for Barbara," she said. "Is that right?"

Jerome nodded. "Yes."

"It took Janet longer to come for her than we thought it would."

"Yes," Jerome said. "She misses you all."

"She was unhappy here. What's your name?" This directness was much like the assuming way Stephen Boyce had taken Jerome's seat in Janet's car. When Jerome paused a beat too long, she went on. "I don't know what all Janet's told you . . ."

"I'm Jerome. She's talked about her daughter—and, of course, her husband. She talks a lot about the old days, this place. She misses this life, I think."

Clay City looked over her shoulder to the women watching. She stared out at the pond.

"Don't let me keep you from anything," Jerome said. "Maybe I'll walk back to the barn. I'd have stayed but the cows made me self-conscious. Those big brown eyes." They both laughed.

"Will's been having trouble lately. I don't know how much you know."

There was no telling what this lady meant or what she was assuming. Jerome watched her eyes, and what he saw was that she was watching his. After a while he pointed out over the pond, down a long slope to a cluster of rough shacks. "What's that?" The ground around the shacks had been bulldozed.

"We've been doing some clearing down there," she said. "When visitors come—or 'temporaries,' we call them, somebody who might want to join—they stay there. Might end up down there several weeks before they're allowed to come up and stay in the lodge." She indicated the house. "That's the lodge. A lot of kinds of people used to think they wanted to live here . . ." She smiled again. "And we, of course, would never know if we wanted them. Now nobody's coming at all," she added after a moment. "Mostly, we're losing people." She avoided his eyes. "Some of them, when they leave it's in the middle of the night. Like they feel they've failed." The pond whipped up a little in an afternoon breeze. She led him down to the edge of the water, where there was a sort of log bench. "Mostly we would get the young ones. They would always be disappointed that certain things here were about the same as in the world."

"Such as?"

"Such as the raggedy ways people relate."

The woods were very quiet except for the gentle wind. He checked back toward the barn.

"You go through times when this life out here is all you need." She shyly laughed at herself.

"I can understand why someone might want to come here to live," he said.

"We're awfully isolated."

"Isolation can be good sometimes, can't it?" He realized as he said it that he'd never lived in any real isolation in his life.

"Stephen thinks we're almost gone. He compares us to an endangered species—he says that at some point the animal gets the hint and begins to aid in the process of its own extinction." She stood up. "Want to look at the river?"

"Maybe I'll walk back to the barn," he said. "I think we should stay close."

"It *is* close," she said.

A cat came out of some bushes nearby, a small gray cat, carrying in its mouth a baby rabbit. The rabbit was kicking. The cat found some soft grass and sat holding the rabbit tight until finally the kicking stopped and it stretched out softly in a bent U-shape hanging from the cat's mouth.

"C'mon. It'll pass the time," she said, and she turned to the women who were still watching from the lodge. "I'm going to the gazebo," she called to them. She kicked off her leather sandals and tossed them toward the porch. The women disappeared inside.

The path arched around the pond and deeper into the woods. "The pond is quite important here at Geneseo," Clay City was saying. She was walking ahead of Jerome, her soft old dress flowing off her hips and down almost to the ground. It dragged among the burrs and scrub, and when something caught on the skirt it pulled away, revealing for a moment her bare feet, reddish and rough.

"Little places like this depend heavily on symbols, and the pond is one of ours. So's the bell, I guess. The pond is spring-fed. The spring is back there in the trees somewhere. Stephen and some of the other early ones used to give talks at the pond. The idea was to inspire the group to the ideas that founded us. One guy taped most of the pond talks and typed them up. Some have actually been published in magazines. I've never read them, but so they say. This is the cemetery." She indicated off to the left of the path. "We don't mark the graves. One man got sick or something, way back when. There's two babies, and some others. We buried a soldier out here in 1974. He arrived in one of those aluminum cans. Nobody knows who he was. They had an extra body, I think."

As he listened, Jerome thought of the sad story of Clay City which Janet had told him. He sensed that the immediacy of the death of her sister was gone. He looked back into the woods. The dead mouldered under this ancient stand of trees.

"Owl," she said. A big bird lifted up out of the treetops to their right. Its shadow passed over. She was talking straight ahead of her. They came into an area of birches, a wonderland of white and yellow amazingly different from the part of the woods they'd just been in. The birchwood, she called it. Then they came out of the trees high above the river. The gazebo was a round, porchlike structure, covered, enclosed at the back. The walls were a gleaming white wood lattice letting the light through in small diamond shapes which gleamed on the green floor.

"We just repainted it last week. Isn't it stunning?" she said. "I wanted to show it to you because Will built it. He's our best builder. He has all the best ideas." From the gazebo platform, she pointed out over the river to the village of New Boston, and the other way toward what she called Lock 17, a dam.

Jerome sat on the bench in the gazebo and looked out on the river.

"Did you see the sign?" she said. There was a small hand painted plaque over the threshold of the gazebo, on the inside. It said "Save the Earth." "Seems a little dated now. When he came, he was one of these big ecology people. You can about estimate the date of his arrival knowing that—1972, right? He had T-shirts with that green ecology flag, remember? Turned out he was more complicated than that. But we're glad he came to us. For a long time he and Geneseo were very close—but he got worse. He beat her up." She looked at Jerome. "Janet—when things started coming apart with Will and all, so did she. She's an alcoholic. Has she told you all this?"

"No," he said.

"Maybe I should shut up. I'm sorry—I keep wondering how you fit in."

Good question, Jerome thought but didn't say.

She laughed. "You're friends with Janet? That's all?"

Jerome shrugged, feeling a little helpless. "I don't mean to be coy, but isn't being friends enough?"

"Yes." She said it quietly. "I mean," she said, "I guess. We'll see."

"I paint," he said. "I've been teaching some out at the college, in Tuscola. And I do a little carpentry with a local construction crew, to pay the rent. I'm not a craftsman like this guy, though." He indicated the gazebo.

"Well, you must have noticed that Janet drinks a lot. People die of it when they have it like she does."

Jerome stared out across the river from the bluff where they were standing. Iowa.

"Tell me," she said. "Do you think she's stable enough for Barbara to be with her?"

Jerome sat there. He did not answer her. He wondered if they hadn't now struck upon the whole reason for this walk.

"What's Janet doing to eat? Does she have a job?"

Again he said nothing.

"Look," Clay City said, "we love this little girl. She's frail, like her mother. She has a lot of friends here who are as close as brothers and sisters. We can take care of her. Don't take her if Janet isn't ready yet." When he didn't say anything, she pressed on. "I'm trying to talk sense with you. We love Barbara very much. We don't know where she's going."

"I understand you," he said. He held up his hand for her to stop. She stepped away from the gazebo and stood looking out on the river. He wanted her to trust him, and he knew she didn't at all. He felt accused of being a party to Janet's problems. He had to think about that one. He realized he would like to have been a friend of Clay City, wouldn't ever be.

"There are only twenty-seven on this land now," she said. "Nine children. There are eleven men and seven women. We've lost eight in two years. We're definitely the whooping crane."

Jerome looked at her. He tried to imagine her, how she'd look and what she'd be like if this commune had not been part of her life.

"A couple of the originals are here. Stephen is the main one. He says he'll be the one to close the door and turn off the lights." She smiled, perhaps having noted that Jerome's guard was up and trying to relax him. "Well, anyway, that's the Mississippi. There are other pretty places I could show you if you had the time. A painter could love this area. I suspect you don't have time, right?" Her tone was cooler now.

Down below, the river stretched before them. At that distance there was no sense of the water flowing, although in the sunlight it gleamed and flashed between colors of blue and brown. She was leading him back toward the lodge, a different route. For some distance, they were climbing uphill. At one point, she passed between Jerome and the sun. He caught a flash of her brown hair in the wind and saw the silhouette of her legs through the veil of thin cotton she wore around her. From the top of the high bank they had climbed, he saw that the Camaro had pulled up to the edge of the trees. Stephen and Janet were sitting on the log next to the pond. Standing off from them, along the edge of the pond, was Barbara. On the hood of the car was a large cloth bag.

When they got to the pond, Clay City hugged Janet, held her a long time. Janet had been crying, and now she was again. Her hair was messed. She was utterly apart from Jerome—it was clear that he didn't belong there at all.

"They'll be taking Barbara," Stephen said.

Clay City looked at him. "Of course they will," she said.

She took Janet's arm gently and they walked together toward the lodge, the other women coming into the yard to meet them. Janet's blue jeans were a contrast to the long old dresses. Jerome was standing several feet from Stephen, and neither of them said anything. Barbara was on the bench, her arms folded tightly around herself. She was taller than in the picture Jerome had seen, and her nose was sunburned and peeled. Some of the other children had gathered there, too. Jerome could see Janet talking with people in the lodge. All he could hear was the wind.

When they came out of the house, Janet and Clay City were arm-in-arm, walking close, talking quietly. They went down to the edge of the pond and bent down over Barbara.

"How did it go?" Jerome asked Stephen.

"This is his daughter."

Jerome tried to hear friendliness in the tone, but he wasn't sure there was any.

"Will knows it's better this way. He's been confused for days, you know. Not because of this. He had a bad war." Stephen bent down, pulled a long blade of grass. "Janet's terrified of him. He's in a room and won't come out. She tried to talk to him. Forget it. It's a bad time, everything at once." Stephen paused a moment. Then he said, "You're an artist, didn't Janet say?"

Jerome nodded.

"We have several here, artists. Quite a number through the years. One older gentleman here helps the whole community financially with his work. He sells through a gallery on the near northside, New Town, in Chicago."

"Is he the one who did the Lennon on the barn?"

"Nah, one of our people put that up there when John was shot." He turned so that he could see it, and Jerome looked back that way, too. "I always think of the eye-doctor billboard in *Gatsby*. The way it stares out across the field. 'In Memoriam.' I guess I haven't really looked at it for a long time. We aren't ordinarily grim around here. Listen," he said then, talking straight at Jerome but not looking at him, speaking quieter to keep from being heard by anyone else. "We want this girl taken care of. If Janet has problems, you let us know, will you? We can come down and get Barbara. We can come and get them both, although I don't think Janet wants to come back. This little girl—she's part of us almost as much as she's part of Janet. We care about her, I'm trying to say. You must let us know. Call me—I'll send money—anything."

"I understand," Jerome said. Again, as with Clay City, he had the impulse to show Stephen that he could fit in here, that he was likable in the terms of this community. But it was a futile notion. He watched the women at the edge of the pond.

Stephen spoke in a southern accent, strong and steady. "They call this an anarchist community." Now he was looking right at Jerome, smiling. "To my way of thinking, you got most of the anarchy out where you live."

"No argument on that," Jerome said. He and Stephen shook hands.

The women walked back up to them, bringing Barbara along, their hands on her shoulders. Barbara had the same kind of wide-open face and level stare, but she also had that pale, frail blue-white skin, blue veins in her forehead and temples, at the corners of her eyes.

"I'll be coming back, won't I?" she was asking her mom.

"Maybe so," Janet said.

"No," Stephen said, and he squatted down to her. "You stay with your mother. We love you, but you stay with your mom, Barbara. Okay?" She was crying, and Stephen hugged her. The bell, far off, was ringing again. "I've got to go," Stephen said, standing up and turning to Janet. He embraced her, saying something to her no one else could hear. Then he waved again and jogged toward the barns, heading for where the tolling sound of the bell had come from.

"Will I see Daddy anymore?" the little girl said.

Janet put Barbara's cloth bag in the front seat of the car. "You will," she said. "Of course you will." She and Barbara both got in the back seat. Jerome started the car and slowly, driving on dry leaves, pulled out from under the oaks. In the rearview mirror there was Clay City waving. Barbara was waving, too, through the back window.

Suddenly Jerome was thinking about where they were going. A time or two he'd stayed the night at Janet's rented trailer when they'd dragged in late from Gabby's. The feeling was desperate and temporary. The trailer was dark inside, and damp—so damp that the borrowed couch smelled and the dark walnut-print contact paper on the bathroom wall was peeling off in a sheet. The little grass that might have separated Janet's from the next trailer down had long ago been fried away by the sun.

"What did Stephen say to you?" Jerome asked.

"He said good-bye. He said Geneseo's going down. It was like he was apologizing. He said it isn't a failure just because it doesn't last forever."

Clay City came forward out of the shade into the afternoon sun. As they went down the long two-rutted grassy path toward the gate, Jerome could see her, still waving. The children had taken a shortcut and met the car near the gate. One of the older boys swung it open wide. He said "See you, Barbara" as the car went by him.

Barbara was crying quietly, her head down in her mother's lap. Once on the road just beyond Geneseo's gate, Jerome looked back toward the clump of trees, and now he could see where the lodge was, and down the hill to the shacks where the visitors stayed, and deep in the trees he saw Clay City one last time, watching them drive away toward the main highway.

South of the Border

LEIGH ALLISON WILSON

From *From the Bottom Up* (1983)

In a car, headed point-blank down an interstate, there is a sanity akin to recurring dreams: you feel as if every moment has been lived and will be lived exactly according to plan. Landscapes and peripheral realities blur and rush headlong backwards through the windows like the soft edges of sleep. And the road ahead and behind you becomes a straight line, framed in the perfect arc of a dashboard.

My sister sits hunkered against the side of the car and fiddles with the radio, careful not to touch my right leg. On a Sunday morning in the midlands of South Carolina all radio stations play either gospel music or black church services. Jane Anne chooses a church service and claps her hands, eyes closed, to the hiccupping rhythm of the preacher, both his voice and her percussion sounding disembodied in the smallness of the Volkswagen. "Take Jesus, oh Lord take Jesus," the preacher says, "take Jesus for New Year's." Clap clap clap goes my sister, clap clap. "Jesus is my friend" clap "Jesus is your friend" clap "Friends, accept Jesus" clap clap. Deep in her bowels she is a fundamentalist, a lover of simple truths and literal facts; her resolution for the coming year is "to see things more clearly." In this she is resolute, commenting often on points of interest as we career northward through cotton fields and marshy bottomland and stark-colored advertisements.

I have no such resolution. While driving I develop an acute myopia and it is all I can do to concentrate on the pavement that blears and dashes like water underneath the car. Outside the world flashes by as if switched on and off in a two-dimensional slide show, one frame at a time, the whole universe condensed to a television screen.

"Look at that!" Jane Anne cries and points frantically somewhere outside. "Look, look!"

"What was it?"

"You didn't even look," she says. She claps her hands together with a violence that means she wishes one of them was mine. "Didn't even goddamn look at what I saw. You probably had something more important on your mind, I'm sure, probably aren't even interested in that cow I just saw with the human face."

"You just saw a cow with a human face?"

"No," she says, almost happily. "I didn't see a thing," and then she stares sullenly out her window.

Just last night my father and stepmother engaged in a domestic catfight over this kind of optical delusion. During a television football game, the Gator Bowl in Florida, they break out in an almost-brawl over forces beyond their control, forces five hundred miles to their south. Clemson, a South Carolina school, and Ohio State are playing and my father perversely roots for Ohio, a state that exists for him only during television football and basketball games. My stepmother was raised in the thick of Clemson patriotism, a twitch at the corner of one eye blossoming into a full-blown spasm, possibly hindering her vision, at every Clemson penalty and first down.

By the end of the game tension is extreme, my stepmother's eye winks rapidly, my father's mien settles like concrete as he stares at a commercial. Clemson is winning, my palms are sweating and slick, my stepmother is exalted, and my father steadily slips into a familiar attitude. Once, eight years ago, he almost hit me when I won a Monopoly game. His is a competitive madness that operates at a slow boil until all is lost, then his expression explodes into a kind of pseudo-apocalyptic blitz. So when a Clemson player intercepts a key Ohio State pass and Woody Hayes, ex-coach of Ohio State, smacks the Clemson player in the face, my father blitzes out saying "Kill him, kill the bastard, Woody." My stepmother blithers to her feet (they sit in identical easy chairs, separated by a coffee table), winks and gasps, arms akimbo and shivering, shouting now:

"You might as well say 'kill me' that's what you mean!"

Blitz over, my father settles back into concreteness while my stepmother marches, footstep-echoes beating into the walls against one another, into their bedroom. An hour later everyone is sleeping heavily and even the television has sunk into a blank stupor. Today she poked her head in my bedroom doorway, flashing a smile birthed and bred in South Carolina and cultivated like white cotton, and told me goodbye before she left for church. She plays the organ for the Methodist Church of Fort Motte.

Jane Anne points out advertisements for the South of the Border tourist complex still an hour and half in the future. CONFEDERATE FOOD YANKEE STYLE, BEST IN THIS NECK OF THE WOODS one sign reads. So frequent are these advertisements that they serve as punctuation along the sameness of the interstate and I begin to despise them because I feel my utter dependence on their familiarity. I come South twice a year, once at Christmas, once in the summer, each time more of an amnesiac experience than the visit before. I am fearful that after another few visits I may go home and never be able to leave, my present and future eradicated by the vicious tenacity of the past. But, truly, I am hypnotized home by the staid reality of what I remember—a somnambulatory reality so familiar and so unchanging that it appears to be the only true god in my life.

"I'd be a fool to stick around," Jane Tressel sings from the radio. My sister has found an AM station. Lips taut and round, she sings along with her mouth forming the words as if molded around an ice-cream cone. The way she sings turns the words into nonsensical baby-noise, but this is also a special function of AM radio, this ablution of meaning into a catchy anonymity. Jane Anne carefully reads several beauty magazines, pining over the structured perfection of the models, always running out to buy new beauty products although she is as frugal with her money as a squirrel in autumn. A stranger, she sits so close to her door that no place in the car could be equally far from me and she eyes the side of my face with the wariness of a stray dog. She could be a nervous hitchhiker, except that she controls the radio. This trip is the first time we have been together alone in eight years. She is a stranger, stranger still because for thirteen years we slept in the same bedroom and now she resembles a kewpie doll rather than a younger sister.

With her left hand, when it is not spiraling around the radio tuner, Jane Anne tosses boiled peanuts between her lips. They look like a pile of swelled ticks, gray-skinned and blood-bloated, in the palm of her hand, and she is soberly emptying a paper sack full of them. I have noticed that she eats in a dazed trance, similar to the manner in which she sings to the radio, as if eating were a habitual duty. She was always a dutiful child, and now she weighs one hundred and seventy-five pounds, has a prematurely stooped back, and the corners of her mouth pucker down in a perpetual expression of bad humor. An unhappy kewpie doll.

Fifteen years ago she was a beautiful, dutiful child. Fifteen years ago I would bring her red and purple ribbons, watch her thread them through her hair. It looked like miniature maypoles, and when she tossed a braid I wanted to grab one and swing out. Today she wears a mud-colored scarf tied tightly at the nape of her neck.

"Why don't you ever talk seriously to me?" she asks and I grip the wheel, staring hard at the car in front of me, abruptly aware of the scores of vehicles swarming the interstate ahead and behind me. Each one is a possible fatal accident.

"What do you want to talk about?" I say warily, my thighs beginning to feel cramped in the immobile space-time of the traveling Volkswagen interior. In the event of an accident, all is lost in a Volkswagen.

"What do you want to talk about?" Jane Anne mimics in a voice that, remarkably, is more like my own than my own sounds to me. She is full of surprises, this sister of mine whom I do not know. "I'll tell you one damn thing," she says, really angry this time, her tongue flailing against a stray peanut, "you may be smart, but I have all the common sense in this family." Snorting, she clings to the side of her door.

This is true. She does have the common sense in our family, a fact uttered and re-uttered by my paternal grandmother who likens me to my Uncle George Wilkins. My Uncle George was so smart, she says, that he was almost an idiot. He died with a moonshine-ruined liver and a cancer that ate from his breast right through to his back, and Grandmother said it would have gone on through the bed and into the hospital linoleum if his heart hadn't stopped first.

He was a geologist and forever poking rocks with his cane, head bent forward, arm flicking, cane flicking, eyes pouncing toward the ground to examine and file away every square inch of land that his feet passed over. Once he broke his nose against a haybaler, never saw it, saw only the gray-black pieces of sedimentary rock that flipped over and under the tip of his cane. But he was a smart one, my Uncle George, and twice a year scientists from Washington came down to sober him up and fetch him back to a laboratory where he performed penetrating geological studies. They wanted him to fly up there, but he always said he did his traveling on the ground. Now he's his own specimen, buried under six feet of sand and sedimentary rock in Calhoun County, South Carolina, and he's not going anywhere.

"I'll tell you another damn thing," Jane Anne says and warms up to one of our childhood wrangles, the kind where neither of us is aware of the reason but both of us will stake our lives on a resolution in our favor. It is our father's blood that swells up at these times, bubbles of madness that break at the mouth. "I'll miss your sweet, sweet eyes," Willie Neal croaks from the radio, "I told you when I left, I couldn't live with your lies."

"I'm sick and tired of you making me feel stupid. You act like I'm still eleven years old, like I'm still your devoted and moronic pawn. I'm nineteen, damn you, I've read Sartre and Camus." She utilizes her French education in all arguments, since I have studied only Latin and vaguely remember it anyway—French is her code language through which she can curse me to my ignorant face. "I've seen Chicago and New York, I've seen Paris and *you* don't even have a passport."

"A passport isn't exactly a rite of passage, Jane Anne."

"Not," she says, "if you don't even have one." Furious now, she sputters like a cat and is just seconds away from a serious assault. Sometimes when we were younger we'd forget what we were angry about in the middle of a wrangle, and so kept on with it anyway, only louder and with more passion.

"Not," she says, "if you travel with your heart incognito like a goddamn ghost. You've been just a barrel of laughs for two weeks."

"Didn't come down here," I say, grim as a soldier, "in order to entertain my family." There is a white Pontiac endangering my rear bumper.

"Then why, in God's name, did you come at all?" Jane Anne kicks the peanut sack; the Pontiac veers to the left and passes safely, though in a glance I can tell that the man inside it is a lunatic.

"I know one thing and don't you forget it: I am as educated as you are, I am as competently conversive as you are."

This, too, is true. In fact, Jane Anne can shift facilely between

Sunday dinner chatter at my grandmother's and mournful sympathetico at my aunt's where my first cousin, Jonathan, is dying of cancer. Both situations strike me dumb.

At my grandmother's Christmas dinner, I deaf-mute my way through the awkward vacuum during which butt-pinching uncles watch football games and bouffant-headed aunts question me as to how many boyfriends I have and my grandmother pounces at odd moments to bark in my ear, "Can't go to school forever!" Normally I wink and grin like a demon, offer condolences for my slovenly personality, giggle madly while my butt is tweaked, and create countless football players who appear and disappear as boyfriends according to my whim. Once I created a rather bookish law student who was poorly received and he disappeared during the course of dessert, an hour later reappearing as a dashing quarterback who was a well-received pre-med. This time, however, I sleepwalk, staring maniacally at each relative until they leave me alone.

"Time to eat!" Grandmother cries, pertly, her presence in its element and as relentless as a Mack truck. Fourteen grown men and women rise as one and throng into the kitchen where dishes of food, festive-colored and bubbling, are lined in perfect rows to be picked over, placed on china plates and retired to the dining room, there to be consumed in dutiful silence. But first comes the continuum in which fourteen grown men and women hang back, hem-haw, pluck at their sleeves or pick their noses, succumb to the cowardliness of not being first in line though for five hours their appetites have been titillated to the peak of a savage desire. For a few seconds we stand like tame vultures and just peer, ravenous, at the untouched food. I believe I will faint from hunger, until I finally find myself at the table, slapping mashed potatoes onto crisply cool china.

"Jane Anne," Grandmother says in her grand commandeering tone, a tone reminiscent of both grade-school teachers and Methodist preachers, "would you please say grace." Jane Anne positively glistens with glee, jubilant while all eyes pin me against the profaned table, potatoes puffed and accusing on my plate.

"For these Thy gifts, Oh Lord let us be thankful," Jane Anne croons, in a strangerly fashion. The surge is on now, compliments and condiments fly across the table, and I sleepwalk through dinner, an attendant to disapproval.

FREE IN-ROOM MOVIES: TWENTY HONEYMOON SUITES I read on a huge sign. In twenty minutes we will pass through the middle of South of the Border, almost into North Carolina. The peanuts have risen once more into Jane Anne's lap, and she nimbly eats them. "It's my last night in town, I'd be a fool to stick around," the radio says. I do not know the performer although his song is appealing in its drowsy insistence. At South of the Border Jane Anne will meet a boyfriend from her school and I will continue north to my school alone. Both of us are hyper-aware of the advertisements, as if they are motes of sand trickling time away. She wants to get out of my presence as badly as I do hers; we are both morbidly afraid of each other. FREE—ADVICE, AIR, WATER. EVERYTHING ELSE REASONABLE.

"Another thing," she says, wrapping up her side of the dialectic before handing the floor to me, "you have been nothing but rude and ill-mannered this whole vacation, to me, to Daddy, even to Aunt Louise. You lack discrimination, that's what you lack."

"Jonathan . . . how is he?" Jane Anne whispers to my aunt. I perch on the lips of a couch, finger wringing finger, my tongue thick as a marble tombstone.

"Dying," my aunt chokes, "dy—ing."

"How long?" Jane Anne looks absolutely engrossed, a dutiful child.

"Days, weeks, God knows when he'll be free from the pain." Solemnly Jane Anne acknowledges the mercy of God with a slow, dazed nodding of her chin. She is gathering momentum for the predictable eventuality wherein my aunt will begin to sob and she can console with a firm and warm arm across the heaving back. But—surprise—my aunt visibly marshals her circumference and pulls herself together with a prolonged sigh. My palms are clammy with the dead and the living.

"Sarah Louise is home," my aunt says, giddy with recovered strength, but poised along some precipice of mental breakdown. Sarah Louise is also my first cousin. "She's in the back bedroom getting dressed." Sarah Louise is in the back bedroom getting dressed, Jonathan is in the front bedroom, blinds drawn, dying. For a while we sit in an uncomfortably loud silence until Sarah Louise comes into the living room. Like her mother, Sarah Louise has reddish-brown hair and a pointed face that articulates itself at the breach of the nose. She looks like a rumpled domesticated animal, exhaustion whitening her cheeks in random places like frostbite. She is looking directly into my eyes.

"He wants to see you, Bo."

"Me?"

"He's asking for you."

Jane Anne shivers and recoils. I recoil, a creeping nausea deep inside my throat; I wish to hell I was somewhere, anywhere, somebody someplace else. When I was two, Jonathan christened me into the family by nicknaming me Bo, a name used only by blood relatives and, to them, a name coincidental with my very existence. Only recently has Jane Anne begun to call me Jennifer, her statement of self-determination. Nomenclature is her forte.

I remember Jonathan in two ways: first, the way he looked at eleven, knobby-kneed and skinny as a fence post, my best friend and comrade. Like rabid dogs we chased the cows on his father's farm until they ran idiotically into their pond water and grouped together up to their buttocks in sludge and cattails. The days I spent with him were always warm and cloudless and kinetic with revelry. We played doctor inside the very room where he now lies dying; he was the first man I ever studied. Once my father found us together and beat me with a leather belt until welts crisscrossed my bare legs and back like textile woof. Afterwards, since we lived in different towns, he grew out of revelry and into proms and long-legged cheerleaders. I saw him last two years ago, a young man so handsome he could send pangs of romance down the back of Ayn Rand herself. Blond hair feathered and long around his neck, the face of a beautiful woman made a little rough at the edges, an unaware body oozing casual strength and grace, the man was unbearably pretty. I believe the mythic Christ, aided by centuries of imagination, could never approach the fullness of reality in Jonathan's splendor.

I stand and rub my hands together and they slide against their own moisture. In times of stress I enter into a semicomatose state like an instinct-driven opossum. Automatically my brain begins to decline a Latin noun, a ae ae am a, ae arum is as is. The room is shadowed and unlit, a thickly-queer smell of medicine and urine and *sweet Jesus* the smell of life itself condensed into a pungent and rancid death-room, without light and without hope. I feel an acute hatred for myself, sweat trickling—an endless beading health—under my armpits: da ta ta ta, a ae am a, this is the way the world ends. Across the room the bed seems to rest against the far wall but surely to God he is not in it, there is no indentation under the quilt, there is only a skull resting on the pillow, a yellow hairless sunken skull.

"Bo," he says, a muffled, anonymous sound, drugged, removed, a physical impossibility save in nightmare. Dipping strangely, the lines of the room combat with a nausea, and I realize my mouth is whimpering and salivating. This nausea moves around the throat like an unconscious prayer. The sting is for the da ta ta ta, arum is as is.

"Bo," he whispers, "I wanted to tell you . . ."

"Tell me."

"It's not so bad."

"Tell me quick."

He coughs without coughing, resting. Two more minutes and

I will go mad and this thought is comforting. Someone is whimpering somewhere.

"Are you still my friend?"

("Fucking Jesus!" Jonathan yells and punches the air with his fist. The cowshed blows up in slow motion, splinters of wood fall like dust on his hair and shoulders. Large pieces of board fly over the fence, landing with dull thuds in the pasture. Down below, huddled up and frightened, Bo studies the delicate white hairs on the back of his right leg.)

"I wanted to tell you goodbye," he says.

(The others said, "Don't tiddle in the pond," but they pay no attention. They are full, with the warm brown water pressing against them, and they pay no attention. Across the water, stabbed by erect cattails, the cows stand knee-deep and black near the pond's edge, tails slapping onto their backs, heads browsing onto the surface then easing back up to stare at pine trees. Bo and Jonathan know that they think of great things, standing there in the water, staring. They tiddle freely and silently into the pond.)

"It's not so bad," he says.

I pretend I haven't heard.

"It leaves."

"Jonathan . . ."

"Goodbye," he says. "I loved you, yes," and then he starts to doze.

"Goodbye."

I return to the living room and begin to cry. My aunt and Sarah Louise begin to cry. Jane Anne stares at me with narrow eyes, her mouth puckered in distaste, then she pats and coos and comforts Sarah Louise. Uncontrollably I want to punch her in the nose, kiss her on the mouth, dash outside to the car, and get the hell out of South Carolina. A past is dying out from under my feet and I notice for the first time the blinking red lights on my aunt's Christmas tree. One two three, one two three they waltz, immobile, on the outskirts of her fir needles. I picture my sister wrapped in red lights, clapping her hands—one two three. When we get into the Volkswagen, she says: "You should have controlled yourself, you shouldn't have cried in front of them. We were guests in their house."

Ramona Stewart sings: "The sun's falling from the sky and night ain't far behind." Jane Anne waits for my defensive remarks, contemplating her retort through a wriggling at the lips, the worrying to death of a boiled peanut at the tip of her tongue. "Sun's falling," Ramona goes on, "night ain't far behind."

"Listen, Jane Anne," I say, glancing briefly in her direction, then staring straight ahead, a cheap power play although my hand and eyes are truly busy. She is filing away the information, noting the brevity and attributing it to arrogance.

"Can't we part as friends, can't we please just forget our old roles and part as friends? Please?"

Up ahead a huge sombrero sits atop a five-story tower. We have arrived at our connection, South of the Border. My sister sits in complete silence, one of her half-dutiful trances, and I pull off at the exit and enter the parking lot of a coffee house that is partly Mexican, party southern, and mostly middle-American slough. Jane Anne's friend slumps manfully against the wheel of a red Datsun hatchback with Wisconsin plates and, suddenly businesslike, Jane Anne is out of the car, suitcase in hand, pocketbook slung in a noose around her neck.

"Goodbye," she says and is gone. I watch while she situates herself in the Datsun, then I pull out of the parking lot, drive up the entrance ramp to the interstate, alone inside the throbbing, hurtling Volkswagen, then insert myself into the welter of anonymous northbound vehicles.

I can go home again, again and again, each episode like a snowflake that sticks to your eyelashes. They melt and mingle with your tears. Take a memory, any memory, and it becomes an inviolable god, a sanity exactly according to plan. But those soft edges—those peripheral realities that blur, those landscapes that shift and rush past—those are the crucibles of emotion, and they flow headlong backwards beneath your feet. I come South only twice a year, once at Christmas, once in the summer. Each time is a possible fatal accident.

Miller Duskman's Mistakes

KARIN LIN-GREENBERG

From *Faulty Predictions* (2014)

Miller Duskman's first mistake was shipping the fancy pizza oven from Italy to Morningstar, Ohio. His second was taking out a full-page ad in the *Star Record* to inform us that his pizza was made from a gourmet Neapolitan recipe. No one wanted his pizza with that burnt thin crust and the cheese made from buffalo milk. Why would anyone want anything to do with Italian buffalos when you could drive five miles from town and find farm after farm with cows producing good, clean American milk? If Miller had done his research, he would have known that in Morningstar we liked our pizza from Joe's, and we liked the crust doughy and thick, the cheese a gooey mix of provolone and mozzarella. We didn't need to see dough tossed in the air. We loved watching Joe push out dough with his stubby fingers in the dented metal pans he'd used for years. And besides, we had no money for twenty-dollar pizzas that wouldn't fill our stomachs. The glass factory had closed down two years before and the broom factory had closed right after that; many people were still out of work when Miller showed up.

I've run the Ladybug Bed and Breakfast for the last twenty-five years in Morningstar. Ask me anything about this town and I can likely give you an answer; people talk to me, tell me things. They stop by for a muffin or a cup of coffee—and mind you, I never charge anyone I know for food—and they tell me what they've seen and heard. And so when Missy Carlton, the librarian, stopped by with the newest Mary Higgins Clark I'd requested, sipped the mug of Earl Grey with cream I'd prepared for her, and said there was a new face in town, I listened hard.

The rumor was that Miller had an aunt and uncle who'd lived in Morningstar years ago, and he'd come to stay with them one summer when he was a child. After he'd grown up and made his money on Wall Street, he decided to come back to Morningstar because of his good memories of that childhood summer. But I'm not sure if that story is true. Miller couldn't have been older than thirty. Most of us have been in Morningstar all our lives, and if a new child, especially one like Miller with a head the shape of a tire swing, appeared for a summer, we would have noticed. And there are no Duskmans in town, never have been. Certainly no one claimed him when he showed up and opened the Brilliance Café on Friendsville Street in the space where Ike's Hardware used to be before Lowe's came to the north end of town and drove poor Ike Bell into the grave. Even those of us who wanted to keep shopping at Ike's had a hard time, since Lowe's was cheaper and had a better selection. We wondered if the stress of losing his business caused Ike's heart attack. We felt sorry about that, guilty, and swore we'd do better about supporting our own.

Miller Duskman's third mistake was building the outside of the Brilliance Café completely out of glass. Who wanted to be watched while eating, like an animal in the zoo? I guess he thought it made the place look cold and modern, like something you'd see in a city. All that old brick and stone downtown, and then the Brilliance Café glowing like some giant ice cube plopped in the middle of the block. I'm not sure how the whole building managed to stay upright; I couldn't see any metal or glue or anything else holding all that glass together. I'm sure he got some architect from New York City to draw up the plans for it, someone who knew nothing about the weather in Ohio, and I didn't trust that the building would stay standing through the windy fall and the blizzards of winter. Every time a storm hit Morningstar, I'd wonder if the building would be knocked over in a gust of wind, and I was always surprised when I drove by it and saw that it was still there. To tell you the truth, that all-glass building was like something magical, and maybe if someone we liked had constructed it, we would have been impressed. But we couldn't believe Miller tore down Ike's Hardware. The structure was sound, the floors made of good black cherry, and the building had years of life left. We watched the trucks from Lowe's deliver sheet after sheet of thick glass. Glass had once been manufactured in Morningstar, and as I watched the men unload the trucks, I thought about the time when our town was busy and people had good, steady jobs.

Construction on the Brilliance Café went on through the spring, and it opened on the first of May. The only people who went were the Lake College kids, checking it out before heading home for the summer. Of course the college kids ate there. They're not really from Morningstar; they're like the tourists who come for the Harvest Festival, except they stick around for four years. Word is Miller put an ad in the *Lake's Voice*, the paper at the college, with a coupon for 30 percent off any pizza. The kids piled in with that coupon and paid with their parents' money. Miller was a newcomer, an outsider, and all his business from Lake College just seemed to prove how much he didn't belong.

Once May ended and the students left, the Brilliance Café suffered. The only customers were the people who worked at the college. I knew Miller had to be thankful for the college's business; I understood how the college could keep a place afloat in

Morningstar. Without the parents and the campus visitors stay-ing at the Ladybug Bed and Breakfast, my business would be slim. But there was one crucial difference between Miller and me: my family has been in Morningstar for generations. My grandpar-ents opened the bed and breakfast in 1927. No one in town faulted me when most of my business came from the college. And I pro-vided a place to stay for those overflow relatives at Thanksgiving and Christmas that just couldn't fit into overcrowded houses—at a discount, always, for people I knew. In fact, I barely made a profit off any of the townsfolk. The outsiders were another mat-ter; they were willing to pay far more than the rates at the Hol-iday Inn in Akron or Cleveland in order to absorb the charm of small town Ohio. If they were lucky, they might even see one of the Amish buggies rolling by slowly in front of the B&B.

Sometimes tourists wandered into the Brilliance Café; maybe it reminded them of home, of the types of restaurants they'd go to in their cities. But most everyone who lived in Morningstar made an effort to steer clear of it. When we saw Miller in town, we didn't say hello. We ignored him or gave him cold looks. And maybe Miller would have given up after a few months, packed up and moved back East, but then Avery Swenson returned. She'd just graduated from Ohio State, had her teaching degree, and everyone thought she would leave Morningstar behind, escape the hurt that'd happened to her here. We were overjoyed when we heard she had signed a contract to teach third grade at Morn-ingstar Elementary. Avery was a girl with options, and she'd cho-sen to come home.

When Avery was four, a semi from Florida filled with oranges barreled down Friendsville Street. The trucker raced through Morningstar after part of I-71 was shut down because of oil spilled from a tanker. The semi killed Avery's mother, who'd been driv-ing home from the night shift at the diner. It had been the truck-er's fault, blowing through a stop sign. Still, now, when I drive on

Friendsville, I think of those oranges rolling on the road after the accident, the force of it so hard that the back doors of the trailer opened, spilling its contents.

Now Avery was an especially sad story. Her father—who'd been a good boy, so smart and handsome—died over in Iraq, the first time we were there. All she had left after her mother's death was her grandfather, but he was forgetful and soon that forgetfulness turned into senility. Even at four years old, Avery could take care of him better than he could take care of her. It must be said that Avery was extraordinary, the smartest girl maybe to be born in Morningstar, and at four she was already reading real books with chapters. It was up to us, then, as a town, to step in, to care for Avery and her grandpa Earl. For the next twelve years, we worked on a rotating schedule, cooking Avery and Earl dinner, packing Avery's lunches, making sure everything was OK. Each Friday afternoon, Missy Carlton dropped off a sack of library books and picked up another sack of books that Avery had read during the week. We sewed her costumes for school plays, took her to Miss Betty's to get her hair cut, and when she was sixteen Logan Pierce taught her how to drive in his Volvo. We'd assigned him the task of driving instruction because we'd heard Volvos were the safest cars.

When Avery was ten years old, she rang the doorbell of the Ladybug one Friday after school. I opened the door and saw her, hair in two tidy braids, white button-down shirt still crisp after a day of school, Mary Janes unscuffed. I smiled. "You don't have to ring the doorbell, Avery Swenson. You're like family. You just walk in whenever you want, day or night."

She nodded but said, "It's not polite to walk into other people's houses. It's trespassing."

"Well, you don't need to worry about politeness, young lady. You're the most polite person I ever met. My Izzy could take a lesson or two from you." My daughter, Isabelle, was three years older than Avery. I'd hoped that they might become friends, but Izzy had no use for Avery; she said Avery was too much of a kiss-up, won every academic prize in school, was every teacher's pet. "Mom," Izzy once said to me, "Avery *volunteered* to go outside during lunch period every day and clap the chalk out of the erasers. She's such a nerd." And Izzy, I hate to admit, was never the teacher's pet, was sloppy and undisciplined, wore her shirts untucked and painted her fingernails blue. She constantly had headphones on and listened to music too loudly blasting out of her Walkman.

"Do you want a snack?" I asked. I ushered Avery into the front hallway and toward the kitchen.

She shook her head. "No, thank you. Would you show me how to make a bed?"

"Make a bed?" I wondered if I'd heard wrong.

"I thought you would be the best bed-making expert in town since you have to make the beds here at the bed and breakfast every day. I can make my bed, but I can't make it *well*. I'd like to learn from you, please."

I understood then what Izzy meant about Avery being every teacher's pet. She wanted to learn to do things that no one wanted to do. What other ten-year-old girl would have made such a request? I looked out the kitchen window and across the street to the stone lions at the gate of Lake College. Beyond the lions was Armstrong Hall, with its gray turrets, its blue and gold flags flying high atop them. I imagined Avery in a few years—at twelve or thirteen—pushing through the solid wooden doors of Armstrong Hall, where the science classes at Lake were held, and asking the professors to teach her how to use microscopes, how to train lab rats, how to use Bunsen burners.

"All right, Avery," I said. "If you want to make a bed with tight corners and fluffy pillows, you've come to the right place. Follow me." I led her up the stairs, and she followed, walking daintily, barely making any noise, so different from Izzy who pounded up and down the stairs dozens of times a day in her unlaced boots.

Avery was an odd little girl, but I, like everyone else in town, could not help but love her.

When Avery was sixteen, her grandfather passed. This death was slow and painful, and we were all grateful when it ended. It was his time. After that, Avery said she could take care of herself. We didn't want to agree with her, but we knew she was a responsible young lady. There was some money, life insurance from her father, a settlement from her mother's death, but we wanted her to save that money for college, so we still delivered food to her front porch and dropped it off before Avery could say no.

Avery was the valedictorian of Morningstar High and received a Presidential scholarship to Ohio State. She'd chosen that over a full scholarship to Lake College. We'd hoped she'd stay and go to Lake. She could mingle with those students who drove expensive cars with license plates from Connecticut, New York, and Massachusetts, and she could prove that Morningstar was able to produce someone who could go head-to-head with those kids from private schools in the Northeast. Now I wonder if Avery had chosen Ohio State so she could have a little breathing room for a few years, so she could get away from us and become her own person. In any case, the scholarship allowed her not to worry about tuition, and it was good that she had money tucked away. She bought herself a car. She could afford books. We were sad to see Avery go to Columbus, but we knew it was for the best.

The person who was saddest to see Avery go was Caleb Barlow. It might not be kind to say that he was slow, but that's the truth. He was the sweetest boy around, gentle, loved animals. He was in the same grade as Avery. On graduation day, Avery gave her valedictorian speech, and Caleb received an award. He was the first student in the history of Morningstar to never miss a single day of school from kindergarten all the way through twelfth grade. Everyone cheered when the principal handed him a certificate. We clapped so loudly and cheered so hard that

Caleb handed his certificate back to the principal and put his hands over his ears, but it was ok because he was smiling, as overwhelmed as he was.

Everyone knew Caleb had been in love with Avery since pretty much the beginning of time. Well, everyone except Avery. Avery never seemed interested in much except her books. On some Friday nights, she and some girls from the track team would go to the movies at the single-screen theater downtown, but most Friday nights she was at home studying. She'd never had a boyfriend in Morningstar, and that was just fine. She didn't need to get herself into trouble that way, didn't need to get pregnant like those trashy girls who lived past Bowman Lane, the ones who sat on their porches eating greasy potato chips out of large bags and hooting at men driving by. Bowman was just three blocks away from Lake College; it was where the town turned from the well-kept faculty houses that surrounded the school to the run-down, dilapidated houses that the students from the college rushed by if they were headed to a movie or the ice cream shop or the bank downtown. Avery's house was only a block up from Bowman, and I was always glad she never let herself drift down the street, never got involved with the high school dropouts.

Caleb followed Avery around town, hanging around her in the library or the drugstore. Avery was always kind to Caleb, but she didn't seem to understand how much he cared for her. When she left for college, Caleb moped around town all day. A couple of weeks after she left, he found a job working for some of the Amish down the way, caring for their chickens. It was good that Caleb had found a job; his father had been out of work and depressed since the broom factory closed down, and at least Caleb was able to bring some money into the house, however little it was. The Amish must have had a sense about him, because they never hired anyone who wasn't their own. When we drove out of town, we saw him walking around on the farms, scattering feed, and we watched the chickens follow him everywhere he went like he was their mama hen. He was so gentle, the way he picked up the chicks, cradled them in his thin hands.

After a few months Caleb started a business delivering eggs for the Amish. He drove an old, bulky Cadillac that had belonged to his grandfather, and he could drive fine, although he always drove under the speed limit. We'd put in our orders, and on Wednesday afternoons he'd drive from house to house, delivering our eggs. I always made lemonade, extra sweet, when I knew he was on the way with my eggs.

Caleb was happiest during Avery's breaks from school, when she'd come back to town. She always took Caleb out to Frost King, and she'd tell him about her life at college, and he would tell her about the chickens and the egg business. He'd order a soft-serve vanilla cone, and she'd eat a bowl of strawberry ice cream, and when she was done, she'd put her chin in her palm and listen to Caleb as if his stories about baby chicks and delivering eggs were the most interesting stories she'd ever heard.

No one was happier than Caleb to hear that Avery was returning to Morningstar. For the week before Avery's return in late July, he gave everyone thirteen eggs instead of the usual dozen, cradling the extra egg carefully on top of the carton as he walked from his car to our front doors. I thought a lot about Avery and Caleb that week, thought about how we hardly knew her anymore. Four years away was a long time. Maybe she had a boyfriend. Maybe she was even engaged. What would that do to Caleb? It would be OK if these things happened far away—we could shield Caleb from them—but what would he do if she brought some boy home with her? It was a relief when Avery arrived home alone. She took Caleb out for banana splits after she found a wire basket filled with six dozen eggs on her porch the afternoon of her return.

After they'd finished at Frost King, Caleb and Avery walked to the center of town and stood outside the Brilliance Café. Caleb waved his arms and crashed his body into the glass building.

He did it again and again, and finally Avery pulled him to her and held him tightly. Caleb was crying, big, heaving sobs, his face sloppy. He had been telling Avery about the birds. Just like the rest of us, the birds couldn't understand that glass building right there in the middle of Friends-ville Street. They flew into the Brilliance Café since they couldn't tell the difference between glass and sky. There were often dead birds on the sidewalk. Sometimes we'd see Miller with a snow shovel, scooping those birds up. He'd slide the birds onto his shovel, carry them to the Dumpster out back, and heave them in like last week's leftovers.

A few weeks before Avery's return, Caleb drove down Friends-ville Street, on his way to deliver two dozen eggs to Mrs. Crenshaw, and saw Miller with his shovel standing over a dead bird. Caleb parked his car crookedly and ran to Miller.

"What are you doing?" Caleb said.

"These birds," Miller said, waving down at three dead blackbirds, "they're a pain."

"You're killing the birds?" said Caleb.

"*I'm* not doing anything. They're too stupid to know not to fly into buildings."

Caleb bristled at the word "stupid." Everyone in Morningstar knew he didn't like it. Years ago, I spanked my own daughter for using the word about Caleb. He wasn't a quick thinker, but he wasn't stupid. He didn't have a brain that cranked fast like Avery's, but there were things he knew how to do, things he was good at.

"Are you going to bury them?" Caleb said.

Miller laughed, hard and dry. "Bury them? Yeah, sure, and I'll have a funeral, too."

"What do you do with them?" Caleb said.

"Dumpster," Miller said, pointing toward the back of the building.

"Oh," said Caleb. He took a step backward and then he began to cry, his mouth open, spit dribbling out.

"Oh, God," Miller said. "Please don't cry." I think this was when Miller finally realized something about Caleb, maybe understood he wasn't just a young punk giving him a hard time.

"Hey," Miller said, his voice softening. "It's OK."

Caleb shook his head, didn't say anything more. He sniffled hard.

"Listen, you want some pizza? Free pizza?" Miller said.

"I like Joe's pizza," Caleb said.

"You and everyone else in town." Miller sighed and put his shovel down on the sidewalk. "Look, I'll buy you a slice of Joe's pizza. Truce?"

Caleb's tears had started drying, but he was still sucking in big gasps of air. "You can't buy a slice. You have to buy a pie."

"Who doesn't sell slices? You can't walk down a block in New York without seeing some place selling slices. What if you just want one slice of pizza?"

"Then you share the rest of the pie with your family," Caleb said.

Now it was Miller's turn to shake his head. "Of course," he said. "Because everyone has a goddamn family around here." His voice was sharp again.

"I have to go," Caleb said, backing farther away, as if he were afraid Miller might hit him. "The eggs in the car are going to get hot."

He turned and headed back to the Cadillac. Miller stood on the sidewalk and watched as Caleb pulled back onto Friendsville Street. When Caleb was gone, Miller picked up his shovel, scooped up the dead blackbirds, and carried them to the Dumpster.

After that, I'd see Caleb slowly driving down Friendsville several times a day. If I stepped out onto the porch and craned my neck, I could see all the way downtown, could see the front of the Brilliance Café. If there were any dead birds on the sidewalk, Caleb would park, slip on a pair of thick leather gloves, and place the birds in a burlap sack.

One afternoon, Logan Pierce, the high school math teacher, followed Caleb, kept close behind Caleb's Cadillac in his red Volvo that Avery had learned to drive in six years before. Logan told me that he followed Caleb all the way to Harding Cemetery, where Caleb's mother had been buried when Caleb was fifteen. Caleb parked in a visitor's spot, and Logan watched him haul a heavy-looking sack out of the Cadillac's trunk. Caleb put his gloves on and grabbed a gardening shovel from the trunk and walked toward his mother's gravestone. Logan got out of his car and followed. He stood under a weeping willow and watched as Caleb dug up a small patch of grass near his mother's grave. Then he reached into his burlap sack and took out one of those small egg cartons, the kind for just a half dozen eggs. He opened it like a coffin and put a sparrow in. Then he gently placed the closed egg carton in the ground. Logan squinted and saw other patches of missing grass near Beverly Barlow's grave and realized it wasn't the first time Caleb had done this. He jogged up to where Caleb was digging another hole for the next grave.

"Caleb," Logan said.

"Oh, Mr. Pierce," Caleb said. "Hello." He blinked up at him.

"You can't do this," Logan said. "People put a lot of effort into keeping this grass looking nice."

"But he's putting the birds in the Dumpster."

Logan nodded and thought hard about what to do. Then he got down on his knees and helped Caleb bury the rest of the birds. When they had smoothed moist soil over the birds' graves, Logan stood, held out a hand to Caleb, and helped him up. "We'll figure something out," Logan said. "We'll figure out what to do about the birds."

Logan went to the Brilliance Café to talk to Miller the next day. He asked him to put bird silhouettes on the window, the kind that let birds understand there's something solid in front of them.

He even brought some silhouettes he'd bought at Lowe's. Miller told Logan he'd spent his life savings on the Brilliance Café, paid a lot for that clear glass, spent an hour each day wiping fingerprints off it, and he wasn't going to ruin all of that with ugly bird cutouts.

"Please," Logan said. "I'm asking you as a favor."

Miller shook his head.

"You really can't?" Logan said.

Miller shook his head again and said, "I won't."

For the next few weeks, Caleb drove by and picked up the dead birds. He'd show up in the morning before Miller arrived and then return in the afternoons when Miller was pacing back and forth between the kitchen and the dining area. Miller had cut back on his staff. There was just the chef and one waitress per shift. Sometimes Miller let the chef go home early because he knew how to cook everything on the menu himself. Someone heard that he'd gone to culinary school in France for two years after he'd made all his money and quit his job on Wall Street.

The only people who still went to the Brilliance Café were from the college, and the only day the restaurant was busy was when Luanne Gilcrest retired from the Admissions Office and the entire office came out for a celebratory lunch. Miller brought pizza after pizza out. He smiled, and everyone noticed for the first time that despite the too-round head, he was handsome when he wasn't scowling. No one in town had ever seen Miller so happy before, so excited. Some of the women from the Admissions Office said that Miller was really a lovely young man, and his attitude problems were just a result of his money troubles and a sense of being unwelcome in Morningstar. They were convincing, but not convincing enough to get me to go to the Brilliance Café, especially in light of the bird issue.

And the bird issue was certainly still a problem. Logan Pierce knew Caleb couldn't keep digging up the soil around his mother's grave like some gopher, so he offered his backyard for Caleb's burials. Of course Mary Pierce was furious about Caleb coming by every few days with his shovel and tearing up her flowerbeds, but what could she do? She told us that someone else had better step up once her backyard was filled. She said this loudly while standing in line at the bank, looking directly at Nancy Stables, who owned twelve acres right on the edge of town. Nancy stared down hard at the check in her hand.

So once Avery got back to town and Caleb explained everything, Avery stormed into the Brilliance Café and gave Miller an earful. Her face got red and she kept pointing at the windows and at Caleb, who waited for her on the sidewalk. It didn't take long before Miller began to nod, saying, "OK, OK, OK."

The next afternoon, Avery sat at one of those long wooden tables in the Brilliance Café with a stack of black construction paper and a pair of scissors. Every once in a while Miller walked by the table and stopped to examine Avery's work. She cut out all sorts of birds, some small, some big with wide wingspans. After a few hours, Miller and Avery stood on chairs and taped the birds all over the glass walls. They laughed as they worked. At one point, Avery reached up high, her shirt lifting to expose a line of belly, and Miller jumped off his chair and grabbed Avery's sides to make sure she didn't fall. After they finished, they shared a pizza, one of those extravagant ones, with morel mushrooms, ricotta cheese, and baby asparagus. The two of them ate it all while sharing a carafe of red wine, drinking until their cheeks got pink.

After that afternoon, things changed. Birds stopped flying into the Brilliance Café. Avery's cutouts did the trick. The more significant change, of course, was that Avery took up with Miller. Maybe we should have expected it. She'd spent four years in the city, and when she returned, we must have seemed awfully quiet and dull to her compared to Miller with his glass building and exotic ingredients. I could show her how to fold a fitted sheet,

Missy Carlton could teach her the Dewey Decimal System, Logan Pierce could explain the Pythagorean theorem. But how could we ever compare to Miller?

Before the school year started, we'd see Avery sitting in the Brilliance Café drinking iced tea and working on lesson plans. Sometimes Miller would stand behind her, massaging her shoulders, leaning down to kiss the top of her head before he went back to the kitchen. In the evenings, after the few customers left, they would dance slowly in the darkened restaurant lit only by a few flickering candles on the tabletops, spinning around and around. Why would Avery so boldly display herself in the glass restaurant? What bothered us most was that Caleb could see all of it. Some nights he walked by outside the Brilliance Café with his gloves and burlap sack, but there were no birds anymore. There was nothing for him to do but walk slowly and watch Avery and Miller and all that love right on display.

We were sure Caleb's car accident in September was because of his devastation. He crashed the Cadillac on Pine Street, smashed right into a telephone pole. If we hadn't known Caleb, we would have thought he was drunk, but everyone knew Caleb didn't drink. The car was too twisted to be salvaged. Caleb, unsurprisingly, was perfectly fine. As a child, he tripped on uneven sidewalks, toppled off his bike, fell off ladders, and there was never a sprain or broken bone. At worst he'd have a few scratches. "That's my miracle boy," his father would say after every one of Caleb's accidents. Even though Caleb was fine, his car was totaled, and this was a problem because Caleb had been doing well with his egg deliveries. We all wanted to help, but what could we do? There were no jobs to spare in Morningstar.

Avery persuaded Miller to hire Caleb as a busboy. She told him it would just be until Caleb made enough money to buy a used car and could get back to delivering eggs. She must have told Miller that it would be impossible for the Barlows to survive with both Caleb and his father out of work. So Miller hired Caleb, and it became his job to spray the windows every morning and make sure there were no fingerprints. He also had to load the dishwasher, wipe down the tables, and sweep the floor. We saw him sweeping slowly and carefully, and we could just see the hurt drip off of him when Avery and Miller were there together.

It went on this way for over a month, until right before Halloween. The Brilliance Café was doing better business because the college kids were back. Miller bought an espresso machine and started serving expensive coffee drinks, and the college kids hauled their laptops to the café and spent hours sipping coffee and typing away. Miller developed a good relationship with the people at the college, and they used him to cater their events, and he seemed to get happier as he got busier. Avery seemed happy too, spending the late afternoons grading papers and drinking espresso at the table right by the front of the restaurant.

Before they headed to Miller's house each evening, Avery and Miller would still slowly dance in the restaurant. We could hear the music they liked to play when we walked by on the street; it was something bluesy, with a syrup-voiced female singer who sounded mournful. It was strange music for young people to like. Sometimes we'd see them sway in one spot and kiss. We still didn't understand how Avery could be so thoughtless, especially since most nights while they danced Caleb was in the kitchen loading the dishwasher. But then, suddenly, the dancing stopped. I thought it was because of a conversation Miller and Avery had at the diner one night while they were eating pumpkin pie.

Miller had a strange way of eating his pie. First he took the crimped edge of the crust off and ate that like it was a breadstick. Then he used his fork to turn the pie upside down and scraped off the rest of the crust and ate that, leaving a quivering hunk of pumpkin on his plate, which he ate with a spoon. Avery laughed, and Miller shrugged and said, "I was raised by wolves."

"I didn't know there were wolves in Brooklyn," Avery said.

Evelyn Anderson came to refill their coffee mugs and said, "Caleb came by for supper earlier. I've never seen that boy look sadder." Evelyn had been Avery's mother's friend, worked side by side with her at the diner for five years before her death, and she didn't like the idea of Avery and Miller together. She thought he was trouble and would complain about him to anyone who'd listen.

"He must be sad about his car," said Avery. "It belonged to his grandpa, you know."

"Oh, honey, that's not what he's sad about." Evelyn raised her eyebrows dramatically at Avery and pointed one sharp red fingernail at Avery, then at Miller.

"Can I have another slice of pie?" Miller said.

Evelyn paused for a moment.

"Please?" he said. He flashed her his too-white, too-straight smile.

"Anything you want," Evelyn said coldly, and headed back to the counter. "You get anything you want."

Avery waited a second, then said, "What was that about?"

"I'm still hungry."

"I mean the Caleb stuff. Why is she mad at you?"

Miller sighed. "You don't know?"

"Know what?" Avery said.

"I thought you were the smartest girl in town."

Avery shook her head. "Come on. Tell me what you're getting at."

Evelyn slid another slice of pie in front of Miller, then went back through the swinging door into the kitchen.

"Caleb is in love with you. And everyone is upset with me for stealing you from him."

Avery laughed, clear and high, innocent. "That's just silly." And here was the thing about Avery: she was the smartest girl in town, got the best grades, whipped through book after book, but sometimes she wasn't smart about the everyday things. Like how she hadn't known volunteering to clean the erasers instead of running around on the playground during recess would make the other children resent her.

"It's not silly to Caleb," Miller said. "You see the way he looks at you?"

"He's like a brother. I've known him forever."

"Then he's probably been in love with you forever."

Avery sat silently while Miller chewed on his pie crust, and finally she said softly, "How could I never have known?"

Miller's fourth mistake was hosting the Halloween party. Every Halloween, the Student Activities Committee at Lake College threw a big party. Usually they held it in the basement of the student center, but it had flooded earlier in the fall, so they rented the Brilliance Café for the night. The students would pay for the space, and they'd put in an order for two hundred pizzas. Miller hired people from Cleveland to help cook and serve. He knew enough not to try to hire anyone from Morningstar.

Each year the Halloween party had a ridiculous theme—Space Robots, Buried Underwater Ship, Japanese Disco—and the students raised money for an entire year to pay for the DJ and decorations. The party in the Brilliance Café was themed Haunted Forest. They were going to clear out the tables and bring in fake trees, the kind they have in the rides in Disneyland so the indoors could look just like the outdoors. They would spread twinkling white lights across the ceiling to look like stars, and everyone would dance under the fake starlight.

For a week before the party, trucks kept arriving with more parts of the forest. First they laid out a thick brown carpet to look like the forest floor. Then the trees came: pine, ash, maple, elm. They were so lifelike that if you didn't get up close and examine them, you'd swear they were real. The day before the party, a white van pulled up outside the restaurant, and two men brought in a dozen owls.

"Awesome!" said one of the Lake students who was helping to set up. "They look totally real!"

A squat man chewing on the end of a drinking straw while carrying one of the owls said, "They *are* real, boy. You understand what taxidermy is?"

"I meant they looked alive." The student reached out a finger to touch the owl's wing, and the man turned in a half circle and shielded the bird.

"Best not to touch it. You're just renting these," the man said.

The two men climbed ladders and settled the owls high up in the trees. Those birds were the perfect touch, all of them staring down with their round yellow eyes watching everything beneath them, making the forest actually look a little haunted.

Miller's Duskman's fifth mistake was taking down those bird silhouettes Avery had made. Miller and Caleb climbed on chairs and peeled the tape off the birds, and then Caleb scrubbed the glass, trying to remove the stickiness left behind. While he was cleaning the glass, one of the owls caught his eye and then another and then another. He waited until Miller disappeared into the kitchen, then brought a ladder to one of the pine trees. He climbed the ladder and softly touched an owl. It was the calmest looking one, its wings tucked into its body, its head slightly tilted. Caleb ran his hands over and over that bird until Miller came back out of the kitchen, holding a can of solvent. I thought he'd yell at Caleb for touching the rented owl, but he just held the ladder steady while Caleb climbed down, and I thought maybe Miller was changing, learning how to be a decent man. After Caleb was back on the ground, Miller showed him how to put the solvent on a rag and rub the spots where the tape had been. The two of them worked together until the glass shone.

On Halloween the weather was perfectly clear. Miller and Caleb had done such a good job of polishing those windows that it hardly looked like there was any glass there; the forest seemed to have sprung up right in the middle of the sidewalk. A few hours before the party was to start, we saw Caleb crouched outside the café holding his burlap sack. The birds were back. And the trees inside, which looked so real, must have been confusing for the birds. They glided right into the window, thinking that within a few feet they'd land on a high branch. That October was especially cold, and the hawks were already in Morningstar, those magnificent birds that liked to sit high on the branches of the bare trees at Lake College. Maybe they thought they'd stumbled upon such good luck to suddenly find a forest full of lush trees. Or perhaps the hawks saw all those owls, perched comfortably on trees they thought were rightly theirs, and they wanted to claim their territory. By late afternoon Caleb had already collected four dead hawks.

Avery came to the café after she'd finished at school. She was dressed as Dorothy from *The Wizard of Oz*. When she arrived, she saw Caleb crouched on the sidewalk with his sack. He stared at her. She looked beautiful with her dark hair in two braids, the blue dress, the sparkling red shoes. Ever since Miller had told Avery that Caleb loved her, she'd acted strange around Caleb, like she no longer knew how to talk to him.

"More birds," Caleb said. He lifted the sack.

"I'm sorry. I'll make more cutouts after the party and I'll have Miller tape them up."

"I could help you," Caleb said.

"Oh, I don't want you to have to stay too late," said Avery. She moved her feet nervously, and she looked just like Dorothy clicking her heels together and hoping to get out of Oz. "You've been working so hard."

"It's ok," Caleb said. "I can help."

"We'll see. Maybe you'll be tired by then."

Caleb said nothing and followed Avery inside, clutching the full burlap sack.

By eight o'clock, the waiters and cooks Miller hired had arrived. Everyone wore brown from head to toe, maybe to make them blend right into the forest. The party wouldn't start until ten, but there was still a lot of work to do. There were balls of pizza dough lined up on racks behind Miller. The pizzas would be made fresh: tossed, topped, and slid into that Italian oven right before being served.

Caleb's job was to collect tickets, which had been sold on campus. All Caleb had to do was stand by the door, take the tickets, and drop them into a basket. At nine thirty he took his post. He held his empty wicker basket, waiting for the first students to arrive. He looked down the street toward the college for a minute, but then his head turned and he stared inside the restaurant. At first it seemed he was looking at Avery; she was mixing a large bowl of Sprite, fruit punch, and rainbow sherbet. But then we noticed the tilt of his neck and understood that he was looking up at those owls up in the trees. He was fascinated by those birds, which seemed frozen halfway between alive and dead.

It was calm for a few minutes, exceptionally quiet, and Avery mixed and mixed the sherbet into the punch bowl, the waiters dried glasses and stacked small plates on the counter, and Caleb stared at the birds. And then Miller crashed through the side door, holding Caleb's burlap sack high in the air. It swung back and forth from the weight of the hawks. Miller got close to Caleb's face and shouted, "What is this?"

"Birds," Caleb said. He tried to take a step back, but there was nowhere to go. He was pressed up against the closed door of the Brilliance Café.

"*Dead* birds!" Miller screamed. The vein on the side of his neck bulged. He grabbed Caleb's shoulders and pushed him hard against the glass door. The bag of birds was still in Miller's hand, and it sagged heavily on Caleb's chest. "I told you to put them in the Dumpster."

"I was going to do that with them," he said, pointing up at the owls inside.

"You were going to learn taxidermy?" Miller said. He pulled Caleb away from the door by his shirt collar, dragged him onto the sidewalk, and then pushed him again, hard, into the glass on the front of the building. "Why do you have to be so stupid about everything?"

The waiters watched what was happening from inside, and Avery dropped her mixing spoon into the bowl of punch and ran outside.

"Miller!" she said. "Stop!"

"Stay out of it," Miller said. Spit flew from his mouth as he spoke. Caleb clutched the handle of his basket. He was shaking.

"Stop it, Miller Duskman," Avery said, grabbing his arm. She spoke to him in the same tone she used when her third graders were cruel to each other.

"You don't understand," he hissed, shrugging her hand off of his arm.

"Please give me the birds," Caleb said.

Miller took the bag and swung it over his head and flung it down the street. It landed with a dull thump. He returned his hands to Caleb's shoulders, pushing him into the glass.

"Do you know what this retard did?" Miller shouted.

"Stop it!" Avery said. "Don't ever say that."

"Please, let me get the birds," Caleb said. He stretched his neck so he could see the sack.

"This idiot," Miller said, "put the filthy dead birds he scraped off the sidewalk in the walk-in cooler. They were sitting on a rack between the asparagus and the eggplants, those nasty dead birds just laid out on the rack like loaves of bread. Do you understand what kind of health code violation that is? I have to throw it all away, the cheese and the tomatoes and the rest of the produce. That's thousands of dollars of food in the garbage! We have nothing now to make pizzas with. We have dough."

"It's ok," Avery said. "We'll figure something out." She looked around her. Some of the students from the college were arriving in their costumes, standing back, worried.

Miller laughed in a mean way. "There's nothing to figure out." He dragged Caleb onto the sidewalk. Caleb let his body go slack, fell to the ground. "You ruined everything."

"Stop it," Avery said again.

"You don't understand, Avery," Miller shouted. "I have nothing. I'm broke. This party was supposed to save my restaurant." He pointed to the students. "You think these kids who sit around for hours and pay for one cup of coffee are keeping this place afloat?" Miller pulled Caleb to his feet and pushed him hard into the front of the Brilliance Café. "You've ruined everything," he screamed into Caleb's face as he pulled him forward by the shoulders and then slammed him back once more into the glass.

Everyone heard the cracking. Everyone, even Nancy Stables, all the way on the edge of town. There was one large crack when Caleb's head crashed into the wall, but then the cracking kept going and going, like the ice on a frozen lake fracturing from too much weight on it. The waiters ran outside, and everyone watched as the cracks spread and spread, from one wall to the next, and for a moment, everything glowed from those twinkling lights inside, the whole thing a map of glowing cracks and crackles. Then Avery swept down and pulled Caleb to his feet and there, right in front of Miller and everyone else, she pressed her lips to Caleb's and remained unmoving for a long time, as if this one kiss could right everything that had gone wrong, as if this kiss was her apology for everything that she could not give him, and everyone watched as Miller opened his mouth to say something but nothing came out. Then the cracking stopped and it was absolutely silent for one second and then the glass walls fell on all sides of the Brilliance Café, and shards of glass blanketed the whole forest, over all those trees and owls, glass plunged into the punch bowl, into the empty cups, and covered the brown carpet that lined the forest floor.

Miller Duskman's final mistake was not fighting for Avery. Afterwards, after the Halloween dance had been cancelled and the Brilliance Café had crumbled and all the waiters had been sent home, Miller wept, told Avery, "This town has changed me. I'm not like this."

Avery shook her head, walked away.

"Don't go, please," Miller said, but Avery continued to walk down the block, her sparkling red shoes glowing in the moonlight. The sound of her footsteps echoed down the street.

I think Avery could have come to forgive Miller if he'd just chased after her that night, had followed her down the street and begged her to understand his side of the story. He could have told her how we ignored him when we passed him on the sidewalk, how we'd boycotted his café. I understand now that the party had meant something to him; he'd prepared for it for a long time, and he'd thought it might change his relationship with the town. But he didn't chase after her. Miller stayed on the sidewalk the entire night, cried until he fell asleep, right there next to the forest that had been rained upon by slivers of glass.

Miller was lucky Caleb had that miracle body. Logan Pierce helped Caleb into his Volvo and took him to the hospital after the Brilliance Café crumbled, and the doctors said everything was fine with Caleb, inside and out. Some people told Caleb he should sue Miller for assault, but Caleb said he wanted to forget about it all.

When the men from the taxidermy shop came to pick up their owls, Logan talked to them, told them Caleb was a good worker and loved animals, wasn't afraid to touch dead ones, and asked if they might let him do an internship with them. "An internship?" said the squat one. "What do you think we are, the White House?" But then he agreed after Logan told him the whole story about the birds and the egg carton coffins and the burlap sack and the cracked glass. "We could use an extra pair of hands, but we can't pay him much," the man said. It was OK, though; Caleb didn't need money to buy a car anymore. Miller had given Caleb his car, had taken care of the paperwork so it could belong to Caleb, and left it parked in the Barlows' driveway and put the key in the mailbox.

So now Caleb had a car and could deliver eggs on Wednesdays and could drive the thirty miles out of town to learn taxidermy on the other days. It was good, we thought, for him to spend as little time in Morningstar as possible. He didn't need to be around Avery. There was something about that kiss that changed everything. Everyone knew that it didn't mean that Caleb and Avery could be together, but it had altered the balance of things.

Two days after the Brilliance Café crumbled, Miller was gone. He'd rented a U-Haul, packed all night, and left. Everyone thought he'd gone back to New York. We all knew he wasn't coming back. He'd loved Avery—we understood that—and Avery had loved him, and if they'd been in another place maybe things would have worked out differently.

Once she'd sold her house to a young political science professor at the college, Avery was gone, too. We realized later that the kiss was really a long, wordless goodbye to the only person that Avery would miss when she left Morningstar. Eileen Cord, who was the long-term substitute the school district called whenever one of the teachers went on maternity leave, took over Avery's class. A week after Avery left, a construction crew ripped up the remnants of the Brilliance Café, and then there was just an empty spot where it had once stood.

———

Right after Avery left, I sent her an e-mail telling her that she'd always have a room at the Ladybug Bed and Breakfast if she wanted to come back to town. "Stay as long as you like. I know you know how to make beds ☺" I wrote. I waited months and months and got no reply. A postcard with an image of a yak on the front and foreign stamps on the back finally came the next fall, and Avery asked me to pass it around to everyone who'd cared for her when she was a little girl. She'd joined the Peace Corps and was in Mongolia, as far away as she could go. She said she hadn't spoken to Miller since he'd left Morningstar; she'd added that part, I knew, because she understood that we'd want to know whether she and Miller had met up somewhere, continued their romance. "Thank you all for caring for me for so many years," she wrote, "but please know that I just can't come back anymore."

I manned the apple dumpling stand at the Harvest Festival that October and passed the postcard around to the people who'd gathered around me. It moved from hand to hand, each person reading quickly and passing the postcard on. No one said anything; it was hard to figure out the right words. We knew we hadn't been hospitable to Miller. He'd seen something in the town, had liked the place enough to open his restaurant here, and we should have been kinder. If we'd treated Miller better, that awfulness never would have happened with Caleb, and we wouldn't have lost Avery.

I looked at the postcard when it returned to my hands, stared at the yak and was reminded of Miller's buffalo milk mozzarella. Then I thought about that Halloween party and Avery's sparkling red shoes walking right out of town. And then I knew we were the ones who'd made the worst mistakes of all.

A Country Girl

MARY HOOD

From *How Far She Went* (1984)

The Misses Bliss kept store north of the limits, a mile past the FFA sign that said Welcome Back when you were going south and Come Again when you were going north, although if you were to stop and ask them the way to Rydal, the one would be sure to smile in pardon of the question while the other would gently reply, "You're now in town." There was not an uninhabited front porch in all the valley on any summer afternoon, so you could inquire for directions all along if you were lost and someone would be sure to tell you, "Rydal is the center of the universe," and it might be that a barefoot girl with a flat-top guitar would stare coolly past you and her uncle, propped against the post hollowed by carpenter bees, would say nothing, having vowed long before not to speak to anyone, not even kin, till suppertime. The dogs, bellying low on the under-porch shadows, would be saving their energy for moonrise along the river. You could pick up one of the little early apples from the ground and eat it right then without worrying about pesticide.

The most famous local citizen was hanged just that much before a reprieve—a sad, legendary thing; there's a farm named for him, and grandchildren. And the second-most-famous person, the lady writer, is dead nearly as long as the hanged man, and buried in her chapel garden beside her daughter Faith. Not that many pilgrims seek the grave anymore. And the house she loved wears antennae, and a twin-engine fiberglass cruiser on its trailer is parked on the terrace where the doctor, who had a presentiment, told her, taking into account the flowered borders, the wide fields, the view: "You have everything but time."

The barefoot girl by now will have finished her singing, not the impersonal, brave gospel singing, but melodies low and private as lullaby. She will have set the guitar aside with a slight discord. And she will sigh, wanting nothing in the world she can name, free to come and go with no more than a lift of her tanned hand, yet burdened, restless, seeking that one thing to strike out at or from. Soon the afternoon train will track across the valley and the colt in Paul Lilley's pasture will race it, pleasant to see. The girl would go that way. There was no hurry.

But when she got there, there were others.

"I live," said the man with the camera, "where you can hear alligators groaning each night in the tidal mud."

The license plate on the car said Sunshine State, sure enough, but that didn't mean there was no rain in Florida, or liars either. The girl shook her head, slightly, in rebuke, the fair hair swaying and settling into order on her shoulders.

"It's true, every word," his wife corroborated, dabbing a dry brush on her canvas. (But you cannot prove alligators by protestation.) How could they say such things in Paul Lilley's pasture and every cricket and June bug singing born two thousand feet above sea level, thereabouts?

"That's all right," the girl told them kindly.

The woman had painted the colt. The train had been too much for her. So the dappled horse ran alone at the back of her perspective, presentably drawn.

"That's how I like," the girl told her. The man with the camera checked his watch again.

"Mother," he said. The sun was in decline.

"I know, I know," his wife sighed, folding up shop. She released the wet canvas from the easel and admired it briefly. "Oh, well, I guess you got the real action with your camera."

"Two different arts. Two different artists. Two separate truths," he said easily, as though he usually talked that way. He cluttered their picnic things into the hamper and recorked the Pontet-Latour.

"You keep this." The woman handed the girl the painting.

"Oh, no, I caint, I mustn't."

"Whyever not?"

The girl frowned in concentration, seeking the exact ethic being jeopardized. "We don't make uneven exchanges."

The man and woman looked at each other in amusement. He got in the car.

"But I want you to have it," the painter protested. "Find something (quick!) to exchange."

The girl drew a deep breath. "Poor Wayfarer," she said, then announced her name, "Elizabeth Inglish," and began to sing a cappella in her low, thrilling way. When she finished, she received the painting from the woman, and they drove away.

"Mercy! I never expected a serenade." The woman snapped her seat belt. Looking back once, she saw the girl still standing there with the painting raised to her eyes as a sunshade.

"Country girl," he said, like a slide caption. Before the dust behind them had settled, they had digested her into anecdote.

The Bliss sisters had directed him here, a stranger. He had their quavering map stuffed in his shirt pocket to keep it from blowing out the window as he rode along. He had no more country sense than to drive on the clay road like a turnpike. His brick-red wake stood tall as a two-story house, slowly settling grit onto whatever laundry happened to be hanging out and seeping into the crevices between the piano keys at the Missionary Baptist Church if Mavis Cole had left it open again after practicing the choir. Anybody who looked could tell some stranger was coming. But May Inglish wasn't looking, she was cooking for the reunion. Horace was at the barbershop swapping lies with the others, and Sophie and Bremen were playing in the branch. Uncle Billy was out in the corn, potting crows. Aunt Lila and them were due in the morning, soon enough. Uncle Cleveland was due any time, and welcome, but at his age you could never be sure. His chair to preside in was already set out in the shade of the beech tree, the sawhorses were aligned to make the picnic tables, and the white sheets for tablecloths were ironed and folded away on the sideboard by the piles of Chi-net platters and bowls. Everybody agreed from the start there was no shame in paper plates so long as you bought the best. It was the same every year: should we or shouldn't we, and where to meet, and what to eat, barbecue, or fry, and every year they arranged themselves under the identical beech tree for the reunion, every year the same with allowances for births and deaths. As the years went on the number of aunts and uncles diminished and the number of cousins increased, but there had never yet in this century been a reunion where Uncle Cleveland wasn't prime mover.

So when Elizabeth looked up from chopping the celery for potato salad and saw two bright tips of a man's shoes (the kitchen was partitioned from the dining room by a fiberglass curtain which was drawn now to fend off the glare from the toolshed roof) she cried, "Oh, it's Uncle Cleveland!" and ran to him. And there stood the stranger with the note pad in his raised hand.

"I knocked and knocked," he apologized. "You didn't hear."

"It's the fan. It lumbers." She nudged it back a bit with her bare toes. The machine rumbled on, ineffectual but soothing. "It's not Uncle Cleveland, Mama," she said over her shoulder to May.

May looked up from her lap of green beans and shook her head. "No, it isn't." May didn't say what is a stranger doing in my house and she didn't say welcome either. She just looked.

"The ladies at the store said here was where to find Cleveland Inglish." He held out the crumpled map as proof.

"You're early, that's all." May dumped another load of bean strings onto the newspaper by her chair. "He owe you?" The remarks were getting down to business now.

"I'm writing a feature on Mrs. Harris—life and works and that."

"Uncle Cleveland did used to work for her some," May grudged. "Off and on."

"But she's dead, years and years!" Elizabeth ran her knife over the whetstone and tested the blade on her thumb.

"She wrote about us," May said. "She got some of it wrong." She bent a bean till its back broke. "She meant well, for all the good it does."

"Are you writing a story story or a true story?" Elizabeth kept her eyes on the knife and guided it gravely through the celery stalks. She never imagined that he might be uncomfortable there, in the doorway, waiting for them to produce Cleveland. She did not realize him at all. She finished chopping and laid the blade aside.

"A true story," he told her gently, as though she were a child. It was the way she listened, yearning for some remark she had never heard, some refutation, some proof.

"I can show you her studio," she offered. He set his tea glass down on the sink apart from theirs so if that made a difference they could tell which was which. "Mama?" she asked in afterthought.

"You're old enough to know better," May said. Maybe she was teasing. Maybe she meant the Posted signs.

"It's not life or death," Elizabeth said.

"Shoes!" May exhorted, but she needn't have, for Elizabeth was already tying on her sneakers.

"If Uncle Cleveland comes in before we're back, ring the dinner bell." She was out of the house and away before the fan had a chance to turn back to her.

The writer's name was Paul Montgomery. She stored it up, but never would call him anything other than sir or mister, though there wasn't a decade between them, just the wide world. They went overland, uphill all the way, and summer had its full go with the trail. "You mustn't resist the brambles," she advised, hearing him tearing himself free, his shirt already picked in a dozen places. "Just back out of them." She demonstrated. He got entangled again. "It's no country for a man with a temper," she agreed as he struggled furiously with the blackberry runner slapped across his back. They could hear Uncle Billy's gun, pop-pop-pop. And the crows laughing. Going under a plum thicket her scarf was torn from her hair. They paused while she retied it. The blueberries were long past prime, but she found a handful and shared with him.

"Almost there," she encouraged. "I can smell the verbena." At the summit they stood undismayed before the fierce sign that proclaimed

KEEP OUT
WHO THIS
MEAN YOU.

"Not us," she said. "Not me." She knew a place where the fence was down. They crossed boldly.

He stood with one arm resting on the warm fieldstone wall that belted the household gardens from the fields. Mint and verbena and lavender and geraniums bloomed pungently at his feet. The last irises were gone to parchment now, and the shasta daisies were taking their turn. Hollyhocks towered over the iron gate to the chapel. It was locked. Everything was locked. The place was like an opera set, and needed moonlight for its true majesty.

Even the graves, as he could see through the gate, looked cute and common. The stone was baking. An undecided lizard, half green, half brown, darted past at eye level on the wall, its blue throat puffing.

"Must be gone fishing," Elizabeth reported, returning empty-handed from her quest for the keys. "Her workroom's back there. We can look in the windows." She led the way. Her quick eye spotted the lizard. She caught him and let him run up her arm and down her arm and away into the sunstruck flowers. The writer peered in the window at the lifeless studio, left as it had been when the enterprise of thought and imagination ceased, decades since. This was oblivion. The bundled papers were yellowed; he could catch a whiff of them, a cellar dankness. The table stood just so in the slant of light, the ink gone to dust in the well. They moved from pane to pane, staring into obscurity.

"Better it had all burned down than this," she said.

"No." He sounded sure.

"It's like my grandmother: she saved my grandfather's love letters, even after he died; she kept them in a sack under her bed. So we couldn't ever pry, she cut them into quilt scraps. Now she's dead and it's Mama saving them and nobody says so but it makes us sad and ashamed and I'll burn them one day, yes I will!"

"This is different," he assured her at once. It made her think of the man with the camera who had said, "Two separate truths."

"I thought the bell would have rung by now." She stood listening. "If he doesn't come till tomorrow, will you be back?"

"Is he sharp?"

"You mean Uncle Cleveland?" She laughed. "You'll be pressed to keep up."

"He must be ninety."

"That don't differ."

"Why did you think I was your uncle? Do I look so old?"

"You're you. Just yourself. Born in God's time and going to last till you're done." She brushed a crumb of moss from her blouse. "It was your shoes. Being new and all, city shoes."

He looked at his unexceptional feet.

"Old folks never wear out their shoes. Not even the bottoms get scratched much. And the tops never crease. You know. And so when I saw them—"

"Well, I never noticed."

"It could break your heart. The same as all these things of hers waiting for her to return." She polished a little twig smooth as a chicken bone and broke it in three. She let it drop.

"Have you read any of her books?"

"After sixteen they caint make you," she said.

They were already halfway down the ridge when the farm bell rang and rang.

"That's Bremen," she reckoned. "God never gave him quittin' sense."

Back at the house she sent him round to the front door like company while she slipped into the kitchen. "Only thing," she said in parting, "Uncle Cleveland's slightly deef." They could hear May and Uncle Billy shouting their welcomes, and the rough monotone of the patriarch's replies.

Uncle Billy told his favorite joke, twice, then went to clean his crow gun. May plumped the pillows behind the old man's granite back and set a glass of tea beside him. Sophie and Bremen, blue jeans damp to the knees from wading in the creek, pressed to the old soul, one on each side of the recliner, showing what they had brought him from the woods, and what had come in the mail, and the oil painting of Paul Lilley's Texas pony the lady had given Elizabeth for a song. The black-and-white cat strolled in through the wide-open door like family and posed at Cleveland's feet, gazing all the way up those blade-thin legs in their white trousers to his vest where the gold chain and Masonic fob rose and fell conversationally. Elizabeth went upstairs and put on the blue dress he had liked the last time, and brushed the tangles from her hair. She announced her coming with each step in her whited shoes from Easter. She curtsied and he called her Priscilla and asked her to sing.

"With or without?"

"Without? What kind of singing is that?"

So she got her flat-top guitar with the little red hearts painted around the sounding hole and she sang as loudly as she could bear to, and he must have heard her. Paul Montgomery did, waiting on the front porch to be remembered.

"Whose red car is that?" Billy was back with a new joke. The kids looked

"'76 Charger," Bremen said. There was a silence, then May stepped in.

"Where's your professor?"

And that's when Elizabeth remembered him and asked him in.

"He's writing about Corra Harris, for the Sunday magazine," she explained to the old man.

"Ghosts, ghosts, ghosts," Sophie and Bremen chanted. They once reported having seen a "spectacle" in that tilting barn.

"Behave," May told the kids, but she let them stay. Billy stayed too, just kept butting in, and Elizabeth, who had heard every word at least once before, went to peel potatoes. By suppertime it had been decided that it was no trouble, none at all, and would Mr. Montgomery stay and eat with them?

He would.

The lady writer got herself mentioned time and again, but nothing much came of it that Paul Montgomery saw. He kept his note pad open just in case. He was a city boy all right, speaking of baby cows and 2% milk. Bremen took it on himself to mimic Aunt Lilah's boy Bud, spearing his green beans wrong-handed and nibbling them sideways like a rabbit. He'd been brought up better, you could tell. It was pure devilment. Aunt Lilah and them had that effect, even long distance. (One year's reunion Bud shot out the glass ball on the lightning rod, on the north one, the most important one by the chimney, and all Lilah Inglish Ames would say was, "Well, well," and go on chewing chicken salad.) Sophie thought Montgomery was "weird," having never been that close to a red-haired man with a mustache. "Vinnie vannie veddy veddy lou lou lou," she jeered at him, eating pickles right off his plate without asking. She was seated to his left, and Uncle Cleveland to his right, so that the writer could shout into the better ear. Elizabeth sat around the table from him while she sat at all. She ate in a hurry and excused herself. They could hear the porch swing creaking and her soft voice singing some sad thing, without the guitar.

"Well, she's just full of summer," Horace said at large.

"Summer don't last long, even in a good year," May said. And she wasn't looking at the sky.

When Montgomery left to drive to his motel on the interstate, Sophie and Bremen sprinkled him with goodnights from their windows upstairs. "Have you heard any news?" Sophie called to Bremen, silly with sleep. "Not a word. What have you heard?" he ritually replied. "Welcome back! Come again!" they chorused as the red Dodge drove off. It was too dark to wave. Only Elizabeth knew that he had decided to come back to the reunion with a camera, and questions for the others. It was more than his deadline he was considering when he said, "I need more time."

In the dark Elizabeth sat on the porch and thought about the colt in Paul Lilley's lower field. She walked out in the moonlight down across the meadow where the lady painter had laughed at her scruples. "I brought you apples," she coaxed, but the horse held aloof, snorting, haughty. "Last chance," she warned, but he was coy. He trembled all over. He trotted deeper into the shadows. "All right." She flung the apples then and ran up the path toward home. The lights were on like a funeral was happening, and those gusts of laughter, and the clatter of pans. She heard the first tentative scratchings of Cleveland's fiddle, and Horace calling her to bring her guitar.

It was just like always. The Inglish population had remained stable during the year so there were no eyes seeking resemblances to the departed and that bittersweet pang when they were discovered. Aunt Goldie was meeker than ever. She sat off to the right of Cleveland's throne, on a kitchen chair; she was neither crumpled nor crisp, just resigned. She had lived a while at the State Hospital when she was younger, had started crying one day at breakfast and couldn't stop; for weeks and weeks she had wept, giving no reasons. When May spoke to her now she looked up, eyes swimming, but had nothing to say. Aunt Lilah and Big Bud drove in about eleven-thirty. Little Bud was going for a three-year pin at Sunday school so they had to hang around home long enough for him to put in his appearance, then they drove directly on. They brought watermelons on chipped ice in a galvanized tub. Lilah's daughter Patty and her groom were already present, joking their newlywed jokes with Uncle Billy. Grant and Tillie and their five drove in not long after the watermelons were set to earth from the back of Big Bud's Buick. And the Bliss sisters arrived, on their canes, with their cushions and scrapbooks. There were more dogs than usual and indistinguishable children seen from time to time dragging first Sophie's Belgian bunny and then Bremen's round and round the springhouse. The elders, in perfect state, arranged themselves by bloodline and years under the beech tree. And all the time there was talk, and renewals, and measurings, and little disputes about what year and just where and wasn't it a Reo and not a Model T? and the tap-tap-tap of May flouring the cake pans and one wife or another running out of the house and setting something on the spread tables and running back in so quick she could almost pass to and fro on one slam of the screen door. The older cousins were stationed along the tables to ward off flies and jaybirds and dogs. Everybody's kind and nobody's kin Johnny Calhoun drove up in his restored Packard after they all had a plateful and a big waxed cup of lemonade and the good hush had fallen where hunger in the open air overcomes sociability. Someone had counted and reckoned there were fifty-four human beings present, or possibly only fifty-three, owing to a confusion about the James twins whose mama, despite psychological advice in *Family Circle*, continued to dress them alike.

"Take out and eat!" they cried to Johnny Calhoun as they'd have cried to anyone venturing into the yard then, friend or foe. But they knew Johnny. He was a chenille manufacturer, forty in a year or so, and wild in the way that made him worth the trouble he caused. He was the best-looking one there for his type, fair and fiery, like Uncle Cleveland when he was a stripling. But Uncle Cleveland had married young and for all time, and Johnny was still free. Mighty free, some said. Patty ran up to him and kissed him right on the mouth and he made faces over her shoulder, brows high and delighted, then winked at Jeff, whose responsibility she was now. Who didn't laugh didn't see. Aunt Goldie eased on up to the house to take her snuff in private. Folks expanded with lunch and love and the elders in their circle nodded and woke and nodded and spoke. If they noticed how Paul Montgomery was watching everything shrewder than a cousin-in-law, they just guessed he was Elizabeth's beau and made him welcome. Welcome all.

It was the custom for Uncle Cleveland as senior to pray over the food before they ate it and the other brothers and sisters of his generation to pray afterward. Uncle Tatum began it now, standing upright, foursquare, hand on lapel, eyes shut tight against the distractions of the younguns tearing back and forth like hellions. Elizabeth stood at the outer ring of the connection, near the childish freedom of the lawn where cartwheels and somersets were underway. It was her wish to escape now, before the music-making. Once they called on her she couldn't say no, not to family. She studied her locked fingers, head down, not to mimic piety but rather to avoid the too-plucking gaze of the aunts. "I'll never love but one man!" they'd all heard her say since she was a babe, and they kept watch to see if she had made a fool of herself yet. Uncle Tatum said, "Amen," and Aunt Goldie stood, shyly, for her own prayer, lost among picnic debris and her own rollicking pinafore collar.

"Oh God," Goldie quavered, and her tears, never far off, began to fall. This was the saddest part of the day, they all feared for her so. "Goldie's next," they thought, and gazed and gazed, memorizing every living detail. Elizabeth slipped farther away, till she could hear no childish voices, no ancient piety, and no music at all. The gray tabby from the hilltop farm crept past her in the long grass.

Elizabeth lay back on the warm earth and sang so lightly that the kinglets and phoebes resting in the bower went undisturbed. She moved her head to the left until the elm shadow lay cool on her eyes. She watched a great satiny fool of an ant, clown-striped, race headlong off a blackberry vine above her. The sun outlined everything in silver. The grass looked like cellophane. And there wasn't a breeze in all the world to turn a leaf.

There was something else about Johnny Calhoun: he was quiet as a cat. He nudged her with the toe of his shoe. "Look what I found," he said, as he said every summer to some girl, to Patty, to all of them, that Johnny Calhoun. She stood up too quickly. It took a moment for the landscape to settle in her thoughts. She stamped her tingling foot, dazzled. She could talk and talk among kin, overheard. Now she couldn't even say boo.

"They were calling for you," he reported. He had stripped off his tie long since; it trailed from his coat pocket. There was razor burn on his throat, below his ear. He eased his collar with one finger.

She shook her head, denying all claims. She dusted her fingers on her skirt. "Lilah can play as pretty a bass run as they'll hear, or need to."

He turned her hand palm up and set a little present on it. "For Christmas or the Fourth of July," he said.

"Oh I caint. I mustn't. I don't have anything for you." It was not so heavy; it was not very large.

"It's yours," he said. "It's for you."

"I caint think," she said. "What do you suppose it is!" She unwrapped it a tag at a time, not to tease him but herself. When she got the ribbon unknotted, she coiled it tidy as a clerk and filed it in his pocket. "Well I don't know," she murmured, filled with exquisite dread. She drew the paper off. A music box gleamed on her upturned palm. It might have been the most precious egg. It took her breath in surmise.

"I'm listening," she said cautiously. He pressed the switch and the melody dripped out, three dozen notes of a nocturne.

"Chopin," he told her.

When it ran down he wound it again.

"Johnny?" she wondered, more to herself than not. Calhoun lit his cigarette and imperceptibly waited. One old leaf on the tulip tree was stricken with palsy. It shook and shook. It might have been any ordinary day since Eden fell. She never did see the hawk, circling the sun. When she looked at it again, the tulip tree was motionless, every leaf in place.

"Johnny," she decided.

The music was over, and the melons devoured, and yellow jackets had come and drunk from the rinds. One of the twins had been stung so the other had to try it. Sympathy swirled back and forth between them as everyone gave advice. Most of the food had been cleared away and the white sheets that covered the plank tables had to be weighted with stones. In the winding-down part of the day everyone got more related somehow, and Paul Montgomery, feeling shut out, shut his notebook for good. He locked his briefcase in the car, then realized that was too citified a thing to do: heads had turned at the rasping of his key in the car door, indicting him, and so he left his trappings lying frankly on the back seat, the windows down, his suit coat on the front seat with the garnered facts in the black book jutting from the pocket just the way Uncle Cleveland's Prince Albert showed, like a handkerchief, in its red can. Montgomery swung his camera around his neck and set off up the hill to the studio for some pictures. He knew his way well enough, but he looked around for Elizabeth, hoping she might come along. She had disappeared earlier and despite several alarms had failed to show. One of the dogs heaved himself to his feet and volunteered for the hike. They set out in the best of spirits. There were massing clouds that would make his camera work more challenging.

He finished the roll of film and, seeing the dogs panting in the shade of the tainted well, he crossed to the spigot at the house and let the animal drink from his cupped hands. He thought he heard the television playing inside; he hallooed and knocked, but no one answered. He paused one last time at the chapel gate and peered through at the graves. Already the first tentative sentences of his article were forming in his thoughts. He turned back down the ridge toward the Inglish farm. The dog suddenly took an interest in something just beyond his view, barked and looked away and did not bark again.

Johnny Calhoun was sitting with his back to a tree, not smoking, not smiling, not speaking. He shook his head to warn Montgomery not to step on Elizabeth's outflung hand still clasping the music box. She lay sleeping, an arm across her eyes to ward off the sun.

Johnny brushed a ladybug from his ear. "We'll be along," he told the writer, neither unnerved nor amiable. Montgomery jogged on past, the camera beating against his pounding heart.

He left without making the entire rounds of all the guests, though he did press the stiff warm hands of the Bliss sisters; he congratulated May on her dinner and nodded to Horace's raised hat, but Uncle Cleveland was asleep again and Goldie was distant.

"Let us hear," someone cried after him from the porch. Uncle Billy already had his chair tipped back against the bee-stuffed post and dozed malevolently. It was Lilah's newlywed Patty who noticed Elizabeth and Johnny Calhoun were both still unaccounted for and when the black-and-white tomcat leaped onto her familiar lap she slapped it away with a remark that made her groom look sharp and Uncle Billy, that impostor, laugh.

The number of tourists driving by and asking after the lady writer's remains increased dramatically in the weeks after Montgomery's article came out. Uncle Billy got so aggravated with the interruptions that he began taking his chair out on the back porch, leaving Horace to direct traffic. Not every Sunday would a literary pilgrim find Elizabeth Inglish on the porch, guitar in hand, waiting for the evening train to pass through Paul Lilley's meadow, but when she was there she stared coolly past the stranger, mute, head held high, as though nothing whether trivial or profound would distract her from her reverie. Some thought she was blind, and walked back to their car to mention it to the others. And some had the impression she was a fool.

Crybaby

DAVID CROUSE

From *Copy Cats* (2005)

Candy was lost and I hoped I might find him somewhere in the graffiti-scribbled buildings of our youth. Or it was *me* who was lost. So I left my wife and daughter and drove north through six states back to that ruined Victorian house on the hill where Cheryl was throwing her never ending party.

I entered through the wide-open back door, walked into the smoke filled pantry, found a beer, and held it like I belonged. People wandered from room to room, sat on the floors, passed around black bottles of wine, pills wrapped in strips of cellophane. Most were strangers—fragile little potheads dressed in secondhand clothes, Hispanic kids from the westside projects, and even a couple of beefy jocks in letter jackets checking out the freak show. They were probably strangers to Cheryl too, people she had met a couple of days before in a coffeehouse or club. They glanced at me as I moved deeper into the house. A few older ones pulled me close and said my name—the name they used to call me. I hadn't heard it in years.

Her letter had said that everything was okay. But it didn't feel okay. The walls in the front room were spray-painted with sunflowers and smiley faces, and the floors were littered with plastic cups, bent cans, scraps of paper, ghostly strands of toilet tissue I broke with my legs as I crossed the room to Cheryl. A band was grinding slow familiar chords in another room. I set down the beer on a windowsill, took her by the arm, and pulled her to a corner, where a couple of skeleton-faced boys were sneaking *manteca*. As she kissed my cheek I said, "He's not here?"

"We don't know where he is," she said and something else that was drowned out by the band's building intensity. A girl was jumping on a caved-in couch, arms tight by her sides and teeth locked in a speed grimace. A few people sprawled on the floor looking up at her, and as the music swelled she turned in a circle, corkscrewing, and they applauded and hooted. Cheryl raised her voice to compete with the music, but there was something creeping and languid in her tone. I wondered what she had taken.

She had buzz-cut her hair and dyed the leftovers bright red, and she looked better than I thought she might, like some of the sophisticated forty-something women who came to my readings and asked me sensitive questions about my history. She put her hand on my back and pulled me closer, my fingers still wrapped around her arm, and for a second I thought we might kiss. "I didn't think you'd make it," she said.

"You knew I would," I said, although I wasn't sure she could hear me over the music. A kid with a yellow scarf wrapped around his shaved skull came over to her, whispered something in her ear, and she pushed a couple of twenties into his palm— maybe for drugs, maybe just charity.

She said something as she looked out over the crowd, and I bent my head closer to listen. She repeated what she had said, evenly and clearly, like it was a line she was practicing for a play. "If you hadn't run away you wouldn't have had to come back." I straightened up and loosened my grip. "Do you at least miss him?" she added clear as a bell.

I realized the music had paused, and I squeezed a few words

into the pocket of silence between songs. "It's not like he died," I said, but maybe he was dead and this was what passed for his wake.

Then I heard it. Someone was singing one of his old songs from the back of the house, probably because they had spotted me. I knew the words—sarcastic and nasty when skittering over a backward Black Sabbath riff, beautiful when sung with an acoustic guitar. I could tell Cheryl remembered it too, because she tilted up her chin and closed her eyes. Someone else joined in, harmonizing badly. *It's the most beautiful river running through the most beautiful town in the most beautiful world in the world. The most beautiful world in the world.*

The party moved around us, past us, and now my mind reeled back fifteen years and three city blocks to the warehouse on Canal Street, where we used to watch Candy smack around a guitar with his revolving-door band. I remembered the coiled energy of his body, the flailing of his right hand, and the nervousness of the little crowd of dropouts, wannabe ecoterrorists, dopers, and ex-lovers as they gathered around him in a loose half-circle. They wanted to see him scratch his fingers along the strings like he was clawing an itch, jerking out chords in spasms and squinting his eyes as if against glaring light.

I wondered if they were waiting for him to step through the door of Cheryl's house right then, the way I had five minutes earlier. We would pull each other close, the room would go quiet, and then with some urging Candy would take a guitar from the band and play one of the old songs. Everything would be fine then, right?

As if I had said these thoughts aloud, Cheryl laughed and slipped my grip, spinning back out to the center of the room and then toward the kitchen. I followed her, stepping over a couple of people staring at the ceiling. "Hello," one of them said as I looked down, and we shared vague smiles.

Cheryl headed outside to the cracked blacktop driveway on the side of the house. People were drinking out there and throwing a soccer ball at the broken basketball hoop. I could see her through the kitchen window, talking to a teenage girl who had come probably because she heard the noise. They were laughing, and Cheryl looked much older then, around the eyes especially. I probably looked older too.

"Hey, hey," someone said from behind me, and I knew the voice. I knew the face too, although he had gained weight and grown a beard to match his stringy hair. I had forgotten the name, but he used to play bass in Candy's band.

"I heard you singing that song," I said. "It's been years since I heard that."

He lifted his head and wiped his nose with his thumb and finger. "I have your book. I haven't cracked it yet. Things have been crazy obviously. Things have been out of control, man."

I tried to get away from him, but he motormouthed after me, through the kitchen and past a circle of people handing around the nub of a joint. He stopped long enough to close his eyes and take a deep drag and then said in a louder voice, "Who would have thought things would turn out the way they did?"

"Nobody," I said. "Not me anyway. Especially not me."

He laughed through his nose, blowing smoke, and held the joint out to me. "His father still lives here, you know. We drove by his place the other day and thought about going in and asking him where the hell was Candy. You know, really lay some interrogation on him. We thought about throwing rocks at the windows too."

My own father was in a veterans' hospital in Providence with a tumor in the front of his brain. I went to see him whenever I drove through Rhode Island, which was not often. He sometimes called me by my brother's name, and I let him, because it seemed to give him some solace, and my brother was even less inclined to visit him than I was. Besides, it was more comfortable to visit him as someone else, like wearing a disguise. The last time I went I sat at the foot of his bed, and we watched television, and he complained about the food and the nurses and said that the other inmates—he called the patients inmates—were trying to steal from him. He had a Semper Fi tattoo on his inner forearm, but it had collapsed into nonsense as he lost weight. His weak hands shook when he held a spoon. Once or twice I tried to talk to him about our past, but I always pulled up short. What did I want anyway? To make this chapped-lipped old man feel guilty? Yes, probably. But the fog in his mind made him safe. It was like a shield my words couldn't penetrate. Then again, maybe it was just an act—his disguise.

"Dad," I said, "do you remember what you used to do to me?" I was testing him, poking around the edges of his memory.

"I used to take you kids fishing at Round Pond," he mumbled. "You and your friends. We would get up so early in the morning."

These were the kind of stories he told now. His cancer stories—that's how I thought of them. And none of them were true. Maybe they were wishes rising from his dank subconscious, pushed free by the pressure of the knot in his skull. I guess I didn't care too much, except that I had to listen to them and consider, at least for a second, that they might be real.

"The roads were so empty, going to that pond," he said. "It was like we were the only people alive out there."

On the television the Red Sox were behind by a couple of runs. The other team had men on first and third but Pedro Martinez was pitching, and he looked as angry as I had ever seen him. He threw one strike, then another, and looked up at the sky—talking to God, I guess—but Dad just called him an asshole and jabbed the remote duct-taped to the bed rail. In the following silence I rubbed his feet and felt the fragile bones of his toes between my thumb and forefinger. His eyes closed and he slept, looking peaceful—like the kind of father who really would have done the things he had just talked about.

"Okay," I said to the man who had sung Candy's song. "What the hell? For old time's sake," and I took the little wet roach between my fingers.

I had been Candy's best friend since middle school, when he was still breaking windows and setting small fires. He had learned to play some primitive songs and then to write them, and by high school small crowds took the freight elevator up nine stories to see him practice with his band.

I remember those days as a haze of noise and motion. The onlookers loved it when his bowling shirt opened and they could see the scar, jagged on his stomach like an old road running across a map. His right arm would pump, his hand shimmering across the strings, and the shirt would open and close and blow like a flag behind him. The windows were always up even if it was cold outside, and the yellow walls would sweat in summertime, and I swear you could smell the fish in the river a hundred feet below.

Candy didn't care, not about the smell or the heat, not about the audience, and not even about the other people in his band, who always seemed to be falling behind. Sometimes he grabbed a smoke and let them catch up or jam on their own, the guitar hanging loose at his waist as he slid a cigarette between his lips. Or he glanced out one of the tall warehouse windows at the traffic speeding below, and then he spun on the ball of his foot and attacked the microphone, barked at it like he was going to chew it up and spit it out.

My favorite song was "Crybaby," and the first time he played it in his bedroom sitting on the edge of his narrow cot the world stopped. "Crybaby," he sang softly, "can't you take a little scrape? Can't you take a little bruise?" He wore a black knit cap on his shaved head, head bowed, and his right eye was freshly blackened, his nose red and swollen. "Turn that frown upside down, Crybaby, Crybaby, Crybaby." The space between syllables opened up and closed, lengthened and shortened each time he sang the word. His hand hung above the same shaky G and then came down, and it rang out like the only G chord ever struck. I don't know how he did it. Maybe it was just me.

"Crybaby, Crybaby, Crybaby." The chords clattered louder, and his voice rose and cracked and bounced around the walls, and it seemed like the song could go on forever. Would go on forever. It was our song, *my* song. I knew what that blackened eye felt like, had worn two myself in the last year.

Later when Candy sang it in public his eyes always found mine in the crowd, if only for a second, and he smiled as he launched into the chorus, and I bet every girl between us thought he was looking at her and only her. Later still the chorus vanished altogether—Candy probably figured the crowd knew that part by heart anyway—and the song grew even more jagged and out of control. That was when he was taking a lot of amphetamines. His newest drummer had a lifeline to unlimited sources in New York, and the stuff just appeared in our pockets.

That's how Candy got his nickname. He would cup his hand to his mouth and swallow and say, "Sweet." We were just kids. Not even twenty then.

"When's the last time you saw him?" I asked as I passed back the joint to the guy who had attached himself to me. "Was he okay?"

"I bet they'll turn it into a movie," he said. "Do you think they'll turn it into a movie?" He was twirling this idea around in his head now, absorbed in the possibilities. "Who would play you?" he asked. "Who would play Candy? They'd probably get people who look nothing like you. Who's enough of an asshole to play your dad? Or Candy's dad. They should get one guy to play both parts. With a mustache and without."

He laughed like that was the funniest thing he had ever heard.

"It's just a stupid book," I said. But what I wanted to say was, "It's just my life." My life it seemed then, with the people who had once occupied it swirling around me, should not have been turned into that book, let alone a movie. It wouldn't have been either if a small press in upstate New York hadn't recognized "something there" in my draft and then been patient enough to bring it through three rounds of edits. They said the subject matter was genuine, the people were real, and I had a distinct journalistic voice. They said it was a story that deserved—that needed—to be told.

"This book of yours, is it popular?" the guy asked, which was a way of asking if I was rich, if he might see me on TV soon.

"No," I said. "It's only been reviewed a couple of places and not very well."

"Oh yeah?"

"Yeah," I said, remembering the day I had spread the paper at the kitchen table and read the first review. "One guy used the words melodramatic and unrealistic. I don't think he believed people like us really exist. And in such abundance." I waved my hand across the undulating crowd, the bobbing heads and shaking bodies.

"Don't worry about it. You'll bounce back. You're a survivor," he said. Which meant, I think, that Candy was not.

"What?" I said with a sneer in my voice.

"The reviews around here aren't so hot either," he added as he looked around for something else to put in his mouth. "Like I said, I haven't read it. I've really never been much of a reader. But from what I hear on the street, you left out the best parts."

He was still smiling but he took a step back. I took a step forward. He wasn't expecting that kind of challenge—especially from me—and he said something under his breath. My nickname. I thought of the source of that name—my father—and those visits to his narrow hospital room. He had not called me that name in a long time, but I knew it was hidden somewhere down deep in his brain, a little smudge of anger and disgust.

"Only my friends call me that," I said, "and not even them anymore."

He began to sing the song again, his voice sweet and mocking. I glanced to my right at a laughing girl. She was holding plastic cups to her eyes like binoculars and looking at the ceiling, looking through the ceiling for all I knew. She was laughing with her mouth open. But the laugh turned into a yell as she turned her head toward us, and the cups dropped from her hands and people were holding me, pulling me backward out of the room. I was dimly aware that I had just thrown a punch, striking the man on the chin and knocking him off his feet. I threw a second half-hearted one at the empty air, and I thought even as they were dragging me away, *what a stupid thing to do. How fake.*

Two teenagers held me loosely by the arms. One of them said, "Peace, amigo, peace," and the other said, "Chill, okay? Just calm down," and I let myself go limp there on the porch. Candy and I had talked about quick acts of violence that might free us, savoring the punches and kicks we'd land, the traps we'd set, the places we'd escape to afterward.

I remember him saying, "They're the same son of a bitch anyway," once when we were standing on a bridge watching the traffic slide below us, and then he made the sound of a car horn, a bleating, painful, comical sound that made a real car beep back. One hand was cupped to his mouth and the other was holding the wire fence, and it seemed that if he had jumped at that moment he would have flown. I would fight his demons. He would fight mine.

This punch had not felt like anything Candy and I imagined. Which is not to say it felt bad. "El loco," one of the teenagers said, and he pushed my shoulder. They looked like brothers—the same pug nose, the same small eyes and jet-black hair—sixteen or so, both of them, about half my age. "Drink this," one of them said. "It'll make you feel better." And he handed me some flat orange soda in a plastic cup. I swallowed it down, dropped the cup, breathed deep.

My knuckle was bleeding just above my wedding ring, and I remembered that my wife had asked me to call her as soon as I arrived. But the idea of talking to her on the phone seemed impossible now—or at least beyond my ability.

I sucked my knuckle and wondered how hard that first punch had connected. The two brothers were laughing, and I had to laugh too—a snort that made them grin and slap my shoulder. Maybe they knew who I was, and maybe they didn't, but they seemed to be treating me with respect. I was a man who had just thrown a dirty punch. That could have been enough to do it. Maybe they hated the guy I hit.

We were cackling like we had just heard the filthiest, funniest joke in Lawrence, Massachusetts. But I was laughing at a different joke, a private one only Candy and I would understand. I was thinking of the little electrical thrill when my fist connected, the way the guy's expression flashed from a self-satisfied grin to childish shock as he stumbled back. Would he wake up the next day with a bruise? Two hundred something pages, two years of my life, a mess of theories and guesswork about motivations and feelings, and it was one lame-ass punch that helped me get into my father's head.

The old house on Primrose had burned down, like the house next to it had years ago, and the vinyl siding of the buildings on either side was blistered and blackened. Enough empty space was there now for a McDonald's or a Burger King. In six months I would probably be able to return and find one. I stood on the side of the road drinking bottled water and listening to the cars pass behind my back as they headed to the highway. This was where Candy and a few of the others had lived and where they had thrown parties like the one I just came from.

It wasn't surprising to me that the house was gone. The landlord owned a number of buildings in town, and several of them had burned down. And this one had almost been destroyed when the house next door had burned. I had told the story in the book, beginning with my waking up on the couch in the middle of the night, the room flickering orange. People were yelling outside, but I was still half asleep, and drunk, and so I sat there watching the flames through the window like it was television. Candy appeared, naked except for a towel, and Cheryl too, and we all watched from the window until the firemen pounded at the door.

"It's magic," Cheryl said, and then the door opened, and Candy went to get his blue jeans and his guitar.

Outside a few people were crying, but for the most part the neighborhood had the atmosphere of a block party, and I remember shoeless and shirtless Candy sitting on the curb and playing songs. Some of the neighbors gathered around to listen, kids feigning disinterest, middle-aged wives checking him out.

Someone passed around cigarettes and cans of Coke and little hard sweets wrapped in yellow foil, and Candy told jokes to the smallest kids, jokes I had never heard before. He played songs I didn't know he knew. "Strawberry Fields Forever," the verses in Spanish for the old ladies. *Es fácil vivir con ojos cerrados, mal entendiendo todo lo que ves, se hace difícil ser alguien, pero eso está bien, no me importa demasiado.* Then he did "Danny Boy," his voice high and keening, like he was making fun of not just our sadness but of sadness as a concept. A few people joined in, including Cheryl, who was drinking a beer and dancing a high-stepping Greek dance.

When this other fire had hit—the fire that leveled his place and sent him off in some mysterious direction—Candy had probably been alone. I guessed that he had not played his guitar on the curb and that maybe he had not played it for a long time. I didn't know if he even owned a guitar anymore.

In the letter Cheryl said she had gone by there the next morning, after she had found out. I'm sure she half expected him to be sleeping behind the convenience store, but he was nowhere to be found. He hadn't been talking to anyone recently, and she wondered if he had moved before the fire had hit. She went home, made a few phone calls, and then she thought of me. She had heard about the book, and I was his brother in spirit, after all. At least that's how she put it in the letter. I folded it and put it away and after three days I had almost forgotten it, but then I got the call from the hospital. They said my father was asking for me, that he was nervous and anxious. After playing the role of the dutiful son—asking the right questions, then telling them I would be there soon—I hung up the phone, took the letter out of a drawer, smoothed it out, and read it again. I left the next day, and here I was, watching the vacant lot where Candy once lived, like something might actually happen if I just stared long enough.

I finished my water and capped it and crossed the street, where I called my wife from the greasy pay phone. A group of kids watched me from their car as if I were up to no good. They revved the engine and clicked their headlights from low to high at their friend as she came out of the store, paper bag in hand. She climbed in, the engine revved again, they backed out into the street, and I was alone.

"Hello?" she said.

"Melissa," I said.

I could tell I had awakened her. She hesitated, and I could hear her breathing before she said, "I thought you'd call sooner. How is everything going up there?"

"It could be worse," I said. "I'm calling from a pay phone. I don't have a lot of minutes on my phone card so we should be quick."

"Right," she said. "Okay. Quick. What are you going to do?"

"I don't know. Maybe I'll head back tonight. It's been a disappointing trip so far. I'm not sure what I was trying to accomplish."

"I'm not sure either," she said. "They called again from the hospital. It's worse."

"I figured," I said, and then, not wanting to head further in that direction, "How's Kayla?"

The phone clicked and I thought we had been disconnected, but then her voice came back to me. "She's fine. She's been asleep for hours. She was waiting for your phone call too, you know."

A car pulled next to the phone and beeped its horn once—a shrill, sustained blast—and then a kid in a baseball cap and oversized leather jacket jumped out of the passenger door. "What?" I asked. "Sorry. I can't hear you. It's noisy here."

"I asked you what you're going to do now. If you're going to get a hotel."

"I'm going to see the old man."

"Good."

"Not my father. Candy's dad. He still lives here." There was another beep of the horn, another silence between us. "Melissa?" I said.

She said, "You sound strange."

"I know. But I'm okay. It's like riding a bicycle, coming back here."

"That's not what I mean," she said.

"I know what you mean," I said. "And don't worry. I love you very much."

"You said it was like riding a bicycle."

"The roads. I was just talking about the roads. Finding my way around."

She seemed to consider this as she took another long breath. Then she said, "I love you too. Like crazy, you know?"

I pictured her sitting up in bed, the phone cord twirled around her wrist, eyes closed as she imagined me at this phone booth, shoulders slumped, holding the phone in two hands. "The same," I said. "The same."

"Then don't worry me."

"Okay. Then I won't worry you. It just all seems so immediate now that I'm back here. It all seems *important*. Like I never left. Well, not really. It's like I left last week and changed my mind." But that wasn't right either. I didn't know what I meant, and I wondered if I would ever be capable of eyeing the truth and hitting it dead center. At that moment Candy seemed to be the kind of person who could do that, and if he was, it somehow meant I was not. "I'm not feeling very well," I said.

"I can tell," she said. "I do trust you. But I feel like I know those people. And I think they're dangerous."

"Just because of some words I wrote down," I said, and I was surprised by the edge in my voice. "That's why you know them."

"Yes," she said. "Because of some words. *Your* words."

"Well, then you don't know them at all," I said. "I'm not sure what I'm trying to tell you."

"I'm not sure either. What are you trying to tell me?"

I took a deep breath. "Just that I need to visit Candy's dad, that I'll be home as soon as possible, and that I love you very much." I hung up the phone and wiped my hand on my pants. The world was splintering into pieces of color, and I wondered what had been in that orange drink I swallowed at the party. The car was beeping again, and I imagined Melissa sitting in the dark bedroom still holding the phone.

We had been married for two years when I began work on the book. Although she supported me, she was perplexed that a person with such an unremarkable past would want to write it all down for . . . who? My father had just been hospitalized, and we still lived close enough that I visited him often. I sat at the foot of his bed and listened to him talk. As the visits continued I realized I couldn't reply the way I wanted to except in private, using a pen and paper and then, after I had filled an entire notebook with scribbles, a typewriter.

"So you didn't get along," Melissa had said once as I worked at the kitchen table after Kayla was in bed. "Lots of sons don't get along with their fathers." I had not told her much except to say that there was friction between us. The details came to her through the book, which she read chapter by chapter, correcting misspellings and grammar with a red pen. That's how she got to know Candy and the rest of them. I wondered if she saw them less as real people, more as my personal literary creations. I was seeing them that way too—as characters I had placed on a stage and given words to speak. It took Cheryl's letter to remind me how real Candy was, how unreal I might be without him. When I had told Melissa, "Candy's in trouble," she had said, "Oh, the boy from the book."

As I stepped away from the phone, I took one last look at the space where the houses had been. All that absence seemed like a fitting monument.

I had figured at least one small thing out. So I had to make a third stop that night.

I could see the blue glow of the television from the back porch. And on the other side of the room a figure sat in a chair, hunched over an aluminum tray. The TV cast light across his body, but I couldn't see his face. It had to be him though, and I knocked on the door. Tapped actually, on the small inset window where a sign had been affixed with masking tape. *Beware of Dog.* He had never owned a dog but had put the sign up to keep people away, and after a while we started calling *him* the dog as much as the old man. Sometimes we called him *bestia* or Frankenstein or even Papa Smurf when we felt charitable. We had end-less nicknames for him, although usually we kept him at arm's length with a pronoun, as in *You wouldn't believe what he just did*, or *Someday he'll get what's coming to him*. The window was stained glass, little red and white fractals forming an angel—too nice for a place like this. It had always looked more like a bird with a bowed head and spread wings. I had considered breaking it once, but thinking about it was as far as I could go.

"Come in," someone called over the TV, and I opened the door.

Every house has its own smell, like a fingerprint, deep and complicated as a story. I remembered the smell of this house—cigarettes, of course, and the thin, bony fish his dad always cooked, and the cheap air freshener he used to try to cover it all up. Someone was laughing on the TV.

I crossed the room and touched the small kitchen table with things strewn across it. Two newspapers, one rolled up in a rub-ber band, the other open to the sports page. A coffee cup. A piece of paper with a few words scrawled across it. Needle-nose pliers. Some coins. A seashell with the tip broken off. I lifted the shell and knew that Candy was there. It was as large as my palm, and I cupped it to my ear, hearing the same ocean Candy had probably heard when he picked it up off Hampton Beach. We always used to go there in the winter, walking up and down the surf with our cold hands stuffed in our pockets.

"Crybaby," someone said. The same voice—snide, nasal. I wanted to hug him. I wanted to pull his mouth to my ear like the opening of the shell and hear that voice tell me everything that had happened in the years we had been apart.

"People are worried," I said.

"Boo hoo," he said and curled his lips the way he used to when he played the guitar. He was balding so that his hairline formed a blunt black arrow down his scalp, and he had gained a lot of weight around his midriff, although his face was narrow and his cheeks sunken. Too much beer and speed maybe. The eyes were the same—small and dark like obsidian—but if I had passed him on the street I'm not sure I would have recognized him.

He was wearing a gray T-shirt and jeans, and around his neck hung a beaded necklace. A gift from Cheryl probably, something that had survived the fire because he had been wearing it. "I'm doing an Elvis," he explained before I could ask the question, and then, "I'm helping out with my dad," like the fire hadn't happened. "He's turned into a puppy dog, if you can believe it. It's ridiculous."

"You probably shouldn't call me that," I said.

"Yeah," he said. "I've read the book. I've read it twice. I bet you didn't think I knew about it, but word trickles down—even to here." He picked up the coffee cup from the kitchen table and put it in the sink, ran water into it.

"I didn't lie though," I said.

"You want something from me," he said. "I can tell."

"Yeah," I said. "I want to know you're all right."

"I liked the stuff about your mom especially," he said. "It was beautiful. It really was. I remember those grilled cheese sandwiches too. You got that all down."

"Thank you," I said. "That means a lot to me."

"But I'm not so sure about what you wrote about me, Crybaby. I was never that pretty. I was never that talented." He snickered and lowered his voice to a theatrical whisper. "It's like you wrote the book to seduce me all over again."

"Can I sit down?" I asked. The kitchen felt small and hot like something was cooking in the oven. I rested my hand on the back of a chair.

"And I thought you and I, we shared everything," he continued, "but a couple of things in there—things your dad did—they were a surprise to me. The cigarette burns. Did you keep that secret from me, or did you make it up?" He lifted the change, rattled it around in his hand like dice he was about to throw, and put it in his pocket. His voice sounded like two voices—one mocking, one loving—and then the two voices split into four and then into eight. It felt like I was talking to a crowd, and I wanted to fall asleep right there on his father's kitchen floor. I sat down instead and put my arm on the table, still holding the shell. The ceiling flew around my head, and the shell turned in my hand like a gear. I could feel it moving slowly, and I decided that it was somehow connected to the ceiling above me and to Candy's mouth and the television in the next room. It was some kind of remote control, but I didn't know how to work it.

"It was inspiring, though," Candy was saying. "I identified with the protagonist." He laughed, and the TV laughed, and I swore I heard his father say, "Shut up in there." So I muttered something about having to leave, that my wife was probably worried about me, that I wasn't feeling well. But I was far below Candy now, as if he was standing on a box looking down at me. I realized my knee had touched the floor.

"You look awful," he said, and he touched my hair.

"I know. And you don't look so good either."

We laughed then the way we used to, and I remembered him once saying, with a fresh triangular bruise on his cheek, "You know what makes him angry? When you look him right in the face and snicker. If you giggle he hates that." We had always compared notes.

Candy had his hands on my shoulders and he was rubbing, working the muscles. His hand slid down to the point high on my chest where my collarbone had been broken. He slid two fingers over the bone nub, the way he used to, and then down deeper into my shirt. "You'll be okay in a couple of hours," he said.

"I know," I said, and I tried to turn around on my knees, little baby steps in a circle, until I was looking at his thighs and distended belly. I hugged him lightly, and he took me by the shoulders and tried to help me stand.

"The problem with memoirs is that they're written by the successful," Candy said. "They're written by the people who get out." One hand rose from my shoulder and touched my cheek. "We're not the same."

"I'm sorry," I said. Or at least thought. I tried to focus on his words instead of on the blaring television. The sound came from above us and underneath us, and I hoped that I wasn't going to be sick. I took a deep breath and smelled his father's breakfast—greasy specks of burned egg and butter and coffee—and remembered something from the book. The thought descended on me like a spider on a web. What had I written? That Candy's pain was a way to measure my own.

"I missed you," I said, or thought I said, and pushed my face forward into the folds of Candy's pants. I tried to move my lips, and his hand steered my head. He made a low humming as I nuzzled him thinking, *he is almost singing*. It sounded like something from the book, as if this would find a place there too, next to our childhoods, like boxes on a shelf.

"I really missed you," I said, and this time I knew I had spoken aloud, because he said the same thing back to me, and then he told me to stop.

I could hear voices from the other room, spoons scraping in bowls, footsteps across the floor. I opened my eyes to darkness, but some light shone through the cracks in the window blinds, and I could see stacks of books piled high on either side of the mattress, red and yellow candles stuck in empty wine bottles, and small piles of sweaters and flower-print dresses. Cheryl's room.

She sat at the foot of the bed, rubbing my thigh through the quilt. I allowed myself to think of my father in his hospital room—to make that awkward poetic connection and then dispense with it. My shoulder hurt. I could still feel Candy on my lips. "Hey, sleeping beauty," she said. "Want some water?"

"Sure," I said, and she handed me the glass she had been drinking from. My throat was dry and my voice sounded deep and weary, but I felt better than I had thought I might. My leg was shaking a little, vibrating almost, which was probably why Cheryl was rubbing it. Her face was marked with red splotches, her mascara was streaked, and I noticed some thin mysterious cuts on her neck, crusted with dried blood. I wondered if something bad had happened the night before, a drama worse than the one I had created with my stupid punch—or maybe connected to it.

"They're eating grapefruit in the other room," she said as I handed her back the empty glass. "It's always good to have fruit and water the next day."

She told me this as if I were new here, but I remembered the ritual—Cheryl cutting the grapefruits in half with a long knife, passing them around, sharing stories from the night before and laughing at our stupidity. I wondered if she still picked up data entry projects whenever she needed money, if she begged her parents for cash when times were tight, who she was sleeping with and if they caused her a lot of pain and heartache. I suppose Candy and I had.

"Thank you," I said. "I could use some. I had a bad night."

"You make your own trouble," she said, and I was surprised by the flatness in her voice. I wasn't sure if she was talking about me or people in general.

I pushed back the quilt and sat up. I was still dressed and my clothes were damp with sweat. "I found him," I said, because I thought that might balance the damage I had caused. This was, after all, why she had written to me, why I had come back here.

"I thought you might," she said. "See how easy it was?"

"He looked bad," I said, as I climbed off the mattress and eyed the cluttered floor for my shoes.

"It's funny how people stay the same," she said, and I immediately resented her for stealing my private thoughts and sharing them with me like they were hers. "When I first saw you last night you were just standing there not talking to anybody, and you had this look on your face, almost serene, and that's when it occurred to me that you are a dad now. I thought, *maybe he's changed*. But of course you haven't."

I bent down and found my left shoe, still laced tightly, and the ball of my sock pushed down inside it. She had taken care of me pretty well when I had returned to her house, telling me I was in no condition to drive and then taking me upstairs to her room, past people talking on the stairs in hushed tones. The party had grown smaller, more serious, and the stragglers seemed like different people—gentle and sincere.

"I don't know what you're talking about," I said to her, as I stretched out my sock and slipped it over my foot, scanning the room for the other half of the pair. The second shoe was going to be more difficult to find.

"That's just like you," she said. "You were always putting yourself in jeopardy and blaming it on other people."

"I did not," I said. "I do not."

"Boo hoo hoo," she said, almost exactly like Candy had done. "His father was worse than yours. Much worse. Everybody here knows that." I didn't say anything, so she added, "And you *had* a mother, at least while you were growing up. Candy just had me." She shrugged and spread her arms slightly, as if to show off this poor substitute.

I found the second shoe behind a fallen stack of books. I must have kicked them over during the night. I began to restack them —old mystery paperbacks and water-damaged philosophy textbooks and thin collections of poetry. "Please do not go through my stuff," she said. "Just leave it, okay?"

"Okay," I said. "Sure."

"I do have it, if that's what you're searching for."

"I'm not searching for anything," I said.

"Sure you are," she said. "You're always searching for yourself. That's what you do."

I stood on one leg and tried to put on my sock as fast as I could, bouncing to keep my balance. She stepped toward me, and I thought she might push me over, but she started going through the books, lifting them and tossing them aside. "It's in here somewhere," she said. A wine bottle tipped and began to roll across the floor, but she caught it and righted it.

Any second she would find it and read my words back to me. I imagined her speaking them in an elevated, pretentious parody of my voice, moving through the scenes, pointing out the gaps, the hidden places. She would find the scene about that first fire, with Candy naked except for the towel, his body glowing orange, and say, "This is wrong. You were in the same bed that night. Why didn't you write that?" She would find another place like that, and then another, and I would bend my head, working the laces of my shoes, and listen.

"Look at this," she said, and she laughed at her discovery, although I could not see what she had in her hands.

"Where are my keys?" I said.

I left that place, traveled the eight hours in six, ready to tell everything. I parked the car, took the front stairs two at a time, opened the unlocked door. Stepping through the darkened house I found Melissa in the bedroom, hands raised to her ear as she gazed out a window. She was taking out her earrings. I crossed the room and wrapped my arms around her.

"He's gone," she said.

Whiteout

HUGH SHEEHY

From *The Invisibles* (2012)

Now the snow poured down so Mason only glimpsed the road between wiper flaps. On the windows the snow built to ridges and fell away, and when he looked out seeking a familiar glimpse of flat, snowbound farmland, there were only individual flakes whipped out of a slurry of descending whiteness. He'd been alone on the road for almost an hour, a privacy he'd used to cry about Wendy at first, though the grief had passed, giving way to a feeling of giddy excitement. He was going home for the first time in thirteen years.

The freeway was closed, and there had been no patrol cars since the announcement, back before the radio voices turned mushy. He doubted he would see one before he reached Mansfield. It was Christmas Eve, and the slashed state budget meant fewer cops all over.

A deejay had described the storm stretching from the Canadian Rockies to the Appalachians, dumping snow on central Ohio until tomorrow afternoon, delivering more white than anyone wanted for Christmas. Mason had laughed. Like a snow globe, the pun contained the entire Midwest. He opened the ashtray and got out the baggie of crushed cocaine. He had it tied off with a twister around a red cocktail straw for easy access while driving, and he took a snort, never taking his eyes from the vanishing and reappearing road, careful to miss nothing.

It was four o'clock and growing dark. In his parents' house the furnace bellowed in the basement. His older brother was opening dessert wine and his mother dusting the cookies with powdered sugar while his father stood by the tree at the living-room window, gazing out on the weather with the military sternness that was his mainmast. That was how it had been thirteen years ago when Mason returned from college at about this hour. He had come in lugging a bag of dirty laundry, prepared to deliver a rehearsed speech about how he'd failed out his first semester. He was not ready to see his mother so happy, wiping her hands on her apron so she could take him by the ears and kiss his forehead and cheeks, or Leonard waiting behind her with a second glass of port, or his father drifting in, a smile breaking through his solemn features. All that week Mason was unable to tell them, and afterward he'd driven back to school and worked in the tire shop, avoiding their calls until he found a job at a resort in Kentucky and started making his way south. No doubt they came looking for him, found the empty apartment they'd been renting. He might have been in Memphis then. It was hard to say, it was so long ago he felt more embarrassment now than guilt—he had been a boy then. Eventually he'd reached New Orleans and called that home, though these last few years, when he was feeling especially rotten and desolate, he'd taken to monitoring his family on the Internet. He thought about calling sometimes, but it felt like a lame gesture, and he was more interested in them, anyway, than in telling the story he sensed they'd want to hear about him.

Tracking them was easy, given his brother's tendency to post family news on his blog, even though no one posted comments save for the occasional fat cousin from Michigan whom nobody saw. Mason had been watching them for some time now. He knew all about them, felt as if their lives had been restricted to a small compartment of his consciousness. Sometimes he felt he might be connected to them in a way modern science couldn't explain. He knew details, his father's heart congestion, his mother's struggle with her bone density. He knew Leonard had lucked into a managerial position at Toyota and was seeing a woman who had a little girl. He had seen pictures online—the woman, Tanya, was good looking, surprisingly so, given Leonard's characteristic dullness and expanding paunch, and the daughter, a blonde child with gapped front teeth, was exceptionally cute. He felt he knew Tanya and her daughter intimately, though he'd never met them, and though people in his hometown frowned on mystical thinking, he sensed that if he kept his mouth shut when he met them they would find themselves mysteriously charmed by him. They had been planning for some time to go to his parents' today and open presents, and Leonard had mentioned it so many times on the blog that Mason wondered whether his brother wasn't really posting secret messages to him. Of course Leonard would never do this consciously; he was too jealous, too attuned to his local frequencies. But maybe some part of him, something spiritual, reached out to Mason while the dumb body labored on. He imagined Tanya's daughter shrieking with delight as he threw her into the air and caught her repeatedly, while Tanya and his parents looked on, amazed by his way with kids, and Leonard unable to conceal his envy. It was not too late, he thought, never too late for family, for even if he had been the troublemaker, he had always been the favorite. Long before his troubles began, he saw himself in the story of the prodigal son. He was the carrier of his family's joy. He reached for the baggie in the ashtray.

They were going to be so surprised. Maybe too surprised. Maybe he should call from his cell phone to diminish the shock of his arrival. There was his father's heart to think about. His mother's ticker probably wasn't shipshape either. He picked up his phone and nearly called, but then he remembered he was driving in extremely hazardous conditions, and then he remembered his earlier reasoning that it would be better to wait until he had stopped the vehicle before he broke a thirteen-year silence. A shiver of pleasure ran from his throbbing head down through his spine and arms and butt. It was a good thing he wasn't any higher.

He glimpsed a passing exit leading up to what must have been a country highway. This couldn't be Mansfield, not yet, and even if he wanted to stop to rest, there was nothing out here but farmhouses and barns and silos scattered over vast tracts of snowy farmland, and if you had asked Mason to guess how many of those structures had been abandoned for decades he would wager more than half, the rest inhabited by couples of a vanishing generation, people so old they were probably already tucking themselves in for the night.

He had to push on another couple of hours at this slow-going speed, which with the coke would be no problem. He would slow and make the gradual turn into his parents' driveway, and the people inside would see the headlights. He had presents, a backseat filled with them, gift-wrapped in shining silvery blue paper and red ribbons this very morning at a mall in northern Kentucky. Shopping had been a revelatory experience. Wandering among the stores, he had been seized by a spirit of generosity and serendipity that felt new to him. He found himself spending twice what he had vaguely budgeted, but it didn't matter; he could always pour more drinks, and people would give him money. That had always been simple enough. He found he had a talent for choosing the right gifts. There was a book on history's greatest military campaigns for his father, a copper-clad sugar boiler for his mother, a new bass fishing rod for Leonard. Though he had yet to meet Tanya, he was sure he knew her better than his brother did, reading beyond the observations in Leonard's blog, and he had picked out a sleek leather jacket for her, figuring her for a size six—if he was wrong, there was always the gift receipt. For the little girl, he had picked his favorite board game, The Game of Life, in which you started out with a single plastic peg representing a person and rolled dice to advance along squares in a road on a cartoon landscape while acquiring a car, an education, a job, a family, and a fortune. While you could choose certain things, like whether you wanted to retire, your ability to do what you wanted depended on luck, the roll of the dice, the card of fate. It was just like real life, Mason thought as he reached for the baggie in the ashtray, except it only lasted an hour or so, and you could play as many times as you wanted, be as many people as you wanted, and there were no real consequences to what you did. Which wasn't like real life, contrary to what the salesman in the toy store entrance had tried telling him.

Just thinking about it made Mason furious all over again.

The guy was from India or Bangladesh or someplace like that, this salesman whose eyes had sought Mason's from across the store filled with children, tired parents, noisy video games, and mechanized singing teddy bears. He was in his late forties, his face clean shaven, his black hair turning white around his ears. He beckoned for Mason to come to the folding table he'd set up in the doorway of the shop. He was sitting in front of a steel box with a meter divided into fields of blue and red. The meter's red plastic arrow rested just to the left of the zero in the blue field.

"How are you, sir?" the man asked in a solemn unaccented voice, as if they had embarked on a costly business transaction. "Enjoying your shopping?"

"Merry Christmas." It occurred to Mason the guy might not celebrate the holiday, but then what the hell did he expect, selling whatever he sold in a mall the day before Christmas? He set down his clutch of plastic bags and put his hands on his hips. He was feeling the need to duck into a bathroom and get the baggie out of his coat's inner pocket. After he learned about this steel box. "This looks like a Geiger counter or something. What's it measure?"

"Stress," the man told him.

Mason laughed. New Age shit—he should have known. "How does it do that exactly?"

The man stood and offered him two small steel rods with steel buttons on their top ends. The rods were connected by wires to the Geiger counter thing. "Take a wand in each hand and let it rest there. When you are ready, rest your thumbs on the indicators on the top of each wand. The meter will determine your stress level and show us with the indicator arrow."

The rods were the weight of supper knives. Mason felt doubtful holding them, pressured to buy something. He wished he had refused to hold them. "These are going to measure my stress?"

"Yes. Rest your thumbs on the indicators when you are ready."

Mason felt nervous. The things were probably rigged so that your stress reading was through the roof. The man regarded him with the detachment of someone confident of his superiority. He was probably selling herbal remedies or something. Mason put his thumbs on the steel buttons and looked down at the stress meter. The red arrow swung rapidly through the blue field and into the rightmost quadrant of the red field and wavered there at a spot between the numbers seventeen and eighteen. Great, he was probably about to have a heart attack right here.

"What the fuck does this mean?"

The man took the wands. "It means you have a great deal of stress in your life."

He thought of Wendy again and felt the clamp of guilt. He was getting irritated with this stranger. It was none of his business. The certainty in the man's voice disgusted him. "How the fuck does this machine know?"

"You carry the stress in your muscles. It stores up in your nervous system and affects everything you do. The process is unconscious, and it determines how you hold your body and a whole host of things, including how healthy you feel."

"That's a load of shit," Mason said. "Let's see you press the buttons."

The man blinked once, casually accepting the challenge, and placed his thumbs on the buttons. The arrow moved past zero into the second quadrant of the blue field. "Do you see? Six point eight? That is a very healthy level of stress."

"According to whom?"

"Dr. Hubbard has written a book that explains it all." The man brought a thick black paperback with the title *Dianetics* from behind the stress meter. "It is all in here."

It was rigged somehow. Mason looked down to see if some kind of foot pedal controlled the stress meter and saw only the guy's brown loafers against the mall's drab green carpeting. "What the fuck do these numbers even mean? This shit isn't real medicine; it's all made up!"

"Sir, you seem to be aware of your stress," the man said coolly. "There must be things in your life that make you feel strain, things and people. You could cut these out."

It had been a while since Mason felt like he could punch someone. He folded his arms to hide his shaking hands. His heart, beating fast, felt sick to its stomach. "What do you know about me?"

"You could one day live stress free," the man said. "Think about it. You would feel weightless, happier than you have ever been. It would be better for you."

"Fuck you," Mason told the man. "You don't know a fucking thing."

He had grabbed his bags then and gone straight to the nearest men's room stall for two quick snorts from the baggie and then had hurried out to the mall parking lot, where the snow was really starting to come down. The coke helped him feel better, and he convinced himself that he should be proud of his response to this unpredictable nuisance. But as he crossed the border into his home state, he began to doubt that his words had made any impact on the salesman, who had been so sure of himself.

"Motherfucking asshole," he said, clearly envisioning the calm brown eyes floating in the man's impassive brown face, then checking to ensure he was still on the road. "Fuck you, mother-fucker!"

When he came to the overturned minivan, the snow flowed down so heavily that he almost didn't see it lying in the right lane. Its red color helped it stand out it in the light of his headlights reflecting off the falling snow. It was past five now, and he had been traveling at just under thirty miles an hour, and he reckoned he had another thirty miles to go. There was nothing out here but farms and a few small stands of trees. He braked slowly until he was hardly rolling and steered his car to a stop near the shoulder. It seemed more likely that he would be stuck in the snow than that another vehicle would come along and hit his car. He switched on the hazards before getting out.

Wind rose loudly along the dark road, blowing snow across settled snow and against steel dividers with a sound like tinkling glass particles. Snow fell in his hair and on his face as he trudged through the slush on the highway. A whirling gust packed snow under his chin and down his collar. Soon it would be too cold for the salt on the roads to work. He shouldn't wait out here until help came, and anyway he was too deranged from coke and sleeplessness to talk to cops. Still he had better make sure someone was coming. He grew nervous as he approached the dark hulk of the minivan, glancing back to see his car's hazards, tiny red lights blinking in the rippling gray quilt of snow.

He went to the front end of the van and knelt in the cold snow by the window, which was mostly broken out, and turned on the penlight on his keychain. The thin light revealed a plaid, blue blanket with a tousled lock of white hair sticking out from under one end. The person underneath shuddered. "Jim? Is that you?" She sounded tired and cold. He wondered if she could move, if the van was at risk for combustion flipped over as it was.

"No, I'm Mason," he said. "But it's okay. I'm here to help. Is Jim your husband?"

After a few strained breaths she said, "He went for help. To find us a phone."

"I have a phone," he said. "I'm going to call 911 right now. Are you hurt?"

"My shoulder hurts," the woman said. "Where's Jim?"

"Hold on," he said. "Let me call them. I'll go find him."

"Get Jim," she said. "Tell him to come back here. It's not safe to be running around out there. He's not a kid anymore."

He walked away from the van to make the call, covering his phone with his free hand to protect it from the snow. He was afraid there would be no connection, but the signal patched through on the first try. A man answered, his voice flat, and Mason wondered whether it sounded different tonight from any other night, heavier, more resentful. Probably not. He'd heard the holidays were an especially violent and sad time of year for many people. Until recently, he had been one of them. He explained what he had discovered on the highway.

The operator wasn't sure how long it would take for the ambulance to arrive. "I'd be able to guess better if I knew exactly where you were. At least you're on 77. Forty minutes? Maybe sooner. It's pretty bad out there."

"That's too long," Mason said. "The man with this lady, he went off looking for a phone. He's got to be lost in all this snow."

"Just stay with the woman," the operator said. "Back your car up to the minivan and wait with her."

"I don't know," Mason said. "The minivan's upside down. Couldn't it catch on fire? Shouldn't I get her out of there?"

"Sir, I recommend you leave her where she is. She may have a back injury. If there's not a fire yet, maybe there won't be. But now that you mention it, you might want to keep a distance from the vehicle."

"Is that your advice?" Mason couldn't believe what he was hearing. A 911 operator should know exactly what to do.

"It's really up to you, sir. The police are on their way. Just sit tight."

He went back to the window of the overturned van and shined his light on the woman under the blanket. She was shivering, and it sounded like she was crying. "Is that you, Jim?"

"No, it's Mason again. I just called for an ambulance."

"Thank heavens. How long did they say?"

"They said soon," he said. "They're coming as fast as they can."

"Where's Jim? Someone's got to get him before he gets too far," she said. "Someone's got to tell him he doesn't need to call."

"Okay," Mason said. "Okay. What about you? Are you going to be okay here?"

"I'm fine," the woman said. "Go find Jim for me."

"Okay, I'm going." He wished he had another light to give to her, to keep her company. He would have given her his keys with the penlight, but it would be suicidal to leave the highway without any way of seeing his tracks. He rose from the window and took a few steps onto the road, astonished by how quickly the snow covered her presence and he felt alone again. He could walk out into the snow, stand right next to the old man, and never see him. He shined his light along the shoulder until he found a pair of half-filled footprints leading down into the shallow ditch beside the road and up the far side to a snow-filed space that was probably an open field. He hesitated, the edges of his feet already going numb. What if the old guy had already fallen or sat down out there, had given up? What if he'd already died? It would be much easier to stay here on the road and wait for the police. It would be even easier to walk down to his car, get in, and drive away. No one could fault him for that. He had already done a great deal here, perhaps saved the life of the woman in the minivan. Those people shouldn't have been on the road tonight; they were lucky he even came along. He thought of the man with the stress meter telling him how easy his life could be if he abandoned his obligations to others. He thought of his parents, of Leonard and Tanya and the kid listening to his hero story, how hollow it would sound if he never told them how he ran away at the last minute. Or what a terrible secret it would be if he never told them at all. Letting out a self-pitying sigh he stepped down into the deep snow of the ditch.

In early November he had come in around dawn and found Wendy. He was tired from working a double, he later told the police, which made it hard to remember details, but the truth was that he had stuck around after the bar was clean with a cool new guy, doing shots and telling stories, making brief retreats to the bathroom to make use of his baggie. The sun was coming up over the low slanted roofs of Burgundy Street when he found his townhouse's front door unlocked and became angry enough to wake Wendy and lecture her about protecting herself and their things.

Only afterward did he notice the disaster area of the shotgun house's front room and kitchen, the takeout containers lying open on the countertop and table, the empty bottles and ashtrays everywhere, couch pillows lying on the floor. It was if they had been living in a crime scene all along.

Since kissing him good-bye at midnight, she had apparently had quite an adventure, bringing any number of people back to the house. She'd even left the little sliding mirror from the medicine cabinet out on the coffee table with powder smudges on top. He went to the bedroom and found the bedclothes in the usual tangle. He tried to stay calm then, telling himself she'd gone back out, was possibly opening another beer right now in one of their friend's living rooms, so blitzed she'd never recall leaving the door unlocked. He was already on his way into the bathroom, pushing open the door, seeing the water on the tiles.

She had been packed into the bathtub fully dressed. Her dirty feet hung over the edge. Someone had tucked her elbows in at her sides, tilted her head back under the faucet. Her hazel eyes looked up emptily. Her clothes and hair were soaked, her pallid face rinsed with water, looking almost clean and innocent but for the marks on her cheeks where someone—a man, he first assumed then and simply came to believe afterward—had slapped her repeatedly to wake her up.

He kept walking long after he could no longer make out Jim's tracks in the snow. He was chilled through the bones of his feet and hands, and his teeth were chattering in his ears. His clothes were all wrong for this mission. By now the paramedics and police had surely reached the scene of the accident, and things were under control. Maybe Jim was back by now, too, standing among the uniformed men, soberly speculating about where the well-meaning, if foolish, Samaritan had gone. He didn't believe this version of things; it was too tidy. He was going to die out here, and so was Jim. They both were going to die out here. So much for the prodigal son, he thought, though something in him refused to accept it.

He reached for the baggie of coke he had transferred to his coat pocket and ran up against a man standing upright in the field. Small but sturdy, the man stood turned away from him, bundled tightly in his old trench coat and hunching against the cold, with tiny drifts of snow piled up on the brim of his fedora. Mason touched his shoulder. "Jim?" he said. He laughed morbidly. "I've been looking all over for you."

When the man didn't respond, Mason tried turning him by

the shoulder. Something under the coat was hard and bulky. He reached out to take the hat, and the head rolled back, revealing the black stitchwork connecting the head to the burlap sack body. The face under the frayed hat brim was featureless sackcloth, frozen stiff and stained with dirt. A wind came up and one of the scarecrow's arms flew around, throwing flecks of ice against his cheeks, and Mason let go to cover his face with his unfeeling hands.

He stumbled forward and saw something large and dark looming ahead, a mass to which the falling snow conformed. He hurried forward, getting closer, fighting through a drift to his thighs, until he came up against the frozen wood of a barn wall. As a boy he used to look at them from the backseat of his father's car, half curious about these relics of the cornbelt days, so many of which had been used as billboards for chewing tobacco. He had never been this close to one. Holding his hand against the icy grain of the wood, he made his way around the structure, hoping to find a house on the other side.

The farmhouse stood in a ring of naked maple trees whose branches were thrashing in the wind. The dark shapes of cars stood in the driveway. A light was on inside, within the front door. He hurried through the snow, falling once, and used the iron railing to pull himself up the front steps. Exhaustion and drug withdrawal were catching up with him. He did not know what he would say when he began to ring the glowing, orange doorbell, which he pressed over and over. After a while, a man opened the inner door and looked out.

It was almost ten when he finally called his parents. He was sitting in the kitchen of the farmhouse, the presents he had picked out for his family laid out on the table before him. The couple who lived there had been very kind, giving him dry clothes to wear and offering to let him stay the night in one of the spare rooms upstairs. After talking with the local sheriff, the farmer had taken Mason in his truck with a snowplow to retrieve his car, which was now parked in the driveway, behind the sedan that belonged to the couple's son and his wife. Mason had talked to the police, who seemed to take his state of mind for confusion and panic and cold. They too had been kind, thanking him for his help. They had found Jim on the freeway, wandering in the wrong direction, confused and upset. He had mild frostbite on some of his fingers and his nose, but he was otherwise okay. By now he and his wife were at a hospital somewhere.

The farmer was a serious man with a strong air of religiosity, and in the course of taking Mason back to his car and offering to put him up he had repeatedly and pointedly made references to God, to whom he clearly felt Mason owed his life. The farmer was courteous but also wary and faintly disapproving, having detected something he didn't like in his unforeseen guest. Now that he had fulfilled his obligations as host, he had left Mason in the kitchen and gone back to the living room, where his grandchildren were up past their bedtimes, opening presents. From the archway to the brightly lighted room came the sounds of paper tearing and the chirpy voices of small children, the reluctant admonishments of moderately drunken parents.

Mason sipped hot tea from a mug, which announced in cartoon font, *The Early Bird Gets the Worm!*, and depicted a smiling bluebird in a nobleman's blouse uprooting a pale worm from the ground. He wanted another bump from the baggie in his coat, but he thought he'd let it wait until he was off the phone.

His brother answered. There was a pause in the space after Mason spoke his name. Leonard said something to people in the background, and suddenly he heard his father and his mother speaking to him. A little girl asking a question and being told to hush. That would be Tanya's daughter. They had him on speaker phone and were trying to take turns talking to him. His father went first, in a voice steady and calm, almost subdued. His mother, too, sounded so careful. To hear their caution made him wince, but he answered their questions as best he could. The connection was poor. He listened to their voices, trying to see their faces through their tones. After a long silence on Mason's end, his father remarked that the call had been dropped, and they should hang up and wait for him to call back.

"Wait," he said, in a voice that sounded desperate to him. He said he was there, though it had already dawned on him that it would be tomorrow before he could prove it to them. He said a few things about the severity of the storm, then promised to tell them his story in the morning. When he hung up, he knew by the sound of their voices that they had not believed him completely. It was not disbelief he had heard, or even skepticism, but an awareness of who he had always been.

He carried the presents up to the guest room as quietly as he could, hoping the groans of the steps beneath him blended into the storm. He was looking forward to another snort, but then he changed his mind, thinking instead to pass out and take the shortcut to the morning. The air in the room smelled like mothballs, and a layer of cold air drifted over the floorboards. He did not bother to turn on the light. The window was dark, crusted with a layer of snow, visible only by the faint violet light outside. He climbed into the bed fully clothed, pulled the quilt to his chin, and gazed at the dark ceiling above. The mattress was narrow and lumpy, and all he could do was lie there and wait for sleep. He thought of Wendy again, and in the painful instant that followed it seemed that it was, this feeling he had run from thirteen years ago, the fear of the way life unfolded in this place, with slow and unflinching inevitability. He opened his eyes and saw the presents lying in a neat stack beside the bed, their wrappings gleaming faintly. After a moment, he remembered what each contained but could not say why he had chosen them. He let out a sigh and felt his body start to relax. Sleep was closer than he had imagined. Tomorrow he would drive home and see his family. Whatever happened after that, happened.

Easy

WENDY BRENNER

From *Large Animals in Everyday Life* (1996)

I'm not even out of Florida and already thinking of my mother: the sun-bleached billboard for House of Porcelain reminds me of the ceramics she took up after my father died. She called it "mastering an art," and she did it so that when she looked at me she would not be so distracted by his eyes, his chin; she wanted to make the hard first months easier. She set up shop on our screened porch, replacing my father's shelves of hardware with ten-pound bags of wet clay and a kiln she assembled from a kit, and soon the porch filled up with coy-faced rabbits and round-limbed, winking frogs. She glazed them conservatively in calm opaques and garnished each with a set of stick-on eyelashes, which she thought was a cute idea and I thought made the animals appear hopeful. When one fell and smashed, with those eyelashes, it was heartbreaking.

She could probably cut a deal with the House of Porcelain people—their billboards boast of "spirited porcelain children" and "fragile crystal relics from a simpler time"—but I can't afford to stop and browse. My plan is not to get off the highway until I'm in Georgia, which is not just superstition, though Georgia sounds safe to me with all its bragging about such harmless commodi-

ties as peaches and pecans. By the time I reach Georgia, I've figured, my mother should be up and eating her Danish, and I can
phone her from some anonymous rest stop and tell her I'm on
my way. Like an athlete, I visualize my successful arrival, picture
her spare house key, which sits in the mouth of a ceramic squirrel that's frozen in an adorable crouch and nailed to the front
steps of her Chicago house. She sculpted the squirrel herself, using neither mold nor model. I picture the highway stretching out
ahead of me, the squirrel at one end and me, a dot, at the other,
like a puzzle in a children's magazine. But there on my left thigh
is a quarter-sized blue bruise from Charlie, and it too is the dot. I
whip along, going seventy, my hand resting lightly on the bruise,
which also goes seventy.

There was a time, just after my father's death, that my mother
would never have let me get this far out of her sight. I was just
starting first grade, so she took a job serving food in my school
cafeteria. She may have been possessive, even compulsive, but I
loved that it was my own mother's hand placing the extra cookies
on my tray. Lunch was like a daily personal gift, somehow connected to my father, whom I couldn't exactly remember. I knew
that she was there *for* me, but *because* of him, and I sometimes
wondered if he had actually told her to give me the cookies. She
stayed on for eight years, and because she was younger than the
rest of the cafeteria staff and served with a mild, surprised look
on her face, while the other women scowled and had drawn-on
eyebrows, my mother was popular. She knew every kid's name
and she made jokes about the food she served. She could afford
to; she had chosen to be there.

When I went off to high school we thought our arrangement
had ended: the high school cafeteria workers had a union and

wouldn't even accept my mother's application. But then she found out the company that serviced the school's vending machines was hiring, so she became the new candy bar lady. Now only the greasers joked with her, the guys in navy tanker jackets who hung out by her machines talking about Auto Mechanics Lab and looking too old to be in high school. They were shiny-faced, actually greasy, and often red-eyed, and they clomped around the halls in black lace-up boots, jingling large bunches of keys that were attached to their belts with heavy link chains. Their girlfriends looked cleaner but wore clunky wooden sandals that made as much noise as the boys' boots and keys, and they went around with giant combs sticking out of their back pockets. They all looked shrewd and unhappy, as though they expected to hear bad news at any moment, and my mother would tell me stories. "Kimmy Forsythe is not as dumb as she looks," she would say to me at home. "She is the sole guardian of her four little brothers, not one but *two* of whom are diagnosed hyperactive." Or she might say, "You should be nice to the Mazzetti boys. They don't even hear how they sound to others, and they have a terrible time of it at home." By now I felt I was indulging my mother, that her job was a way of ensuring that *she* was okay. One of us needed to feel that one of us was safe, but the roles had grown hazy, as roles will do.

Occasionally some guy I'd never spoken a word to would bump into me in one of my classes and say, "You got a nice ma." This always embarrassed me—I had it easier than the Mazzetti boys and I knew it. I wasn't jealous of my mother's attentions to them, and I didn't secretly want to run away with them, or marry them, or be them. My friends and I ignored the greasers and laughed a little at their girlfriends' clothes, but mostly we did our homework and went to movies and our boring jobs. I was a weekend hat-check girl at a Holiday Inn and was already thinking of going on in art, not for the rebellion or the romance, but because of how simple my mother made ceramics look. I was never one to look for trouble.

I remind myself of this as I pull off of I-75, finally, safely into Georgia, at a stop called Arabi, which I know only because it's written on the rusted pay phone in front of the gas station. Beyond the station there's just an empty road curving away into the high tree line. "I'm coming home," I tell my mother. "I'm on my way right now."

"That's odd," she says. "I mean, not strange that you're coming, but Charlie just telephoned for you here." She and Charlie have never met, but they know each other's phone voices.

"I didn't tell him I was leaving," I say. "He's the reason I'm coming."

My mother doesn't say anything for a moment. Finally she says, "Well, I told him I didn't know anything about where you were, since of course I didn't. What time will you be here?"

"Late," I say. "Or in the morning."

"Wake me up if you want," she says.

I fix my hair for a minute in the silver reflection on the phone's coin box before walking over to the little cinder-block building to pay for my gas. Inside, a large man with a face the color and texture of stone sits behind the counter, watching a newscast on a black-and-white wall television. He nods and takes my money. On the TV a man is speaking in Chinese, and a translation appears beneath him: "We couldn't determine whether here is a detective."

"They're everywhere," the man says to me, sliding me my change. "When you least expect it, expect it." He might be talking about detectives, communists, the Chinese—it's impossible to tell. "You traveling alone?" he says.

"Not far," I lie.

"Be careful, that's all I'm saying," he says. I thank him and back out, keeping my eyes on a spot on his shirt.

Georgia is a lengthy drive, south to north, and it keeps getting foggier and hillier. I listen to all-talk radio and learn unlikely things, that "alfalfa" is Arabic for "father of all foods," that racehorses aren't allowed more than seventeen letters in their names, and that in Tokyo lonely old people rent actors to play visiting sons and daughters, actors who are trained how to laugh and how to say goodbye. These all seem like fine things to know for now—if nothing else, they are things I didn't know while I was with Charlie. They make as much sense as anything. Life, I think, is like one of those games where everyone sits in a circle and each person must, in turn, remember one more item in a series. You have to remember the whole series each time, in order, or else you are out.

Early this morning I tiptoed out of the bedroom, my smallest muscles tensed. But Charlie didn't wake up; his face remained puffy and unmenacing in sleep. I went out to my car, expecting determent: slashed tires, a dead battery, anything. I remembered once when I was a child and my mother had planned a driving trip, packing up the car the night before, as I had now. In the morning when she opened the driver's side door, a kinglet flew out—the tiniest, most perfect bird I'd ever seen. This morning, now that I was finally leaving, I expected and even hoped for something like that to happen, but there was nothing to stop me, to make me think. The best I could come up with was the raspberry Danish someone had splattered all over my windshield a few days earlier, when I'd been withdrawing my savings from the bank. I hadn't taken it personally, because the parking lot was crowded and I was inside for half an hour, but when I mentioned it to Charlie, leaving out the part about my savings, of course, he said a woman had probably done it. He said a man wouldn't mess with something as petty as a sweet roll. "A man would've bent your rearview or broken off your antenna," he said.

I told him he was wrong, that women had respect for things like Danishes, and men didn't. He just laughed, the way he kept me from ever being right about anything. I remember still thinking stubbornly: A woman wouldn't do that to a Danish.

What I can't remember is when I got used to being wrong so often. It started with such minor things—what kind of dish drainer we should own, whether to keep his clock radio or mine by the bed, which was the superior brand of corn flakes. I had no experience with bullies. We'd met at someone's backyard party by a kudzu-covered wall where I'd chosen to drink, and his awful confidence had probably only seemed wholesome, as solid and natural a part of my happy evening as the beautiful green-and-rock wall. I don't even remember when we began to speak, or what was said. It didn't seem like an event, which was probably why I trusted it. I knew if something seemed too good to be true, it probably was, and I put no stock in Princes Charming. My life was solitary and easy then. I was stagnating happily in a futureless position as a keyliner for a commercial line of do-it-yourself books, walking home from work each night with bits of sentences and diagrams stuck in my hair. I still grinned at geckos and cypress trees, even though I'd lived in the South for the three years since college and those things should have been routine. I would sit and watch my lionhead goldfish for ninety minutes at a stretch, talking out loud to him and feeling every bit as satisfied as I would if he had understood me. I had peace and I trusted in it.

Charlie, at first, seemed to fit into my life so easily; he kissed me like it was just another way of breathing. He hugged me tightly and with purpose, the way you hold a child who's just come home from summer camp. We would be kissing and I would open my eyes and his would already be open, as if he were waiting for me. He worked in a distant and glamorous department of my company, in public relations, and when he spoke about us, he spoke with great confidence. He spoke as if it were only a matter of time before most people agreed with him about most things. He laughed at hesitation and uncertainty in any form, and when he talked he made small, finalizing gestures with his large hands. I had been content with the banal—my fish, the Spanish moss, an occasional barbecue—but Charlie brought need, strong desire, and he did it with elegance, with grand finesse. "How this turns out," he said frequently in his salesman's voice, "is up to you." "Whatever you want," a phrase of indulgence, became, over time, imbued with menace. I wasn't sure *what* I wanted, having never wanted much. Now, the more I wanted him, the more inevitable, immutable we seemed. It wasn't long before I couldn't remember ever *not* wanting him, ever being happy without him. Why was I arguing with him, why was I making myself so unhappy?

On one Sunday morning, the morning after the first really bad time, we sat side by side like peaceful grandparents on the sunny second-floor landing outside our apartment's back door. I kept getting distracted by the faint humid wind blowing beneath my legs and by my sore scalp, which felt in the sun as though it were heating from within. My whole body felt hungover, though we had not been drunk. Sitting between us on the concrete, like some Martian child, was a small roll-on bottle of Absorbine Jr. which Charlie had gotten from the 7-Eleven after breakfast, when I'd complained. He'd been silent, dabbing the cool medicine on my bare back and arms, the sore places from the night before where he had yanked me or where I'd pulled too hard to get away, and now the sweet minty smell steamed up from me, both foreign and reassuring. I hung onto the smell as though it really were a child, or a gift, as though it were the first thing about us.

The day wobbled along around us, the fight of the night before looming everywhere and yet seeming unreal, comic, impossible to apprehend, like the balls and blobs of mercury from a broken thermometer, shaken from their context—dangerous, but in a way you could neither believe in nor ignore. We said little, both of us apparently wanting his apologies behind us. I had forgiven him hurriedly, feeling while doing it a rush of instinctive relief not unlike getting my head above water after a long submersion. That anything else lay down there still, beneath my relief, was not a possibility I considered.

After a while a neighbor's cat trotted by, carrying in its mouth a women's pink cardigan sweater, as though this were a sensible thing for it to be doing. A short unnatural laugh came out of me, and the cat's eyes shifted my way for an instant, then back at the sidewalk, the cat itself never breaking stride, the sweater sleeves swinging on either side of its stuffed jaws. I put my sore head down and laughed, great gulping laughs like gasping for breath. "You see?" I heard Charlie say. "That's what I mean."

"What are you talking about?" I said. I didn't sit up.

"Look at me," he said, and then I did. His face was awash with sincerity. "The way you see the world," he said.

I tensed, my whole body ready for the accusation, for more of the same. But he surprised me.

"You're so easy to love," he said. "It would be so easy for you to find someone else who loved you."

His face, without its usual salesman's varnish, was disconcerting. He was scaring me. "Stop it," I said. He was reminding me of being alone, answering a question that had not been asked, and now the question, not the easily spoken answer, was what seemed true. The world without him whirled before my eyes, like some terrible rushing tide. There was something wrong with me, something wrong. "Please stop talking," I said, and held onto him for dear life.

And even now, a dissonance holds me upright, a faint but draining sense that something, like a tire or fan belt, may not hold. I grasp at things I learned in college, Jung saying when we couldn't stand to keep going forward we would go backward instead, looking for someone besides ourselves to blame. I remind myself wisely, over and over, that *Charlie* is the responsible one here—Charlie's anger, Charlie's strength, Charlie's two hands. It is physically impossible to spit in one's own face, I tell myself cleverly. And: It is part of the syndrome for the woman to feel it is her fault. That there is even a syndrome, that this happens everywhere, without reason, should comfort me, but it doesn't. The interstate stretches placidly ahead, shaded by a sweep of high clouds. The question sits, motionless, in the back of my mind: why I let this happen, what weakness in me caused this. Or is it something my mother should have seen in me, but forgot to see?

She never had counseling or went to any support groups when my father died, though her friends and relatives all urged her to. "Vocation and avocation," she said. "That's all the therapy I need." Once, in a stack of papers on her nightstand, I found a newspaper clipping about a group for new widows and widowers. The article featured a man who shaved his legs and held them in bed at night, "just to feel some soft skin," and a woman who wouldn't throw away her deceased husband's Jockey shorts. Anything you needed to do was okay, the article said. I was eleven or twelve when I found this, and it became a source of high, secret hilarity for my friends and me. We weren't laughing at these people's tragedies, it was just the Jockey shorts, though if my mother had seemed tragic, the article might have struck me differently. But she had begun selling her figurines in shopping centers and plazas, and sometimes taught pottery to small groups of women on our porch. And she laughed with me about the women after they left, saying one looked like she was carved out of a butcher's block, another should know better than to wear halter tops—these poor women who had nothing better to do than to take her class, these were the ones to feel sorry for.

It did seem odd that she didn't date, but by the time I noticed, *I* was dating, and much too involved to give my mother's lack of love life a second thought. And by that time, too, she was busy looking after the greasers. The boys I went out with, of course, weren't nearly as dramatic as the greasers; even then I chose regular boys who wore sweaters and had confidence in their futures, nothing for my mother to worry about. Senior year I went out with a Latvian boy I knew from Art Council who wore five earrings and always had some kind of foreign cigarette going when he came to our front door, but my mother liked him so much she gave him one of her homemade ashtrays for Christmas, a turtle with a sly, flirtatious tilt to its head. "There are worse things than smoking," she said, and did not elaborate. And the Latvian boy was, after all, harmless.

"Why don't you get a boyfriend?" I asked her finally, my first time home from college on a break.

"I hate old men," she said, smiling. "You know that."

I wonder now if she knew something I didn't when she made that remark, if she was trying to tell me something important about us or just making a joke.

It's well after dark when I stop in Seymour for coffee and mouthwash. Charlie always insists on Listerine, says it's "superior" even though gargling with it is actually painful, and I wish he could see me buying this tasty, sugary green brand. I want him to see me being kind to myself, and suffer. What I wish for, simply enough, is not his repentance, but his suffering. Memory and grudge are twin swamps to watch out for, I think. Even animals may be sus-

ceptible—my goldfish may be swimming in hate right now, wanting to kill me for leaving him alone with nothing but Charlie and
a scallop-shaped vacation feeder. But somehow I doubt it, and
I can now see why the fish and I always got along so well, the
way he went along so easily, pumping waves of unconsciousness
through his gills, never knowing or owning up to a thing.

Once, with Charlie, I came close to living in that state forever.
While it was happening I was thinking about my Walkman and
how it stopped tracking the tape after I dropped it on concrete.
I was picturing tiny wires coming apart, shaking loose, picturing this while Charlie held my chin and cracked the back of my
head against the floor, over and over. And suddenly all I knew
was that I didn't *want* to be unconscious, sunken into myself, my
brain a fallen soufflé. At that moment I promised someone, God
or Jung or whoever was out there, that I would work harder and
be kinder and stop wearing mascara and take more responsibility, whatever it took. It was my fault that this was happening, my
fault for loving my lazy, easy life. "You asked for it," Charlie was
probably saying—it was what he always said—and I believed him.

I doze in my car for an hour in the lot of a Hardee's. I dream
that I am facing Charlie, just a few feet away from him, and
I'm holding a gun. I'm fully dressed and sobbing, but the three
women behind Charlie are nude and nonchalant. Charlie laughs,
knowing I am afraid to shoot, that I don't even know how. He
starts walking toward me, slowly, slowly, smiling, enjoying this. *I
have no choice*, I cry at the last possible moment, and fire, falling
as he falls, to the ground. Just like that, he's dead. I am crying so
hard I can barely see, barely catch my breath. The nude women
look on, disinterestedly. *It wouldn't have bothered me to do that*,
one of them says.

Rain wakes me—not the noise, but the quality of it. In the
South the summer rains are violent, but routinely so; they come
down daily in friendly torrents. Up here the storms are more
random. The raindrops are smaller and meaner, and they pelt

you according to some unseen plan. My windshield looks like it's breathing. It reminds me of *The Last Wave*, where that poor guy discovers he's the harbinger of the apocalyptic tidal wave. Of course, he figures it out too late and it's all inevitable anyway, his image having been carved in stone by aborigines before he was even born. The first sign he gets is the rain, though, and soon the water is everywhere, surrounding his car and seeping into his home, and when he finally understands, it is both too early and too late for him to do anything.

I am at a Hardee's, I remind myself, a Hardee's in southern Indiana, thinking about the riddle of fate. I turn on my wipers and merge back onto the highway, judging that it will be near dawn by the time I reach my mother's house. The easy authority of the talk-radio host reassures me. "I'm here to tell you: zoning is liquid," he tells a worried caller, and the caller begins to sound a little less worried.

It isn't light yet after all, when I get there, but it's not quite dark either. When I drive around the cul-de-sac the neighbors' security bulb flashes on, as it has for years. Somebody must be landscaping the copse in the center of the cul-de-sac, I notice, because it doesn't look any thicker. My mother's miniature pickup truck is parked in the center of the driveway. As I pull up I realize my big old Chevy will fit neither behind it nor beside it. "No problem," I say aloud. I know the hiding place for her truck keys. I stop where I am, in the street, and turn off the ignition. It still feels like something is running underneath me when I get out. The pavement feels like it might have a motor in it, vibrating slightly against the soles of my shoes. An early morning redwing sounds a single hoarse note. I slide my mother's truck keys out from beneath a clay pot of marigolds that sits beside the front steps.

The problem, once I'm in her truck, is that it's a stick shift, something I've never learned to do, and I can barely keep my eyes from blurring into sleep. I fumble with the clutch uncertainly, then fit my hand around the heavy grip and move it in a direction that feels right. The truck coughs and dies and rolls backward and I jerk my left leg up in surprise, banging my bruise against the dash. I brake hard and too late, and the truck's back end slams the side of my car with a final, metallic jolt. And that, apparently, is as much as I can take—my tears come boiling up, and I wrap my arms around the steering wheel and press myself into it, sobbing, sobbing. And then my mother is there, barefoot in her old Lanz nightgown, smelling of bacon, clay, and lotion soap, reaching in for me. "Oh, honey," she is saying. A long time goes by before I'm ready to go inside, but when I do finally look up the sky has begun to lighten, the house has begun to take on tentative colors.

At the last minute there is something that makes her hesitate. We'll look at the dent later, she says; first things first. But as we're walking up the driveway she looks quickly back over her shoulder at the truck. "What is it?" I say.

"Nope," she says, shaking her head. "Nothing."

"Mom," I say. "What?"

She looks at me closely for a moment and moves a lock of my hair. "Nothing," she says finally. "I just left a couple of new bud vases in the back. But it doesn't matter, honey—they weren't anything special."

"Mom," I say. "Come on. Let's go see how bad it is." I head back to the truck and she hurries up behind me.

"Honey," she says, "it really doesn't matter. I can always do those little bud vases. I'll clean it up later."

I put my foot on the bumper and hoist myself up into the back of the truck. The vases are wrapped in a canvas tarpaulin, and the bundle has slid to one end of the truck bed—it's smashed up next to a box of gardening tools. I open the canvas gingerly, expecting a mess, but the bud vases, for whatever they're worth, are still in one piece. I look up, relieved, but she has already turned her back. I can see the blond hairs on her arms lit up by the sun as she moves evenly toward the house, and I marvel at how young she looks still, as though nothing bad has ever happened to her.

A Country Woman

MONICA MCFAWN

From *Bright Shards of Someplace Else* (2014)

There is a country woman now among us. We can see her from most of our backyards. Whatever you lack she will exemplify in your view—that is, if you are slothful and prone to depression she will be whistling and weeding in the single place in her yard that you can see from the recliner you have not left since last night. If you are needy and rattled when alone you will catch a glimpse of her through her window sitting down with a three-course meal she made for herself. You might even hear the music on her radio—old bluegrass—and hear her sing along. If you are lacking in purpose and passion, you need only see the peppy flick of her muck boots on the sidewalk as she heads out for the day.

"With these two hands and a day's time, I can move a mess of earth," she likes to say, but only to those of us who become impotent thinking of the brevity of days. She is referring to the koi pond she's digging, which she plans to stock with "offspring of her daddy's fish farm salmon," a losing proposition considering salmon's need to migrate, but it seems like a dreamer's envious boldness to those that hear this particular detail. If only they could throw themselves into something so hopeless with such aplomb!

She is at all the parties. To invite her is to send the message: I can face up to my faults. A kind of sweet torture is to engage her in conversation in a corner after having a few glasses of wine. The country woman speaks of many things: her family, the farm, weather changes, ham hocks, apple butter, the orneriness of old roosters as opposed to the sass of old hens . . . None of it means anything to you—why should it?—but the telling is full of charm and homespun wit. Things you clearly lack, if she's displaying them. The only recourse is to keep listening until she loses her charm, thereby affirming yours. It is a convoluted game, and the longer you listen, the more you are entertained and delighted, the more you wince at your own delight, and the more the country woman tries to amuse, sensing your discomfort and trying to alleviate it . . . you end up drunken with your arm around her shoulders, drooling compliments in her ears, as if by foisting your admiration on her you will somehow take on her traits. It is like taking a rubbing of a gravestone with a pencil and paper—the closer you press the better impression it will leave.

It might seem most logical just to avoid her, to keep the shades down and the eye averted, and this we try. One neighbor invests in heavy drapes, tightly locking blinds, and tall wild hedges for her front walkway so she can avoid seeing the country woman in the few steps from the driveway to the front door. And indeed if you walk fast with your head down you need never see the country woman in full. You might hear her whistle as she reams her gutters with a toilet brush or peripherally see the flash of a tartan plaid work shirt through a thicket, but the county woman herself is never again manifest.

Then as sudden as "sow-to-trough" (her saying) she is gone. The flash of her yellow raincoat through the gap in the drapes, the squelch of her Wellington boots, the sound of burning, cooking, nailing, feeding, mucking, whetting, basket braiding, carcass cleaning, pie frying, and meat baking (her order): all this came quietly to an end, as if the country woman had scuttled away in secret though she was the one from whom we hid. We listen for her like the clear tone of a bell long after being struck, a kind of warbling vibration that held us in thrall while we waited for it to cleanly end. Had she gone back to the country? Would she be back? Hers is the most palpable of absences, a not-aroundness so forceful that even her yard, left intact, is ragged, as if something had been rent from it—the pond and roosters and wheelbarrows seem too small for the space they take up, rattling stand-ins for something larger that once fit flush. The neighbors open their windows and beat their drapes with brooms and look around as if relieved but there is a great unease: one could avoid the country woman but not her absence. It was more here than what remained.

Big Where I Come From

PAUL RAWLINS

From *No Lie Like Love* (1996)

How many stories begin with a young man getting off a bus with a bag in his hand to walk toward the old family home while the murky sky begins to rain?

This is not my story.

I hire a limo, waiting at the airport. I read the New York papers, and the driver does not even try to make conversation.

I am big where I come from.

"Don't tell anyone I'll be in town," I have to warn the family. "You'll cause a stir."

I have a secretary to keep track of my days and everything I have to sign. And she loves me, too. She looks like Wonder Woman, wears those heavy glasses and sheer blouses knotted with smart ties at the collar. She's busty and efficient, my right hand.

"Get me tickets out tomorrow," all I have to say. And she looks right through my clothes from behind those specs.

"Sure," she says. "First class?"

Skirts. Always skirts around the office.

I spend millions over the telephone. I buy a ranch I've never seen. T-bills, old bonds and notes.

"Give me an option," I say. "Give me seventy thousand shares preferred."

Give me two more hands, twenty-six hours in a day.

I sell the ranch at a loss for taxes.

"It's got water," I say. "Two lakes and a potable spring."

How do I know? Do I get out to Marlboro Country?

I win big on the margin.

"Brenda," I say. Wonder Woman. In the doorway she looks nine feet tall. "Afternoon flight. Late. We've got court when?"

"Tuesday."

Tuesday. Give me two Tuesdays in a week. Trade them off for a Monday morning and Friday all day long. The amount of business done on a Tuesday would loosen the joints in your knees.

I could sell nineteen thousand units, thirty-five hundred shares, and a Kentucky stable right now.

So I do.

And when it's time to leave.

"Brenda," and she's propped against the door frame, her best foot forward, with her four-hundred-dollar hand-sewn-out-of-Louisiana-thunder-lizard shoe dangling off her toes and my ticket in her hand.

"Mind the store."

I come into town for my brother the Dope's birthday. My brother is thirty-three and cannot catch on. He has tried used cars, securities, beef, marriage, real estate. My mother threw him out of the house and he came back in disguise and tried to rent the basement. She says to me now, "Can't you take care of things like you did with your father?"

I didn't have him killed.

I said to him, sitting there on the corner of a blown-out cardboard box with an empty bottle and my mother's purse between his feet, "Why don't you go now? I think you've done enough."

He said, "Aw, I don't know."

I said, "Why don't I take you?"

He shuffles down the beaches of Bermuda now, lingering on in the final stages of chronic failure.

I took the check down once in person.

"You," he said. He stood there grizzled and one lens of his glasses cracked like a cube of ice in a glass of cold water. "I know you, hunh?"

Now it's the Dope's sleazy ex-wife who sweetens up and comes to the parties when I'm there.

"I read about you in the papers," she says like she's some whiskey boss's moll, a bright spot on the sun. Like she reads anything other than the TV guide.

And my other brother, Jackie.

"Aw, Pauly, remember the old days?" he says. When he could stand me. Then he goes out to the kitchen to stand at the sink and look out the window while he drinks.

It's my mother I come to see.

I come to fight with my mother because we've always fought, and it's the one thing in life I count on to be sincere.

"Pauly," she says, "you've sold your soul."

"And look what it's got you," I say. The woman has pearls by the bucket in a house with rotted carpet and front steps that melt away like bread in the rain.

"I don't go out," she says.

"Sell all and give to the poor," I tell her.

"Physician," she says, "heal thyself."

"Do unto others," I remind her, "and hang onto your receipts."

There was a time before success when I was spiteful.

I was going to buy this town, every crumbling brick, foreclose, and let it molder and decay. All this I swore in anger. I'd cut wages to invite the aimless and the seedy. I'd close warehouses and packing plants and open bars and all-night video arcades. I was younger, wounded by wrongs and rejection. I'd sell it to the Japanese.

Good sense in the form of an enormously fat man in flowered yellow and orange bathing trunks brought me around to hearing reason.

"Why bother," he said while he watched a half-nude coed hold her nose and come flailing off the high dive, "with what time will do for you?"

"Ah," I said, "good things come to those who wait."

"Not at all," my mentor said, and he heaved himself out of his chair to take the wet girl a towel.

"What then?" I said. A penny saved? A fool and his money? Waste not, want not? The Siamese laws of progress and entropy? I studied it out while he got the girl a drink, and I concluded that he meant just what he said.

When I'm in town, I don't stay at the house.

"I didn't expect you would," my mother says. "I didn't even make up a room."

I sleep five hours a night. I tell my mother this and say that I wouldn't want to keep her up.

"Keep up who? We could sit here and watch Carson," she says. It's Leno now. Same difference.

Even at the hotel, I have bad dreams. The Dope gets the number to my Gold Card; his ex-wife gets in bed with me. My other brother strokes a hammer in the basement, waiting for my breathing to turn heavy and regular.

What they would be at home under the frilly jalousies and the fetid envy I don't imagine. If I die in bed, it won't be there.

Even so, at 2 A.M. I am up on one elbow in bed and calling Marilyn on the phone. She is a mother now and a light sleeper. She picks up after three rings and says hello in a voice accustomed to answering the call to service.

"Would you come here now?" I say. I only phone when I'm in town.

"No, Pauly," she says. "How are you?"

"Is Harlow there?" I say.

"He's in Milwaukee till next Wednesday," she tells me.

"I don't want you to send things back if you don't want them," I say.

"I don't want anything, Pauly."

In the long pause that follows my not answering, I note that any hotel room under one hundred dollars a night smells the same. They all have the polypropelene cups wrapped in sanitary plastic in the bathroom. They all have traffic outside the windows.

"Are you still living in New York?" Marilyn says. She's settled back into her bed now, I know, in a sensible nightie with the phone tucked under her chin and the covers pulled up. I know this because she's told me. Ten years ago she had a bedside phone in her room she could throttle in half a ring when I came off swing shift excited with schemes and screwed up tight on ambition and avaristic energy. I would rattle on while I marked up the East Coast papers and rallied numbers into marching order in my head, and she would pop off minor questions now and then or hum a little to reaffirm her interest.

"New York is the land of kings and queens," I say to her tonight. "When are you coming?"

"I'm not," she says. "How are you doing these days?"

"Bigger than I've ever been. Out of bounds."

"'Living large,' isn't that what the kids are saying nowadays?" she says.

"I'm still a size forty." It's worth a little laugh.

"That's something," she says. "I wish I was." This is rhetoric. This is not flirtation.

"I've got a new number," I tell her. "You can reach me by fax."

"I don't need it," she says.

I give her the number and I tell her good night.

Marilyn is amazing just where she is. She might be the most expensive thing in the world, and I want not to have her. It's a good thing to practice denial.

My mother prestidigitates a homemade birthday cake for the Dope and reminds me that she doesn't play favorites.

"All you have to do is come get it," she says.

(Brenda, make a note: 19 July—Birthday. Stop off in Nowhere-ville, pick up cake. Arrive in Chicago 9:17.)

"Ma," I say, "we celebrate birthdays in New York. I have friends there."

"You think I don't know that?" she says.

"Last year the staff threw me a surprise dinner at some swanky bistro uptown. I don't think I knew all the people. Low-ballers pitch up at these things to scout for favors."

"All I said," she says, "is if you want a cake you can come home. Two layers, chocolate with chocolate frosting."

"I don't eat so much cake these days," I say.

"I thought you'd have it and eat it too," my other brother, Jackie, says. He slaps my shoulders and sniffs back at his hay fever. "Aw, you're living the good life, Pauly," then he's out to the front steps with his glass.

The Dope's high school buddies duck out of work about three and come over to barbecue in the late Friday afternoon. They've never made it out of town. They've hung around to inherit their fathers' businesses, watch their wives develop stretch marks, and go to Chicago for convention or lodge maybe once every two years. They look to me to corroborate all the fantastic stories of the wily, madcap world outside their own front yards as told by one of their number who works as a salesman on the road.

"I can't say," I tell them. "I've never been to Sioux Falls." They love this, and all offense is lost. Irony to this crowd is a chance coincidence in sports or cars, a recent football score that corresponds with a high school game on the same date in 1977.

"Weird, hunh?" somebody named Danny says.

"Hey, Pauly," somebody asks, "how long it take you to make your first million?"

"Yeah?" he says when I tell him. "How long would it take for you to make mine?"

I give him a surefire scheme for one point two in twenty-four months if he has the venture capital.

"Yeah, Pauly," he says, "you live the life." They all nod, the sons of upholsterers and appliance salesmen, one fireman, and a small-town bureaucrat and part-time restaurateur. They nod and fold their hands around longnecked bottles of beer like so many wise Jews at Iowa's own wailing wall made up of the peeling white fence that keeps the yard from being outside itself.

"You got the breaks, Pauly, can't argue that. You got Lady Luck for your own lovin' mistress."

"You're the man," Danny says, pointing at me with a half-empty longneck and awed by his own thought, "who could bring major league sports to Iowa."

Back inside, the Dope's ex has ambled by the house in bad faith and under false pretenses. They are making nice for Mother's sake, but she blows me kisses from the hallway.

The Dope would take her back, and this to her is something twice as good as credit if he has anything she needs, which is mostly sport or a coffee cup to spit in.

I call Brenda at the office twice for a heavy hit of merchandising, some contact with the monied world, but I can't get through. I watch the Dow like these sons of farmers' daughters watch the weather. When I stop moving, two yokels shake me down for offhanded stock tips, and a neighbor steers me to the breakfast nook and confesses bankruptcy. He's got his head bowed, and if he had a hat he'd have it in his hands. The wallpaper around us is crazy with sunflowers.

"Mama," I say when the car arrives, and she locks on me in a squint like she's a pitcher waiting on the signal from the plate. I hold both hands out. "No weapons," I say. I hug her and she tells me that I have no heart.

"You did all right by me," I tell her.

"It's easier for a camel to pass through the needle's eye," she reminds me.

I've heard it all. I kiss her cheek. "St. Peter holds my table."

I'm at the airport looking with the flight attendant at my ticket— my one-way ticket—when I hear the world start to rip like a zipper in a piece of tin.

Brenda answers this time. "Hey, baby," she says. Wicked laughter. "What do friends say, 'What's yours is mine'?"

There is blood from the nether regions pumping up my body and a fever starting above my upper lip. Lust is cheap compared to this, pure pornography. For a moment I know no fear.

"You're so beautiful," I tell her.

"You're bankrupt," she says.

Wonder Woman. Nine feet tall.

"If you ever need a favor . . ." She laughs, and there's another voice in the background—anyone I know?—and the sound of ice in glasses. Here, marooned in the forsaken wastes of middle America, a man behind me with a name tag that says "Wallace" is serving up my shredded company credit card and asking please if I could follow him a moment.

I allow myself a minute to consider options.

"Certainly," I say.

The word is out with the morning papers and twice around town by noon. I've been on the phone from Brussels to Hong Kong, woken up old neighbors and accomplices and a distant cousin of the fraternal order who loan-sharks part-time in Atlantic City, all to find I don't have a friend or favor left in this whole world.

By two o'clock I have given up on scrambling, and three thousand milligrams of aspirin are mixing with the rolls of antacids and breath mints in my stomach to form a hardpan layer blocking my intestines that will be soluble only in alcohol. My situation is this: an unwise overextension of some powers of attorney for the sake of convenience and throwing up small clouds of smoke for the bloodhounds of the Department of Internal Revenue has left me with two shirts and my old room back.

While I ponder on my fall, my brother Jackie sits down and pushes coffee in a white ceramic mug across the table to me. He looks both sober and sincere, with his hair wet down and a clean shirt.

"So what happened?" he says. I check his face for sarcasm, but all I see is a close shave.

Later, the Dope's ex calls him to take in a matinee, and my mother takes a pill and a nap, the kind where she lays on her back with her toes pointed up, snoring a Sousa march and swearing that she's never closed her eyes. I tell her Huck Castleman has already been around to offer me a job hawking used cars. He says he doesn't want to see me going to the competition, which there isn't any of in town, unless you want to drive a harvester or a kid's bike to church and down the freeway. He's told me to sleep on it over the weekend; he's not going anywhere.

I bring up the subject of my father's little pistol.

Ma says to me, sitting at the foot of her bed and not yet tipped over, "This will be the best thing ever to happen to you."

"How's that?" I want to know. I've had a shower and I've got on a pair of Jackie's stretch-fit slacks and my old 4-H windbreaker open over a T-shirt.

Ma lies back and scoots herself up the bedspread with her elbows.

"You just wait. There's things in this world you can't buy with money. Families band together when the wolves are at the door."

"That's because they can't get out," I say.

"Just you wait."

Saturday night I spend alone under a blanket in a web lawn chair in the backyard. My brothers and I grew up out here, sleeping under homemade tents and running wild with the neighbor kids. The world turns more slowly this far west, and the nights are long and quiet. I don't recall ever seeing a star in New York City, though you could buy a view there, too, if you wanted one. I don't recall that I ever looked or that I ever cared.

All this I've left behind.

Such is the bed I made.

Sunday afternoon I am sitting on the front porch explaining leverage to a neighborhood hound when Marilyn comes by. In a yellow sundress with a straw bonnet in her hands, she is the picture of all that's good in Iowa and the heroine of a hundred musicals. Starting with her shoulders, I see in her my favorites of geography and every place I've planned to go. She is healthiness and vigor, the rose that's found in cheeks. She is apples, she is peaches, she is lemon.

In another time she is queen, and another she is virgin. And then a maiden moonlit on a balcony, and then a high school girl shooting basketball in gym class. And now a woman and a wife at twenty-nine with her brown feet bare and her sandals in her hat.

She's heard.

She's not offering adultery, but she's inviting me for dinner.

"Why don't you come, Paul?" she says.

In her kindness, which I will take for pity, I find everything I need.

"Thanks," I say. "No."

I can feel bottom now beneath my feet and the air charged with the static of imminent magnificence and currency. I am ready once again to eat the weak and test the alchemy of turning baser metals into gold. I know the sleight of hand of futures shares, the finer points of interest rates, and the eight-fold path of real estate. I know buy low, sell high, corner, hedge, shelter, trade, boom, bust, profit, loss, location, location, and location. There are no great men, only great deals.

And when I find two nickels to rub together, stand back from the heat of molten metal and the flash of a rising star.

I can't wait till Monday morning.

The World Is My Home

SIAMAK VOSSOUGHI

From *Better Than War* (2015)

Just before he approached the young man and young woman walking on the college campus in Dresden, Germany, in the late evening, Arvin Khiavchi thought, Even if we don't find a place to stay tonight, the world is my home. As long as there is a sun beginning to set, and a group of Arab students playing soccer on the grass, and a German man who gave us a ride today from Berlin, the world is my home.

The young woman, he figured later, must have agreed with his assessment, because when he asked the couple if they knew of any hostels in the area, she said, "You can stay with me."

How does a thing happen like that? Should I start drawing some conclusions about either myself or Germany or the world? he thought.

He went to tell his friend Allie Dagneau. He was on a pay phone calling hotels.

"Everywhere is full. Do they know of a place?"

"Yes."

"Where?"

"Her house."

They laughed and didn't understand it and proceeded to go on their best behavior. They didn't understand when she took them to her house and gave them two warm beds. They didn't understand that night when she and the young man took them to a restaurant inside a castle. They didn't understand the next morning when she woke up early to go to the bakery to bring them fresh bread for breakfast.

But Arvin's surprise was that she could see something in them that went with her taking them in and showing them the city. Not that there was nothing to see. He knew there was something because all that he and Allie were concerned with since they'd left Utrecht was everything. And he and Allie were concerned with everything before then, but when two good friends were concerned with everything in motion, that was it—it was the last word. There was no getting closer to living than that, and his only surprise was that she could see it so quickly and clearly, which he felt a little bad about because maybe he shouldn't have sold people so short.

"Would she have done this for any two guys?" Allie said that first night when they were in their beds.

"I don't know. It's too much to think about."

"What do you mean?"

"I mean it's obvious to us that we're two guys to take in. We rode in the back of a van driven by a goddamn traveling video-game salesman coming from Utrecht, and we almost slept in a field that night. We met my cousins in Hannover, and we listened to their dreams. And we didn't say a word from Berlin to Dresden because the man driving us didn't speak a word of English and we didn't want to exclude him. Can she see all that? I don't know. It beats the hell out of me."

Allie laughed.

"Is the world a beautiful place?" Arvin asked.

"It might be."

"I know I ought to be glad to hear you say that, but you know what it sounds like to hear you say it? It sounds like work."

"What kind of work?"

"The kind that is going to make who we are when we're traveling be who we are when we're just living in one place."

"You think it can be done?"

"I think it's the only choice."

The next day she took them to a museum, and by then it didn't seem strange anymore. They were three friends, and it would have almost seemed stranger if she *hadn't* taken them in. She talked with both of them together, and at different times she talked with each of them alone, and at those times they each fell a little in love with her, as a way of understanding her. A young man ought to fall a little in love with a young woman who would do that, they thought.

They clowned around a little bit for her, exaggerating their personalities, telling embarrassing stories of each other that seemed less embarrassing far away from where they'd happened. Her laughter was beautiful, because she looked like she was not overflowing with it as she might've once been. The whole thing was nice, because they knew if they stayed here, one of them would feel enough to want to know exactly what the story was with the young man she'd been with on the first day, but for a couple of days, it was okay.

Arvin and Allie didn't think anymore of whether she would do this for any two guys. It was enough to be in it. No matter who they had been and what they had been doing to make her invite them home without a second's thought, their only job was to keep being and doing it, and since they hadn't been *trying* to be anything other than who they were, the worst thing they could do was to start trying now.

In the afternoon they went by train to a spot she said would be a good place from which to catch their next ride. Allie fell asleep on the train. Arvin looked out the window and saw an area outside the city with rows of beautiful gardens and what looked like very small houses beside them. He built a whole vision of who he imagined lived there: they were all people who'd come to the conclusion that gardens were more important than houses. It was a fair enough conclusion, he thought, having already seen a few European cities and having seen the same lostness and vastness he'd seen in American cities. The townspeople had all decided that it was worth living in very tight quarters if it meant being able to step outside to the immediate presence of flowers and vegetables and fruit trees.

Arvin asked the young woman about it. She explained that they weren't houses. They were plots that people in the city rented to garden, and the little houses were their sheds. She told him that her dream was to one day have one of the plots, only there was a very long waiting list.

"That is what I like to do," she said, "something with my hands, something with the earth. I don't really like to do anything else. If I had my choice, I would read a little each day. I would go and see my grandmother. But mostly I would like to work with the earth, to make something, to produce something. I am studying psychology, but I don't know what I would like to do with that."

All these girls in America that I felt sad for, Arvin thought, and along the way I was assuming that my sadness was confined to America. I didn't know they were thinking the same things in Germany. I didn't know they were dreaming of days of reading and seeing their grandmothers and gardening.

Sometimes the world felt too big to be his home. If there were girls wondering and dreaming like that in Germany, then they were doing so everywhere. He couldn't sit and listen to all of them. Even when he sat and listened to one of them, the world was just barely his home. It was the infinite depth of one person, more than miles they had traveled or distances between cultures—that was the greatest obstacle to the world being his home. Yet somehow it was the greatest opportunity too.

Having Allie around was good, because some time later when they were standing on the side of the road again like they had gotten used to doing, he could tell Allie about the young woman's dream, and then the two of them would carry it together, like a water bucket they were carrying between them, and even if his side would be a little heavier sometimes because Allie was distracted by something along the path and would end up carrying his side too low, Arvin was still happy to be carrying it with someone. It was an opportunity to see exactly what he carried, in step with the day when he could carry it by himself.

They came to a spot by the train station where they said goodbye. They thanked her for everything, and they wondered if they would ever see her again.

After she left, Arvin told Allie about the poetic vision he'd had, of the people living in little houses beside their gardens.

"What do you do with a vision like that when you turn out to be wrong?" Arvin asked.

"It still counts," Allie said.

Arvin didn't tell him about the young woman's dream. They were very good friends, and it was enough to know that he could. And he was beginning to think that if the world was really going to be his home, he was going to have to get used to its mystery; he was going to have to get used to doing something like listening to a young German woman's dream and holding it somewhere where he didn't have to answer it, where he didn't have to collapse at the thought of all the dreams of the young women he didn't know, all the dreams of the young women who were now old women, and the men too, both young and old. He was already good with everything he saw, even seeing visions that weren't there, but he was going to have to get just as good with everything he didn't know and couldn't see and would never be able to touch and would certainly never be able to tell somebody about and would most certainly never be able to always have a good friend like Allie around to tell either. He was going to have to get good at something infinite, but the infinity he had come across a few moments ago made him think that it was possible.

CONTRIBUTORS

ED ALLEN is the author of two novels, *Straight through the Night* and *Mustang Sally*. His short story collection *Ate It Anyway* won the 2002 Flannery O'Connor Award for Short Fiction. His poetry collection *67 Mixed Messages* was published in 2006. He is professor emeritus of English at the University of South Dakota and now teaches in the low residency creative writing program at University of Alaska, Anchorage.

WENDY BRENNER is the author of two books of short fiction, *Large Animals in Everyday Life*, which won the Flannery O'Connor Award, and *Phone Calls from the Dead*. Her stories and essays have appeared in *Best American Essays*, *Best American Magazine Writing*, *New Stories from the South*, *Oxford American*, *The Sun*, *Allure*, *Travel & Leisure*, *Seventeen*, *Guernica*, and elsewhere. She is a recipient of a National Endowment for the Arts Fellowship and teaches writing at University of North Carolina, Wilmington.

DAVID CROUSE is the author of the short story collections *Copy Cats* (2005), winner of the Flannery O'Connor Award for Short Fiction, and *The Man Back There*, as well as numerous other short stories and essays. *The Man Back There* (2008) was awarded the Mary McCarthy Prize. David lives in Seattle, Washington, where he teaches in the University of Washington's MFA Program. His new collection of short fiction, *When I Was a Stranger*, is currently looking for a publisher.

PHILIP F. DEAVER (1946–2018) was the author of *Silent Retreats*, which won the 1987 Flannery O'Connor Award, as well as the poetry collection *How Men Pray* and the novel *Forty Martyrs*. His short fiction was published in such literary journals as the *Florida Review*, the *Kenyon Review*, the *New England Review*, and the *Missouri Review*. It was also anthologized in *Prize Stories: The O. Henry Awards*, *Best American Short Stories*, *Best American Catholic Short Stories*, and *Bottom of the Ninth: Great Contemporary Baseball Short Stories*. Deaver taught in the English Department at Rollins College and was permanent writer in residence there. He was also on the fiction faculty in the Spalding University brief residency MFA program.

TONI GRAHAM, a Flannery O'Connor Award winner for *The Suicide Club* in 2015, is the author of two previous collections of short stories: *Waiting for Elvis*, winner of the John Gardner Book Award, and *The Daiquiri Girls*, winner of the Grace Paley Prize in Short Fiction. She teaches creative writing at Oklahoma State University, where she serves as editor and fiction editor for the *Cimarron Review*.

MARY HOOD is the author of the novel *Familiar Heat* and three short story collections, *A Clear View of the Southern Sky*, *And Venus Is Blue*, and *How Far She Went* (winner of the 1983 Flannery O'Connor Award). Hood is a winner of the Lillian Smith Award and a two-time winner of the Townsend Prize for Fiction. Her work has also been honored with the Whiting Writers' Award, the Robert Penn Warren Award, and a Pushcart Prize. A 2014 inductee into the Georgia Writers Hall of Fame, Hood lives and writes in Commerce, Georgia.

KARIN LIN-GREENBERG's story collection *Faulty Predictions* won the 2013 Flannery O'Connor Award, and it also won gold in the short story category of *Foreword Reviews'* 2014 INDIEFAB Book of the Year. Her stories have appeared in literary journals such as the *Antioch Review*, *Epoch*, *Kenyon Review Online*, *North American Review*, and *Shenandoah*, and she was a finalist for the *Chicago Tribune*'s 2018 Nelson Algren Award. Her many writing honors include a MacDowell Colony fellowship and an appointment as Tennessee Williams Scholar at the Sewanee Writers' Conference. She lives in upstate New York and is an associate professor in the English Department at Siena College.

KIRSTEN SUNDBERG LUNSTRUM is the author of three collections of short fiction, *What We Do with the Wreckage* (winner of the 2017 Flannery O'Connor Award), *This Life She's Chosen*, and *Swimming with Strangers*. Her short fiction and essays have appeared widely in journals, including *Ploughshares Solos*, *North American Review*, *One Story*, *American Scholar*, *Willow Springs*, and *Southern Humanities Review*. Lunstrum has been the recipient of a PEN/O. Henry Prize and fellowships from the MacDowell Colony, the Sewanee Writers Conference, and the 2016 Jack Straw Writers Program. She teaches creative writing and literature and lives with her family near Seattle, Washington.

BECKY MANDELBAUM is the author of *Bad Kansas*, winner of the 2016 Flannery O'Connor Award for Short Fiction and the 2018 High Plains Book Award for First Book. Her work has appeared in the *Missouri Review*, the *Georgia Review*, the *Rumpus*, *Necessary Fiction*, *Hobart*, *Electric Literature*, and *McSweeney's Internet Tendency* and has been featured on *Medium*. Originally from Kansas, she currently lives in Washington's Skagit Valley and teaches at Seattle's Hugo House.

C. M. MAYO is the author of several books on Mexico, including *The Last Prince of the Mexican Empire*, a novel based on a true story and named a *Library Journal* Best Book of 2009. Her collection *Meteor* won the Gival Press Poetry Award for publication in 2018. A native of El Paso, she is member of the Texas Institute of Letters.

MONICA MCFAWN is a writer, artist, and performer living in Michigan. Her short story collection *Bright Shards of Someplace Else* won the Flannery O'Connor Award for Short Fiction as well as a Michigan Notable Book award. She is also the author of an art and poetry chapbook, *A Catalogue of Rare Movements*, and her drawings and animations have been shown in galleries around the country. McFawn is a recipient of an NEA Fellowship in Literature and Walter E. Dakin Fellowship from the Sewanee Writers' Conference. She is an assistant professor at Northern Michigan University, where she teaches fiction and scriptwriting. When she isn't writing, drawing, or teaching, she trains her Welsh Cob cross pony in dressage and jumping.

CHRISTOPHER (KIT) MCILROY lives in Tucson, Arizona, where he is an author-in-residence for the Tucson Unified School District. His story collection *All My Relations* won the Flannery O'Connor Award in 1992. Between 1987 and 2010 he developed and implemented writing programs for the non-profit ArtsReach, which served Native American communities in southern Arizona. Some of those experiences were distilled into the non-fiction *Here I Am a Writer*, which was published in 2011.

PETER MEINKE's latest book of short stories is *The Expert Witness*. His collection of essays *To Start With, Feel Fortunate* received the 2017 William Meredith Award (Poet's Choice Press). With his wife, the artist Jeanne Clark, Meinke published a children's book, *The Elf Poem*. He has published eight books in the prestigious Pitt Poetry Series and is currently the poet laureate of Florida. In 2015 he received the Lifetime Achievement in Letters award at the SunLit Festival, St. Petersburg.

PAUL RAWLINS's fiction has appeared in *Glimmer Train*, *Southeast Review*, *Sycamore Review*, and *Tampa Review*. He has received awards from the Utah Arts Council, the Association for Mormon Letters, and PRISM International. He lives in Salt Lake City.

HUGH SHEEHY teaches creative writing and literature at Ramapo College of New Jersey. He lives in Beacon, New York.

SIAMAK VOSSOUGHI is an Iranian-American writer whose collection *Better Than War* came out in 2015. The collection was shortlisted for the William Saroyan International Prize for Writing. He has received a fiction fellowship from the Bread Loaf Writers' Conference. He lives in San Francisco.

LEIGH ALLISON WILSON has published two collections of short stories, *Wind: Stories* and *From the Bottom Up*. Her flash fiction, stories, and essays have appeared in the *Georgia Review*, *Harper's*, the *Kenyon Review*, *Mademoiselle*, *SmokeLong Quarterly*, the *Southern Review*, the *Washington Post*, and elsewhere. Her work has been read on NPR's *Selected Shorts*. She is a professor in the creative writing program at SUNY Oswego.

CPSIA information can be obtained
at www.ICGtesting.com
Printed in the USA
LVHW091650131019
634067LV00001B/57/P